LIZ ALLISON & WENDY ETHERINGTON

WINNING IT ALL

HQN™

Recycling programs
for this product may
not exist in your area.

ISBN-13: 978-0-373-77402-9

WINNING IT ALL

Copyright © 2009 by Liz Allison and Wendy Etherington

NASCAR® and the NASCAR Library Collection® are registered trademarks of the National Association for Stock Car Auto Racing, Inc.

This edition published by arrangement with Harlequin Books S.A.

® and TM are trademarks of the publisher. Trademarks indicated with ® are registered in the United States Patent and Trademark Office, the Canadian Trade Marks Office and in other countries.

www.HQNBooks.com

Printed in U.S.A.

Dear Reader,

It's hard to believe our journey with the Garrison family is coming to a close. As we wind up everything with Bryan, we look forward to sharing his story with you, even though we're sad to see the trilogy end.

If you've been following us all along, you know Bryan has issues (and if you haven't, don't worry—you'll catch on quickly). He's been through a career-ending injury and a contentious divorce, and watched his parents' marriage fall apart while he was struggling to keep the family racing business the best in NASCAR.

After much nagging and encouraging by his family, he's finally agreed to seek help for his continued pain resulting from his accident. But physical therapist—and push-up challenger—Darcy Butler isn't exactly what he's expecting. Lovely and tiny, she doesn't seem strong enough to handle the volatile Bryan, but he finds out quickly just how wrong perceptions can be.

As a widow, Darcy has experienced her share of love and loss. She blocks her emotional pain with work and looks forward to the challenge of getting Bryan back in shape. But when she still has so much healing to do herself, can she really help a man who no longer believes in the power of love?

Thanks to all the readers who have hung in there with us throughout all the books! It's been a joy to share our fictional, behind-the-scenes peek into the exhilarating, high-speed world of NASCAR.

Race on!

Liz and Wendy

To Lesa France Kennedy, whose love, dedication and passion for NASCAR racing exemplify the heartbeat of this trilogy.

WINNING IT ALL

PROLOGUE

January 2005

"I'M SORRY, Mr. Garrison, but the news isn't positive."

Seated in front of Dr. Neil Epstein's desk, Bryan Garrison drummed his fingers on the wooden arm of his chair. "How bad?"

"While the damage to your knee is significant, with a great deal of physical therapy, I think there's a good chance you'll have nearly complete mobility. It's your head injury that concerns me most."

Bryan resisted the urge to raise his hand to the bandage covering his forehead. Like the cast on his leg, there were moments when it was difficult to believe the flaw was actually there.

"Eventually, you should go on to lead a normal life," the doctor continued, his hands folded calmly on his desk. He met Bryan's gaze directly.

"I don't have a normal life," Bryan said.

"I'm aware of that, of course." Epstein sighed. Regret filled his eyes. "The neurological trauma is too severe. Your racing career is over."

Even as the verdict echoed through the room, the grandfather clock in the corner ticking as loudly as a bomb, Bryan shook his head. "No."

"I know this news is difficult for you to hear, but your head injury is severe enough that any further exposure to your job could kill you."

Annoyed, Bryan waved that aside. There were always risks.

Epstein narrowed his eyes and leaned forward. "Even a minor incident on the track might be too much."

"Might?" Bryan leapt on the word.

"A mild concussion, a hit that would barely cause another driver to feel dizzy... It's not fair or right, but those are the facts."

"No." Bryan lurched to his feet, glaring at the doctor, intimidating him as he had hundreds of competitors over the years. "What about therapy? Exercises? Another operation?"

Epstein rose, then walked around his desk, leaning back against the mahogany surface.

His calmness only increased Bryan's rage. How could he so quickly and easily tell Bryan his life was over? This couldn't be happening. Not to *him.*

"Certainly therapy will improve your memory and motor functions," the doctor said. "But no operation currently practiced will change your condition. I can't give you medical clearance to race."

Bryan clenched his fist. "Then I'll find a doctor who will."

Epstein shook his head sadly. "You won't."

"I'm the defending champion!"

"I know. I'm very sorry."

Blood rushed to Bryan's head. He actually swayed on his feet.

Epstein grabbed his arm. "Sit down, Bryan."

Bryan jerked his arm away, but he sat, because he knew he'd pass out if he didn't. Though one more humiliation would hardly affect him after all the ones he'd endured over the last few weeks.

He was supposed to get the first garage stall all season. He was supposed to strut into Daytona qualifying with all the promise of repeating his championship season. He was supposed to be respected and admired. He was supposed to be great.

"It's a miracle you're alive," Epstein continued. "Anyone else involved in that highway pileup, anyone without your reflexes and instincts, would have died and taken several people with him. If only—"

"If only the old couple hadn't hit me at the end of the crash. I know. I read the police report." A thousand times.

"I wish my diagnosis could be different. You're a racing champion. Nothing can ever diminish that accomplishment."

Pushed beyond the limits of his pride and fighting to deny the truth, however gently and definitively it was delivered, Bryan leaned his forearms on his thighs and hung his head. "My family's counting on me. We race. We don't have anything else."

"You have each other." The doctor paused, then added quietly, "I understand you have a younger brother."

Bryan laughed harshly, tunneling his hand through his hair. "Cade's not ready to take over my ride."

Bryan had tested the car over the season break, but he could get anyone to test and give the engineers the data they needed for the all-important opening race next month. Cade was too busy having fun. He should be allowed to have fun, not be buried under responsibility.

Thank God I lied to Nicole and told her to go to lunch with her friends.

He'd convinced his wife this appointment with the doctor was a routine one. She'd suffered as much as he, becoming his nursemaid, helping him walk to the bathroom and dress himself, driving him to his appointments. Because he could do none of those things on his own. He was a disgusting, pathetic shell of the man he'd been. He didn't know how she could stand to look at him.

He couldn't even look at himself.

If he wasn't a race car driver, what was he?

CHAPTER ONE

February 2009

A CHIP THE SIZE of Lake Lloyd on his shoulder, Bryan Garrison walked through Daytona's busy garage area.

They needed more speed.

He nearly laughed aloud at the ridiculous wish. Every team wanted, needed, *craved* speed. Wasn't that why they were all in this crazy business?

Still, he'd like his team's practice times to be better.

"What are you doing here?" a familiar voice called from behind him.

Clenching his jaw, Bryan turned to face his brother-in-law, Parker Huntington. "Walking."

"You're supposed to be in the hauler, interviewing."

"I don't need a physical therapist," he muttered, ignoring the pain in his knee as he dodged a war wagon of equipment being pushed toward pit road. "I'm managing fine on my own."

Parker raised his eyebrows. "Are you now?"

Parker knew he wasn't. And the humiliation rolled over Bryan anew.

His family had coddled him and nagged him, then outright demanded he see a professional about the continuing pain and stiffness in his knee. In a weak moment, he'd relented. So Parker had him interviewing physical therapists at the track. At Daytona. Less than a week before the opening races.

'Cause, gee, he didn't have anything else to do but make sure Cade and his teammates had cars worthy to race in the biggest event of the year. To be a strong, supportive leader for his teams. To uphold the Garrison family tradition of trophies and championships.

Legends of excellence. Success was expected, not hoped for.

Garrison Racing International had won the NASCAR Sprint Cup Series trophy last year with a longtime driver, who was now running only a partial schedule and training a developmental driver. Their newest full-time driver, Shawn Stayton, had finished fourteenth last season and clearly had more successful years ahead. The third driver in the GRI stables, Bryan's younger brother, had missed winning his first championship by only sixty-four points.

Bryan intended to have that trophy again—this time with Cade's name on it.

And if that was all he had to worry about, his life would be blissfully, pleasantly single-minded. But, no. He had physical therapy interviews. And family to deal with. And now in-laws.

Though supposedly firmly single people, both his brother and sister had gotten married in the last two years, and now Bryan had to bear the burden of romance. In fact, love was so full in the air, he was surprised the clouds hadn't blossomed into baby cupids, their bows pulled back, their faces wreathed in smiles.

Disgustingly trite for a completely, utterly temporary emotion.

Aggravation, obligations and heartache were all love got you. He and his ex-wife's divorce attorney had made sure of that.

Still, he was doing his family duty. Didn't he always? He'd already met with Beverly and Amy, both young women straight out of college. Knowing he'd have them screaming for their mommas inside a week, he'd sent them on their way.

He'd also interviewed a Swedish exchange student named Sven, who, given the size of his hands and biceps, would someday give a helluva massage to society chicks in upscale spas, but he wasn't really Bryan's type.

Then he'd met a former army sergeant, Mack Bowman. Mack was a no-nonsense guy built like a pit bull who barked orders even when he was simply making conversation. This was someone Bryan could relate to. No small talk. No fear he'd be offended by Bryan's short temper. A guy who understood the pace and commitment of racing, since his brother was the hauler driver for another team.

Bryan had decided to hire Mack. All he had to do was get rid of the last interviewee.

Suddenly he saw his perfect opportunity to do so, plus make his brother-in-law break the news. "I want to hire Mack," he said to Parker.

"You still have to interview Darcy."

"No, I don't. Tell her the job's been filled." Considering the business settled, Bryan started to walk off.

Parker stepped in front of him. "Surely you're not going to dismiss her without the courtesy of a simple introduction."

Bryan sighed. His brother-in-law, for all his polite manners and blue-blood vocabulary, had a rod of titanium for a spine. And he was determined as hell. Who else, really, could have managed to charm Bryan's stubborn sister?

"You need to give Darcy a chance," Parker added.

"She's a widow."

"So?"

"Love and pain are the last things I need."

Parker sighed. "I seriously doubt Darcy will burden you with her personal troubles. She's a professional."

Bryan increased his pace. "Yay for her. I want to hire Mack."

"Darcy is lovely, smart and extremely competent. And she needs the job."

Fighting a wince, Bryan kept moving. He already

had anger and regret living with him every day. He didn't need guilt to move in, too.

But they didn't call him "Steel" for nothing.

"I don't need to know about the drama," he said briskly to Parker. "Can she do the job?"

"She can. She's simply had a hard time dealing with her husband's passing," Parker continued. "She needs a change and—"

Bryan held up his hand. "I thought you weren't going to tell me her personal troubles."

"No, I said *she* wouldn't."

Next thing, Parker would launch into a story about how this poor woman was devastated and she would be unable to get out of bed unless Bryan gave her a job. Arguing with the man was futile. As head of Huntington Hotels International, Parker charmed, schmoozed and worked deals with everybody from high-powered corporate executives to the waitstaff at his restaurants. "Fine," Bryan said, feeling like a sap. "I'll talk to…"

"Darcy." Parker gave him a confident smile. "Darcy Butler."

Bryan started to turn away, then stopped. "What's so great about her?"

Apparently, Parker had been waiting for this opening. "She's firm, but kind. Smart, but not a know-it-all."

"Unlike *some* people we know."

Since Parker knew this comment was directed at

him and he was used to the ragging, he simply nodded and moved on. "She's specialized in athletic rehabilitation, and she can handle herself." He paused, looking amused. "Around you or anybody." He slid his hands into the pockets of his charcoal pants, which looked neat, pressed and comfortable, despite the oppressive heat. "We're also friends. She's the therapist who helped Allen get back to work so quickly last year."

One of Cade's pit crew members had been hurt in Pocono, but after several months of therapy, he was back, fit and ready for the new season. Despite his pessimism, Bryan was impressed. "If she's a friend, and you set up the interviews, why all the others?"

"If I presented you with a *fait accompli* you'd have balked."

Fait... Hell. Who said stuff like that?

Still, he got the gist. If Parker had rolled Darcy Whoever out on stage as his already-cast therapist, Bryan would have rejected her outright. Ornery? Definitely.

But then that was practically the Garrison family motto.

Bryan addressed the one detail he could deal with. "If she helped Allen, then she understands racing, right?"

"Her uncle is a NASCAR official, and her husband was a firefighter who used to volunteer at the races in Concord." He paused, his voice quieted. "He died about two years ago, fighting a fire in a local furniture store."

"Sorry to hear it."

"She just needs a change of pace." Parker's gaze met Bryan's. In addition to the obvious determination in his eyes, there was now a hint of humor. "Oh, and she's a great cook."

"Why didn't you say that to start with?"

"The way to a man's heart…" He started off. "It's nice to know the cliché hasn't died."

Yeah. That would be true. If I had a heart.

Shrugging, Bryan headed toward the NASCAR Sprint Cup Series No. 56, Huntington Hotels International hauler.

Great. Now I can add commercial hack to my aches and pains.

He spoke briefly to a couple of crew members from another team, then waved at a fellow team owner. Their expressions varied from giddy to annoyance. The races being run in the next week were the most important of the season. Money, prestige and momentum would greet the ones who performed well. Frustration and humiliation awaited the rest.

The qualifying races would be held the next day, and all three of NASCAR's national series would race through the weekend. Everybody had a prediction on the weather, track conditions and what their competitors had under the hood.

Though gray clouds rolled in the sky overhead, the

scent of grilled meat permeated the air. Team chefs, many doubling as hauler drivers, were gearing up for the lunch hour—which really amounted to about ten minutes. It was make or break time, but it was also a kind of homecoming. Back to the routine. Back to what they all loved.

After exchanging brief greetings with several of Cade's crew members, Bryan slid open the hauler door. The interior hallway was small—most of the space was occupied by locker-type bins full of equipment—but there was still a gathering of people around the microwave waiting for popcorn with all the anticipation of the next world peace treaty.

Though Bryan said nothing, conversation died. The guys backed against the walls to let him pass. Nobody looked directly at him.

One thing was for certain…when you were pissed off all the time, and didn't bother to hide that fact, working your way through a crowd could be an actual pleasure.

He walked down the hall, toward the cab of the hauler, then opened the door to the office/locker room/den. "Ms. Butler, I'm Bryan Garrison, I'm hoping we can—"

His words ground to an abrupt halt. The *get this over with quickly* part of his sentence died suddenly in his dry throat.

She's tiny was all he could think.

Tiny, blond, golden-eyed and lovely. She looked

like an elf. A fairy sprung straight from the pages of a children's book.

She extended her hand, taking his in a surprisingly firm grip, those huge, deep, tawny eyes focused intently on his face. "Good afternoon, Mr. Garrison," she said with the faintest hint of an accent he couldn't quite place. "I appreciate you seeing me. I gather you're a busy man."

"I—" He cleared his throat. His knee hurt before, but now he wasn't sure how long it would support his weight. What was wrong with him? "Yes, I am. The qualifying races are tomorrow."

"Aye." Pausing, flushing, she looked away. "Sorry. *Yes,* I know." She shrugged as her gaze slid back to his. "I spend a lot of time with my Irish grandparents. Their Old World language is a habit I can't seem to break."

"No need to." In fact, he found the music of her voice both arousing and comforting. He shook his head and extended his hand toward the sofa. "Have a seat."

"Thank you, but you're the one who should be sitting." She grasped his hands and, seemingly without exerting any force at all, managed to maneuver him to the corner of the sofa and slide his injured leg along its length. "Is your limp always this pronounced?" she asked, reaching for the throw pillow on the floor and propping it beneath his knee.

"Well…" He hadn't been limping. *Had he?* "No. I mean, I'm—"

"Fine?" She smiled briefly, then dropped the bulg-

ing black bag she was carrying to the floor and knelt to search through its contents. "You, Mr. Garrison, are *not* fine. Your knee is severely wrenched, you're in pain, and I bet you're surly about it."

Bryan narrowed his eyes. A move that had caused grown men to cringe.

But Darcy Butler wasn't even looking at him.

"I. Am. Not. Surly," he said, biting off each word.

She looked up at him, her full lips shining with pink glossiness. "Naturally." She approached him with a plastic pouch that she bent in half. It made a popping sound, and he knew, from lots of experience, that it was releasing a freezing gel. "Isn't that better?" she said gently as she laid the pack on his knee.

He closed his eyes on a wince, though he knew the cold would help in a couple of seconds. "Sure." Forcing himself to look at her, he added, "I'm supposed to be interviewing you, so—"

"I don't know how you can even concentrate, the pain you're in." She laid her hand on his chest and pressed him down, so that his head rested on the arm of the sofa. "Why don't you rest a bit, then we'll talk later?" She rose. "I could fix you some lunch."

As she turned to leave, Bryan literally looked around for the control he'd somehow lost. *"Stop."*

She glanced at him over her shoulder. Her eyes were sparkling with humor, as if she knew he was frustrated, and she knew she'd caused it. "Yes, Mr. Garrison?"

He lifted his head. "I—" Damn, she was cute. "Let's talk now."

"Sure." She crossed the room again, sitting cross-legged on the floor in front of the sofa, so that she had to tilt her head back to look at him.

He wanted to offer her a seat on the sofa, to recall some of the manners his mother had drilled into him all these years, but she'd rushed on already.

"I expect you've seen my résumé. I have a master's degree in physical therapy and extensive experience in sports medicine, rehabilitating elite athletes specifically. For the last three years, I've managed the rehab clinic for a group of orthopedic surgeons, who do a great deal of work with the local university's athletic department. My uncle is a NASCAR official, so there's a handy reference. Oh, and Parker and I have been friends, well…I guess almost a year now."

"You're a racing fan?" he managed to ask, unsure why she made him feel so good and so uneasy at the same time.

She pursed her lips. "I guess. It's all a bit loud for me, though."

"Loud?" She had to be kidding. "Who's your favorite driver?"

"Mmm. Don't really have one of those." She angled her head. "Is that a requirement?"

How did this woman have a NASCAR official in her family and not know the basics? "Yes."

She studied him for a moment. "You're a driver, right?"

He fought against the bitter memories that surged through him. "Used to be."

"Well, if you hire me, I'll be working for you, so I guess *you're* my favorite driver."

"But I don't drive competitively anymore."

"So?"

He wasn't sure why the idea that someone could still be his fan and advocate—when he'd been forced to the sidelines long ago—gave him comfort, but it did.

Anyone who'd followed his career had pretty much transferred their loyalty to Cade. He was happy about that. His brother was the future of Garrison Racing now. That was the way things should be.

But he couldn't deny the excitement he felt when someone asked to talk to him, to have *his* signature on an older piece of racing memorabilia. He'd signed hats, shirts, cards, body parts, autograph books, car hoods, even baby bibs in his career. He used to take them for granted.

Now, he treasured every one.

"My brother, Cade, can be your driver," he said finally.

"You're the boss."

"But I'm not. Not yet anyway. I have several candidates to consider."

"Naturally." She laid her hand over the ice pack on his knee. "Better?"

If he said no, would she go? And the more important question—did he really want her to?

A few minutes ago he was set on Mack. He opened his mouth to tell her to leave, that the interview was over, and he'd already decided on his therapist, which she definitely *wouldn't* be, but the words froze in his throat.

For one thing, his knee *did* feel better. Relieving the pressure of standing was cathartic, but the ice pack was heaven. For another, she both intrigued him and worried him. Many men might run the other direction from a woman like that, but he was impressed someone had broken through his defenses so quickly and so effectively.

For the last few years, his state of mind had alternated between numbness and anger. Intrigued confusion was nothing if not a nice change of pace.

"Mr. Garrison?" she asked, her probing goldenbrown gaze focused on his face.

"Don't call me Mr. Garrison. That's my father." He considered his dad's bachelor pad and recent tendency to date overly endowed blondes named after fairy-tale woodland creatures, then waved his hand. "Actually, don't call him that, either. I'm Bryan."

"Whatever you say…Bryan."

The sound of his name in her lilting accent sent odd waves of warmth through him.

Which he ignored.

He levered himself to stand, disconcerted to find her suddenly beside him. Though her head didn't reach the top of his shoulder, she held his bicep and forearm in a firm, confident grip. If he was about to fall, she could never catch him. He was twice her size. He'd crush her.

"Let's go to my motor home," he said, wondering about the sudden racing of his heart, which had to be anxiety, not desire. If he did hire her, this was a professional partnership, not a personal one. Besides, he was through with personal bonds. "We'll have lunch and talk."

"What do you want?"

His gaze slid the length of her. *"Want?"*

She angled her head. "For lunch."

What he wanted, he realized at that moment, didn't have anything to do with food. He searched her face. "What're you offering?"

She laid her hand on his chest, to support him, or maybe hold him back. "Grilled chicken or tofu." She smiled. "You have a preference?"

He frowned. Tofu? Surely she was kidding.

CHAPTER TWO

GLANCING AROUND at the full-size convection oven, titanium fridge and iron-grated stove top, Darcy hoped to calm the fluttering in her stomach by marveling at the luxurious, if compact, kitchen in Bryan Garrison's motor home.

Well, really, at this point, she was still marveling at the motor home itself.

Plush carpeting and tile, leather seating area, cherry side tables and dining table, flat-screen TV, computer station in a alcove off the hallway.

Her only issue was with the color scheme—best described as *dark*.

Navy, black, dark gray, more black. From Parker, she'd learned Garrison Racing was legendary for their cars painted candy-apple red, but nowhere was that color evident in the company president's personal space.

"It's…lovely," she said, turning in a circle, wishing she was better at lying.

He shrugged, his broad shoulders looking capable of taking on anything, even if his limp and the pained lines drawn into his handsome face belied that illusion. "I'm here more often than I'm home during the season, so it has to be comfortable."

She set her soft-sided cooler, which she'd brought in case she needed to audition her culinary skills, on the counter. She considered her low-fat protein, vitamin-infused, no-processed-food and low-sugar diet critical to a successful rehab. "So, chicken or tofu?"

"You don't have to cook," he said. "I've got stuff in the fridge."

As he opened the door and leaned over to study the contents, she fought the urge to wave her hand in front of her face and catch a cooling breeze. Now that those intense gray-blue eyes were no longer focused on her, she felt the need to give in briefly to her *good grief, he's gorgeous* thoughts.

The view of his strong profile didn't help get her mind back on business.

But with immense effort, she focused on how she could help him. He was carrying too much weight around his middle and arms. His black T-shirt strained a bit across his chest and his hip-hugging jeans were somewhat tight. While none of that took away from his attractiveness, any extra weight on his knee wasn't a good thing.

"There's leftover Chinese food, leftover meat loaf and…" He held up a plastic baggie with a big hunk of meat inside. "Steak." He smiled, which warmed his brooding face. "I've got some hoagie rolls and cheese. Melt it all in the microwave. It's really—" His smile fell away, as he no doubt noticed her horrified expression.

"You can't seriously be considering eating that?"

"It's not tofu, of course, but it'll do in a crunch."

She glanced at the meat, doing her best not to shudder. "I'm not opposed to a bit of red meat," she said neutrally, though she was very concerned about its quality. She believed in organic, no-hormones-added lean protein. "Do you mind if I ask where it came from?"

"Off the grill, two nights ago."

"No, I mean, where did you buy it?"

"The grocery store. My motor home driver likes—"

"I'm sorry. I should have been more specific. Where did the beef come from *before* the store? Was the herd grass-fed or at least grain-fed on a one-hundred-percent organic farm?"

"How should I know?"

She pressed her lips together. She really did want this job. Her uncle and friends were right. She'd let herself fall into a rut, dipping for months at a time into depression. She needed a mission, a cause, a purpose.

And whether he acknowledged it or not, Bryan Garrison needed her expertise. After glimpsing the contents of his refrigerator, she was even more convinced. But to get hired, she had to be tough, as well as smart. "I'm concerned too much high-fat meat will make you unfocused and sluggish."

He shrugged. "I have no problem with being unfocused and sluggish." He laid the meat on the counter, then retrieved orangey-yellow processed cheese slices—

Darcy closed her eyes. She couldn't watch what other insidious items he pulled out.

"It's not as if I'm driving," he continued. "I don't have to worry about being sharp."

Her eyes flew open. Naturally, his pain wasn't all physical.

After working with many other accident victims and injured athletes, she'd known that was true before she'd even met him. Still, she hadn't expected the deep, dark hurt she sensed in Bryan. She hadn't expected the answering ache of remembrance in her own heart.

She laid her hand over his. "*Please* let me prepare lunch."

He narrowed his eyes, and her stomach resumed its fluttering. "I don't eat tofu."

"Then I'll make chicken." She glanced at the steak, trails of blood pooling at the bottom of the bag, and barely suppressed another shudder. "Okay?"

His gaze held hers a moment longer, then he dropped the bag and turned away, flopping on the sofa across the room. "Fine. I like when a woman cooks for me."

And she'd just bet he had women lined up to do so—even with his surliness.

She turned toward him. She'd hoped to ease in the toughness, but maybe it was better to lay out the rules early. "I'm not a woman."

His gaze slid down her, and somehow he made her feel both annoyed and complimented by his perusal. "Oh, but you definitely are."

"I mean, I'm not a woman in this situation. This *professional* situation. If we're going to work together, you have to think of me as your coach. I'm here to get your body back in shape, to strengthen your muscles, to renew your spirit—"

He laughed. "Renew my spirit?" His eyes hardened to icy chips. "You're kidding, right?"

"No." She strode toward him. "To heal the body, you must heal the spirit."

"I don't need healing."

At the core of his pain was self-pity. She knew. She'd been there.

Empathy wrought cynicism. Sympathy increased distance. And pity, well, pity brought about serious, white-hot fury.

But strength respected strength.

It was something she understood—and her potential client might, as well.

So, with a gentle, comforting smile planted on her lips, she crossed to him, reached down, laid her hand over his left knee and squeezed.

Pain racked his face.

"All healed up, are you, mate?" Knowing that was

all the hardness she could manage for the moment, she released him. "I think not."

He glared at her. A muscle pulsed along his jaw. "Get away from me."

Instead of backing away, she turned, heading back to the kitchen. She pulled a fresh ice pack from her bag, popped the cooling gel, then tossed it to him over her shoulder without looking. She heard him catch it and was relieved the fast-food, heavy-on-the-red-meat diet hadn't completely dulled his reflexes.

Forcing cheer into her voice, she dug into her cooler of ingredients. "I'm making grilled rosemary chicken, if that's okay."

He said nothing, and she fell into the familiar, comforting rhythm of cooking.

Thankfully, the stovetop featured a grill on one side, so she didn't have to ask where the gas or charcoal grill was stored. She could handle either, but she'd rather let her client—well, *hopefully*, her client—stew in his anger for a bit. Once she'd fed him, he'd be in a more agreeable mood.

She peeked over her shoulder at him, noting his piercing stare, mixed with pain and barely suppressed rage.

Well, maybe not.

"WHY DO THEY call you Steel?"

Bryan glanced across the table at his would-be therapist and shrugged. "They don't anymore."

"But they used to."

He wasn't sure whether he respected her kindness or her relentless determination more, but both had intrigued him. While his brain and pride kept telling him he wanted meat loaf, or maybe a cheeseburger, he had to acknowledge the grilled chicken and vegetables were tasty, if not completely filling.

Rabbits would probably be thrilled.

Still, hiring someone else was probably the best idea. He needed someone to respect his space and fall in line with his philosophies and way of doing things. He had the feeling that Darcy I've-Got-Tofu wasn't that person.

And, yet, another part of him knew if she left, he'd never see her again.

"I have a hard head," he said finally, shoving aside his questions. "Or so I thought."

His head injury was the reason for his forced retirement.

Ironic.

Ironic, anyway, if you happened to be an overly sensitive, morose poet. Pathetic if you used to be a champion race car driver.

"Your head seems pretty hard to me," she said.

He toasted her with the glass of iced tea. "Same to you."

She nodded. "Determination is a requirement for my job. Like you, I expect."

"But I don't get to do my job anymore."

She looked confused. "But you're the president of the company, aren't you? The leader? You certainly need determination to keep a successful business running."

"I meant my job as a driver."

"I'm sure that couldn't have been easy to give up. But we all move on, don't we? Life changes, so we must, as well. New challenges, new goals, new—"

"I didn't ask for my life to change," he said, glaring at her.

She shrugged, and the brief ripple of hurt that crossed her face echoed in his gut. "Who does?"

This woman had issues. Issues she might even have convinced herself were over. But since he was an expert on pretending the past didn't matter, that he could absorb life's twists and turns without flinching, he didn't think so.

She was bad for him.

Though she had a spine and lovely golden eyes. Though she could cook—if only he could convince her to devote some time to perfecting steak, roasts or meat loaf.

He had to focus on the race season, and she'd be a distraction. Plus, it was long past time for him to take control of this interview, to make her realize she wasn't the top candidate on his list.

Was she a candidate at all? Determination aside, could this cute, delicate blonde really handle herself with him and the life he led?

He rose from the table. "This job is tough," he said, his tone short, knowing he needed to make it so. "The hours are long. The pace is fast and brutal."

She simply nodded.

"It's a traveling circus. And if you're not winning, the rewards are few."

Her gaze flicked up to his and held. "Whether you win or lose, Mr. Garrison, you still have pain."

Not if you run hard and fast enough, he thought, though he recognized she was talking about physical, not emotional, pain. "You're willing to be on the road every weekend? Won't your boyfriend be annoyed about that?"

Her eyes narrowed. "If I had a boyfriend, he certainly wouldn't dictate my schedule, or what my job entailed."

He almost smiled. She certainly didn't lack fierceness.

"My uncle has been a NASCAR official for nearly two decades," she continued. "I'm not here for the rush or the fantasy of glamour. I understand it's not about private jets and cocktail parties with sponsors. I realize there's blood, sweat and tears in every roll cage, engine, tire and spark plug." She lifted her chin. *"I get it."*

"I'm not easy to deal with," he said, knowing he needed to warn her.

"Yeah, well, neither am I at times."

"We're not compatible."

"We don't need to be. We'll be working together. Nothing personal."

She was saying the things he wanted to hear—no drama, no fuss, no connection. Why didn't he believe her?

Admittedly, it wasn't so much her he didn't believe, it was himself.

Except for his sister, he was around men all the time. After his divorce, he needed his life to be that way. But there were moments when the sound of a soft voice or a passing whiff of perfume reminded him of the man he used to be.

Which only pissed him off more.

"I was planning to hire a guy who used to be a sergeant," he said.

She cleared the dishes from the table. "You certainly could use some discipline."

Though he ground his teeth, he took the dishes from her hands. "I'll do this. You cooked." Surprise flickered through her eyes. "I may lack discipline, but I'm fair."

She moved aside so he could rinse the dishes. "I'm sorry if I was abrupt. I was just telling you how I see things. There's no point in pretending now, then confusing you later when you realize I'm a hard-ass."

"You don't look much like a hard-ass."

"My size throws a lot of people off."

His gaze slid from her face down her tiny frame. "I'll bet."

"I have four older brothers who are easily your size. I can hold my own with them. I can certainly handle you."

The word *handle* set off a sensual spark in his brain, but he tamped it down. An attraction to his therapist wasn't a complication he needed. He closed the dishwasher and leaned back against it, crossing his arms over his chest. He wasn't in the same shape he'd been as a driver, but he was fairly certain he could lift her over his head without breaking a sweat. "Can you?"

"Ay—" She flushed. *"Yes."*

"Don't be embarrassed. I like the Irish. It's cute."

"Cute?" Clearly, he'd said the wrong thing. Flames leapt into her eyes. "I'm cute, am I? After a few of my weight training and cardio sessions, I bet you won't think so."

He nearly laughed. "I can handle your sessions. No problem."

"Oh, can ya now? How about a push-up competition? I'll bet you can't do twenty-five." She smirked. "I can."

Could he do *a* push-up?

He hadn't worked out in over four years. "What difference does it make whether *you* can do push-ups or not?" he asked, making sure he sounded as annoyed as he felt. *"I'm* the one in therapy."

"My job requires a certain physical competence. You don't believe I have it." She pointed at the floor. "Let's go. Twenty-five, military style."

Knowing he was trapped by his pride, he reluctantly dropped to his knees, then crawled into position. She watched him with a faint smile on her face, as if she knew he was already in pain, though he'd barely moved.

She mirrored his position, and they began.

After four, his biceps were burning. After six, his arms shook. After nine, he collapsed, panting. He stopped her at fifty.

"I'll let you know about the job," he said when he could talk, still lying on his back on the floor.

Barely winded, she jumped to her feet and held out a hand to help him up. "Could you please do that as soon as possible? I have an interview with Chance Baker this afternoon."

Bryan stiffened. Just what he needed in this mess—a reminder of his family's fiercest rival and the man his ex-wife had shacked up with. "What's wrong with Chance Baker?" he asked, not at all ashamed when his heart beat a little faster over the idea that something *might* be.

"Nothing," she said. "He's interviewing for a chef and personal trainer." She smiled, and she couldn't know how the vision of a hearty and healthy Chance struck him so harshly. "I wonder how many push-ups he can do?"

CHAPTER THREE

HE WOULD PROBABLY HIRE HER simply to spite the Baker family.

Or possibly so he could force her to sign a confidentiality clause, so that the story of the push-up competition didn't get spread around the garage.

As Darcy walked through the driver/owner motor home lot toward her next interview, she had a spring in her step and she was thankful for Parker's tips and information about both Bryan and racing in general. Pretty soon she'd be on the road every week. She could escape her little house of memories and pain in Mooresville.

She *had* to get away. She had to put some distance between herself and her well-meaning family—her kind, but ultimately suffocating, former in-laws.

They all wanted to coddle the grieving widow. They all understood. They all wanted to help.

What they didn't understand was that the way to help her was *not* to coddle her.

And she definitely didn't want people reminding her that it had been two years and she needed to "start getting out again." That she needed to move on with her life. That she needed to open her heart and find someone to love again.

She didn't want to think about Tom at all.

If that was running from her problems, well then it just was. She wanted to work. Her work fulfilled her, kept her moving through her day whether she really wanted to or not. Ultimately, she didn't care who hired her or why, as long as "Steel" or the Bakers did so.

Though she didn't follow racing with the rabid enthusiasm of most fans, living around her uncle and in racing country her whole life, she knew her NASCAR history. The Bakers and the Garrisons had been mortal enemies since 1973, when Joe Baker had bumped Mitch Garrison out of the way in order to win the famed February race at Daytona. Garrison had retired without that coveted trophy, and the rivalry had intensified now that Chance and the youngest Garrison, Cade, were racing against one another.

And Bryan's ex-wife was living with Chance.

From the tales she'd heard about drivers, she figured Bryan was more ticked off that Chance had sideswiped Cade more than once last season than he was about his divorce.

But then it was also possible his wife's abandonment and betrayal had destroyed him, and that her leaving, more than any other event, had turned him into the distant, bitter man Darcy had encountered.

Terrific. Bonding over desertion sounded fun.

As she rounded the corner to the next row, she saw Parker exiting one of the motor homes. "How did everything go?" he asked as he approached, brushing his lips across her cheek. "Do you have a minute to talk?"

She glanced at her watch. "Sure. My interview with Chance isn't for another thirty minutes."

Parker's charismatic smile fell away. "Chance Baker?" When she nodded, he shook his head. "Oh, no. You can't work for The Dark Side."

She laughed. *The Dark Side.* Really. These rivalries were crazy. "Sure I can. My uncle told me Chance was looking for a trainer, so I decided to work in a meeting with him today."

Parker braced his hands on her shoulders. "You need to get away that bad?"

"I need a change."

Nodding, he led her to a bench beside the infield playground. His striking green eyes were focused on her face. "What will it take for you to come to work for us?"

"Are you attempting to bribe me in some way, Parker Huntington?"

He grinned shamelessly. "Yes."

She wasn't exactly sure how she and the CEO of an international hotel chain had bonded, but they had.

He'd flirted shamelessly with her in a bar last spring, and over drinks, they'd become friends instead of potential lovers. She'd also worked for Garrison Racing briefly the year before when one of their crew members had been hurt before a race, which ultimately had given Parker the idea to request her help with Bryan.

Convincing him to start the interview process had apparently taken some time, and, as Parker had been dealing with his own personal life, it was only now that the search for a PT had begun.

"I thought the hiring was your charming brother-in-law's decision," she said.

"Charming? I know sarcasm when I hear it." He shook his head. "I never should have let Bryan handle the interviews on his own."

"He was okay." Gorgeous, angry, compelling, brooding, really broad shoulders—

"You have such a way with words," Parker said, breaking into her runaway thoughts. "*Okay* perfectly encompasses Bryan Garrison."

This was not a path she wanted to explore. She wanted to keep Bryan in her carefully constructed box marked *client*. She was still trying to keep the stitches around her heart intact. She didn't have the strength to take on somebody else's emotional pain.

"So…" She smiled at Parker. "About those bribes. What are you prepared to offer to keep me on your side?"

"I'll think of something. Anything." He leaned back against the bench. "How about Team Nutritional Consultant? We could offer you…"

He named a figure that had her jaw dropping.

"You realize you people take these rivalries too seriously, don't you?" she managed to ask.

"Naturally."

"How about I see the interview through anyway? Just for the sake of professionalism."

"If you really want to." He shrugged. "I don't know what I'm worried about. Nicole will never let him hire you."

"Nicole, Bryan's ex?"

Parker studied her. "Yes. You're too attractive for her to let you hang around."

Though she knew there were family issues and old wounds involved, she couldn't help but lift her eyebrows. "She's *that* insecure, and she's dating one of NASCAR's hottest bachelor drivers?"

"Not the brightest girl."

"She won't hire me because of my face. Bryan won't hire me because of my body." Seeing the slow, speculative smile bloom on Parker's face, she added, "He doesn't think I'm tough enough. He wants to hire some army sergeant. Doesn't anybody care about my *actual* abilities?"

"I do, of course," he said smoothly.

"Uh-huh. Let's talk about something else. How's married life?"

In August, Parker had eloped with Bryan's sister, Rachel. And while some whispered skeptically about how nice it must be to have a multimillionaire sponsor in the family, Darcy knew they were deeply in love.

"Wonderful," he said. "Racing interferes with the romance, but we manage. How are you doing?"

"Fine. Gets easier every day, doesn't it?" Smart man that he was, he obviously didn't believe her, but he said nothing. "I guess your hopes are high for Cade this season."

"He wants that championship so bad he's turning crazy."

"Right. And you're just sitting behind your desk, casually signing checks, not thinking at all about that shiny trophy somebody's going to get in December?"

"So maybe I want it nearly as bad." He clenched his fist. "GRI won it last year, of course, but I want it for Cade. We *need* it."

She turned away from the bordering-on-maniacal passion she'd seen on the faces of so many people around racing over the years and instead watched a pair of boys scramble up the playground's ladder. "People don't always get what they need."

He laid his hand over hers, where it lay on the wooden bench. "They do if they want it badly enough."

Unexpectedly, tears clogged the back of her throat. Grief was like that. It swamped her at inconvenient moments, squeezing her heart when she wanted nothing more than to harden it, to just...*move on already.*

She rose and paced away from him for a moment until she got herself back under control. By the time she turned around, her eyes were dry and her voice steady. "I haven't even gone over to The Dark Side and already I'm morose."

He smiled. "See, the best place for you is with us."

"Hmm, well, maybe you could convince Chance to hire the Sarge, then Bryan could hire me, and everybody would be happy."

STANDING IN THE LIVING AREA of his motor home, Bryan glared at his brother-in-law. "I'm not happy about this."

Parker sighed, leaning back into the sofa cushions. "You're just tense because it's race day."

"Not about that. About the physical therapist."

"Six months ago," Parker began, "you wouldn't even talk about working with somebody. Two months ago, you said to find somebody. A month ago, you changed your mind. Two weeks ago, you told me to set up interviews and hire whoever I thought was most qualified. Then a few days ago, you decide you want to do the interviews yourself. Pardon me if I'm getting a little dizzy."

"I don't want my personal business getting around the garage."

I don't want anybody's pity, Bryan added to himself.

"Darcy will sign a confidentiality clause," Parker said. "She's very professional and certainly not indiscreet."

His brother-in-law's formal speech usually made him smile, but today—for reasons he couldn't quite pinpoint—Bryan was uneasy. "I don't like it."

"So you've said. Is it her particularly?"

Bryan recalled Darcy's elfin face and mulish personality. She was…competent. And he wasn't letting himself think of her beyond that. "It's the whole idea. It's not like I'm ever getting in another race car. Why bother with all the hocus-pocus?"

"Darcy doesn't work magic. She works your body. Hard." Parker leaned forward, bracing his forearms on his thighs. "You've let yourself go, Bryan," he said, almost hesitantly, as if he'd been wanting to say something for a long time and had resisted. "You don't look like the president of a successful racing team. You look worn down, tired, much older than you are."

Bryan slid his hands into the pockets of his jeans. He worked up a glare, but he knew Parker was simply being honest.

"After what you've been through—the pain and disaster, I can understand," Parker continued. "But it's time to pull yourself up. To reclaim your life."

How could Parker sit there, whole and healthy, and preach? "My life will *never* be the same," Bryan said, staring down at Parker.

"No, I suppose it won't," he said calmly. "But you have to try to find a new one. I hate seeing you give up without a fight."

"I'm not—" Bryan looked away. Part of him *had* given up. And the rest of him didn't care.

"I recommend Darcy," Parker said, his tone brisk

now. "But if you won't work with her, I can find you someone else. Though it'll take time."

Did Bryan really want to go through the whole interview process again? It wasn't like this was a big decision. Anybody qualified could work him through a few exercises several days a week. In fact, after he got the routine down, he probably wouldn't need a therapist at all.

Darcy was as good a choice as any, he supposed, as long as she didn't push too much of that rabbit food on him. And as long as she didn't stand so close he could smell her citrusy vanilla perfume.

"Additionally," Parker said, "I'd like to point out that after scaring off all the current potential candidates, you're left with only one option, so I think you should offer her the job before you run her off, too."

Bryan nearly smiled. Winning a negotiation with Parker never got any easier. "The army guy wasn't scared."

"No, he simply chose to take another position."

Before Bryan could question Parker about when that had happened, Cade flung open the door. He strode inside and paced beside the sofa. "How much longer 'til the green flag?"

Bryan glanced at his watch at the same time as Parker did. "Thirty minutes less since the last time you asked," they said together.

"Driver introductions are in an hour," Parker added. "Plenty of time to relax."

Bryan shook his head. Relaxation wasn't in his baby brother's vocabulary.

The drivers' meeting was over. Now was the time for the competitors to be with their families, go over last-minute details with their crew chiefs, get their race-day face on, get pumped up for five hundred grueling, exhilarating miles.

Bryan remembered his routine well. He hadn't liked a lot of noise or people around. Which had greatly annoyed his wife, who liked parties and socializing. He liked to settle down, lie on the couch, go over his strategy slowly in his mind. Sometimes he'd even counted the beats of his own heart.

By contrast, Cade was like a rubber ball bouncing against a cement wall. All nervous energy and intense anticipation. No doubt he'd driven his wife, Isabel, nuts, and she'd kicked him out of his own motor home.

"I thought you were supposed to be entertaining Mom and Dad," Bryan said, at least glad to focus on somebody else's issues instead of his own.

"It's too weird."

"They're fighting again?"

"No. Worse. They're really polite. And they each have dates."

"Dates?"

"Mom is still seeing that florist from my wedding. Dad is seeing a dermatologist. And they're all such good, polite *friends*."

"What's wrong with that?" Bryan asked. Anything was better than Mom crying and throwing bitter looks at the man she'd been married to for over thirty years. He, Cade and Rachel had had a brief moment of peace when their parents had danced at Cade's wedding last May, but since then his parents had lapsed into tense silence whenever they were around each other. Friends sounded terrific.

"Just you wait," Cade said, still pacing like a madman. "You'll have to deal with them during the race. Why do you think I'm so anxious to get in the car?"

"You're always anxious to get in the car," Parker pointed out.

"And I'm not dealing with anybody," Bryan said. "I'm sitting on the pit box beside Sam." He had no doubt that Cade's taciturn crew chief wouldn't question him about moving on with his life or comment about whether or not he looked old and tired. "Parker can handle them."

Parker's eyes widened. *"Me?"*

"Sure," Bryan said. "You're Diplomatic Guy. And part of the family. Convenient for us." He nodded at Cade. "We're not good at that stuff."

Cade stopped pacing abruptly. "I can be diplomatic. Charming, even."

"Used to be. At least with every hot blonde and brunette at the track. But since Isabel's the only woman you look at now, that's gone out the window."

"But people still like me," Cade protested.

Bryan shook his head. Sometimes he wondered about his brother. Fast on the track, but not so much otherwise—at least at the moment. "You really wanna argue this? Diplomatic Guy is the one who has to deal with Mom and Dad."

"Oh, right." He resumed pacing. "You think we can dump this on him?"

"I'm right here, you know," Parker put in, rising to stand next to them.

Bryan and Cade both looked over at him. "You could get Rachel to help," Bryan said, feeling a spasm of guilt for shoving family problems on their sponsor, even though their sponsor *was* family now.

"Probably," Cade added.

Parker squared his shoulders confidently. "Of course I can. As my wife, she's obligated."

"Right." Cade grinned. "I dare you to tell her that."

"I've got twenty on Rachel," Bryan said.

His brother-in-law smiled, and Bryan immediately regretted his bet. Any woman within glancing distance of that crafty, charismatic expression would bow at Parker's feet. Bryan had actually seen it happen. Even normally strong and practical Rachel had been known to sigh, blush and giggle in his presence.

Though it was strange, she didn't seem to mind.

"Oh, she'll help." Parker slid his hands into his pants pockets and rocked back on his heels.

The speculation in his eyes wasn't something Bryan wanted to consider in relation to his sister. How Rachel negotiated favors and paybacks with her husband wasn't any of his business.

"It's perfectly healthy for your parents to date," Parker continued. "What are you two so worried about?"

Bryan met his brother's gaze: Cade nodded. "Have you happened to notice a trend in this family lately?" Bryan asked Parker.

"A romantic trend?" Cade clarified when Parker looked blank.

"You mean, two weddings within three months of each other?" Parker asked. "I don't see what's so terrible about—"

"About falling into the clutches of that sneaky naked baby known as Cupid?" Bryan choked out a laugh. "That's because you're still a newlywed."

"Yeah, and we can't have our parents—" Cade stopped suddenly and narrowed his eyes at Bryan. "Hey, I'm still a newlywed, too. There's nothing wrong with being in love with your wife. Just because your marriage didn't work out is no reason to put down the rest of us."

"Hear, hear," Parker said.

Cade looked thoughtful. "Still, the idea of Mom and Dad…remarried to other people."

"It's weird," Bryan agreed. "We need to put a stop to this wedding trend."

Parker smiled. "Afraid you'll be walking down the aisle next?"

"No way." Bryan scowled. He was through with women—long-term anyway. "Let's stay focused on the topic at hand. You'll deal with Mom and Dad today?"

"Will you hire Darcy?" Parker responded.

I walked right into that one.

Bryan sighed. "Sure. Fine."

It was gonna be a helluva season.

CHAPTER FOUR

SINCE HIS DRIVERS HAD finished fifth, sixth and tenth at Daytona, Bryan arrived at the local airstrip the next week for the flight to California with a reasonably positive outlook.

Which, for him, meant he wasn't openly ticked off.

He ignored the ache in his knee as he climbed the steps to the GRI company jet. After a brief greeting to their longtime pilot, who hovered in the doorway and sipped from a coffee mug, he turned—and nearly bumped into Darcy Butler.

"Good afternoon, Mr. Garrison," she said brightly, even cheerfully.

Her unexpected appearance, happy tone and lovely face immediately sent Bryan's mood south.

Somehow, she immediately sensed his aggravation. She angled her head. "Surely you got Parker's e-mail that I'd be flying west with all of you today?"

He hadn't even turned on his computer today. "No. I've been working in the shop all day."

"Well, I believe we agreed we'd start our training this weekend, so here I am."

As he stared into her amazing eyes, his stomach tightened. "I need a beer."

But as he started toward the cooler, she shoved a plastic cup with a lid and straw toward him. "I made you a protein shake."

"I want a beer."

"But you *need* a protein shake."

She was blocking his path and didn't seem inclined to move. As small as she was, he could have moved her himself, but he *had* hired her. He also felt a moment of embarrassment, since he hadn't taken the time to make sure she had travel arrangements to California. Obviously, Parker had covered for him. Again.

He took the shake and sipped. Bananas and something else tropical he couldn't identify. It didn't even taste that bad, though he would have preferred the beer. "Nice," he said, hoping that would satisfy her and she'd move away and let him be alone.

"It's banana and mango. Parker said you'd probably prefer this one."

His gaze slid to hers, and he felt the attraction for her like the sharp pain he normally attributed to his knee. "And Parker knows everything."

"No, but he's intuitive." Her lips tipped up slightly. "For instance, he knew you'd conveniently forget your therapy this week and need him to make sure I actually came along on the trip to do the job I was hired for."

Bizarrely, Bryan had to suppress the urge to laugh. "He's good at details."

"Yes, he is." She pressed her hand against his, urging the plastic cup toward his mouth. "Drink. You'll feel better."

Though he didn't see how that was possible, he did as she asked.

As his dad—and the dermatologist girlfriend—Cade, Isabel, Parker and Rachel walked on board, Bryan was able to retreat into the background. At least until he talked to Isabel about an upcoming charity event she'd committed the entire family to attending.

"You need a date," she said firmly, crossing her arms over her chest.

"What the hell for?"

She glared at him. "For appearances."

"I can appear just fine on my own."

"I don't think so." She slid her fingers over his stubbled jaw. "You're a little scruffy."

"So?"

After looking away for a moment, her gaze linked with his. "You've been letting yourself go lately."

Again with the personal grooming tips? What was with this family lately?

"I'm busy," he said tersely, but quietly, casting a brief look at Cade and his dad, who were standing a few feet away and laughing about a recent radio show discussion of the Garrison/Baker rivalry. "I have goals and responsibilities to this company. I accomplish those. Aren't we the reigning NASCAR Sprint Cup Series champions? Aren't we the top—"

She held up her hand. "We are. But you don't look like we're on top. You look like…"

"Like what?" he countered when she didn't elaborate.

"Like you've been on a three-day bender."

All the air left his lungs. This was Isabel, his marketing guru, the woman who'd stabilized his playboy brother, who'd been a rock of support to the team, who'd given everybody much needed levity and dry wit when two GRI teams wound up competing against each other for the championship last season.

He bit back his anger and shock. "I had no idea you felt this way."

"Sure you did. You just didn't want to listen. Shave, find a suit, comb your hair and remember you're *supposed* to be in charge."

His blood pressure rising, he pressed his face close to hers. "I can be in charge without a shave or a suit."

"You can," she said, never flinching. "And if that was the only issue, I wouldn't care less what you wore. But I want *you* to care, Bryan. I really think you need to care."

Ignoring the kernel of truth in her words, he clenched his jaw. "I care plenty."

Her eyes blazed with intensity. "Good. Because Cade wants that championship, and I'm going to do everything to make it happen except drive the car myself." She turned away, then glanced back. "And I'd do that if I could."

No pressure there.

Bryan walked to the back of the plane, grabbed a beer bottle from the cooler and slumped into a seat.

So it would be his fault if his baby brother didn't win the championship? Did Isabel not think he wanted success for his team—his *family?* She was entirely too demanding. Sure, she was good at her job. Amazing even. But if she thought for one second that he didn't want, need…*crave* success just as much as all the Garrisons, she'd been staring too long at logo-imprinted highlighters.

Within seconds, Darcy had plopped down next to him. Again, he had the sense that the woman had escaped from some child's fairy-tale book.

"I see you found the beer," she said, somehow throwing just a hint of censure into her tone.

Like he was a kid attempting to eat ice cream before dinner.

"I did," he said, then deliberately took a long drink.

Lately, with his brother and sister paired up with their spouses, he sat alone or with his father during the flights to the tracks. With his dad's date throwing a wrench in that plan today, he was stuck with his therapist.

Not stuck with. It wasn't exactly torture to talk to her or be in her company. But a brief look into her golden eyes made his muscles tighten.

Maybe it was torture.

He was no good for a woman like her—calm and

positive and lovely. His anger would poison her. On the other hand, being a widow, she probably wasn't eager to get involved with anybody, either. She probably kept an emotional distance from—

Stop. Get involved? *Seriously, dude, just stop.*

He wasn't getting involved. He'd hired her to do a job.

At the direction of the captain, they buckled their seat belts for takeoff. In a few moments, they were airborne. No long lines on the runway or jolts, jerks and rattles like on a commercial flight. Everyone's hard work at GRI had afforded them many luxuries.

Hard work he was a vital part of, dammit. What was with Isabel nagging him? Questioning his commitment?

"Did you and Isabel have a fight?"

His beer bottle halfway to his lips, he lowered it at Darcy's question. "No. I—" He glanced at her. "How do you know Isabel?"

"Parker introduced me to her months ago. I've met everyone in your family, except for your dad. Does your knee hurt?"

"No. Well, no more than usual. I should have introduced you to him."

"Yes, you should have, Mr. Garrison. But I can do it myself later."

He drummed his fingers on his thigh, then took another sip of beer. "Didn't we already decide not to call each other Mr. This and Ms. That, since…"

Her eyes twinkled. "Oh, come on, *Bryan,* you can say it—*since we'll be working together.*"

"Are you always this…" He trailed off, unable to articulate just what she was.

"Pushy?"

"I don't think I'd have said that."

"Demanding?"

"Maybe."

"Honest? Efficient? Perceptive? Yes, yes and yes." She smiled. "You'll get used to me."

His gaze, seemingly of its own accord, slid down her. In her leaf-green, terry-cloth warm-up suit, her light blond hair pulled back into a ponytail and her lips painted a glossy pink, he didn't see how he'd ever get used to this fairy creature as part of his daily life.

"When we get to the hotel, we'll do some yoga exercises that should help the stiffness in your knee."

He wanted to ask how she knew his knee would be stiff later, but there was a much more important word in her statement. "Yoga?"

"Absolutely. It's essential to any rehab program."

"How is humming going to help?"

She rolled her eyes. "That's meditation. You could use a healthy dose of that, too. It would help the bags under your eyes."

Bags under his eyes? Honesty was an understatement with this woman.

"Yoga is both a physical and mental discipline of asanas—or postures," she continued. "The controlled breathing manages stress, increases lung efficiency and even calms your central nervous system. The training—along with my diet regime—will give you long, lean muscle tone. You'll gain more flexibility in your hamstrings, back, shoulders and hips. It might even give you a positive frame of mind."

She's trying to kill me.

She patted his arm. "Don't worry. It won't hurt." Then her eyebrows jumped together. "At least not much."

WHEN DARCY STEPPED OFF the jet on the grounds of the L.A. airport, she breathed deeply of the balmy Southern California air. It was terrific and bracing, and she couldn't wait to work Bryan through the yoga routine, which would enable both of them to get rid of the negative energy and confinement of the flight.

She accompanied the rest of the family to the two SUVs that had been rented for the weekend. Being so far out west, the motor homes weren't accompanying them, so they were all staying at Parker's Beverly Hills hotel. In addition to accessibility to the on-site fitness center, he'd thoughtfully rented suites, so she and Bryan would have room for their workouts. Darcy had also consulted with the chef over the phone, so she could start her client's nutrition regime even though she couldn't physically do the cooking.

As the bags were loaded, she introduced herself to

Mitch Garrison, Bryan's father, a two-time NASCAR champion. Even for a casual racing fan, the moment was surreal. He was a man admired and praised by thousands, maybe millions, yet she felt an immediate connection and was drawn to his easy charm.

"So you're going to whip my son back into shape?" he asked.

"He's in good shape, sir," she said, only slightly exaggerating. "I'm going to help him alleviate his pain, so he can work with more efficiency."

"Glad to hear it. What's your plan on making that happen?"

"With cardio, weight training, yoga and diet. Low fat, high protein, whole grains and limited sugar."

Mitch's mouth turned up on one side. "With *my* son?"

"Yes."

"Bryan."

"Of course." Though she realized her ambitions were lofty, she was curious about Mitch's take on Bryan's commitment to getting better. "What—"

"Well, hello, Mitch."

Darcy looked over to see a man about Mitch Garrison's age, with brown-going-on-gray hair and dark brown eyes, standing beside a younger, extremely attractive couple, who looked bored.

"Baker," Mitch said stiffly.

The air thickened, and Darcy sensed the people around her stopping, as if waiting for something and

unsure whether they would be called to action. She'd
heard of the tension between the Bakers and Garrisons, of course, and, in that moment, she also realized
who the young couple was.

Chance Baker and the former Mrs. Bryan Garrison.

She'd never actually met Chance or Nicole in Daytona, since Parker had intervened somehow and
gotten them to hire the army guy, while she went to
work for the Garrisons. Would the animosity between
the families now include her? As silly as that seemed,
Joe Baker was looking oddly at her and Mitch's date.

"Who ya got with you, Mitch?" Joe asked.

Mitch looked as though he'd like to be anywhere
else, talking to anyone else, but he forced a smile.
"My friend, Leanne Tew, and one of our integral GRI
staff, Darcy Butler."

Joe rocked back on his heels. "They're a little
young for you, aren't they?"

Darcy nearly gasped. Instead, sensing another stare,
she looked over her shoulder and directly into Bryan's
eyes. His jaw was clenched; his face had turned to stone.

"Let's go, Dad," Chance said. "What're we hanging around these losers for?"

Nicole, seeming oblivious to the tension in the air,
focused on the man at her side. She never even
glanced in Bryan's direction.

Darcy had the urge to hug him. Or slug his ex-wife.

"We weren't such losers last year," Mitch said, his
tone carefully light. "Were we, Chance?"

Chance's expression turned petulant. "Got lucky is all."

It was like a middle school playground rumble, people circling, taking sides, throwing out cheap shots. And yet the emotions, the conflicts of the past and present, were very adult.

Joe Baker smirked, as if agreeing with his son. "You got better taste in women, too."

In that moment, Darcy really understood the deep animosity between the families. Before now the whole thing had seemed somewhat irrational, probably overblown by media and opposing fans. She'd assumed the Garrisons didn't like losing—to the Bakers or anybody else.

Now, she got it. Now she realized just how personal and thorough the bad blood ran.

In a silly way, she also finally understood the passion and devotion NASCAR fans had for their drivers. Your driver was the one you pulled for no matter how long the odds. He was the one whose T-shirts and caps you plunked down your hard-earned money to buy. He was the one you defended no matter who had dared insult him.

For someone—actually three someones—to be so crass and insensitive to *her* driver was absolutely inexcusable.

"Really, Mr. Baker?" she asked, making sure her voice dripped with fake syrup. "Seems to me you guys got the one the Garrisons threw back."

Then she turned on her heel and marched to the nearby SUV.

After climbing into the backseat, she put on her seat belt and crossed her arms over her chest in defense of her pounding heart. She knew her face had turned red.

What had she said? What had she *done?* She'd been employed by these people for less than a week. She hadn't even officially begun her job. Now she'd probably get fired and have to go back home to her smothering in-laws, overly concerned friends and empty apartment.

She slumped down in her seat as Cade and Isabel got into the front seat, then Bryan sat in the back beside her. She assumed Parker, Rachel, Mitch and Leanne were heading to the hotel in the other SUV. At least she didn't have to have Bryan fire her in front of Parker. With his elegant manners and composed demeanor, Parker was no doubt regretting recommending her. Maybe she'd never have to face Parker again. Maybe she could slink off with her suitcase to a local motel, then fly home tomorrow.

"I can't believe you said that to Joe Baker," Cade said as he started the engine.

Darcy wished she could melt into the floorboard. She didn't dare look at Bryan. "I'm so sor—"

"Stop," Cade jumped in. "Don't ruin the moment." He glanced in the rearview mirror and met her gaze with an amused look in his bright blue eyes. "Nice work."

"Hear, hear," Isabel added. "If only I'd had a camera to capture the shock on that twit Nicole's overly Botoxed face."

Darcy swallowed. "You guys aren't mad?"

"Mad?" Isabel twisted around in her seat. "Hell no. I think this moment calls for champagne."

"Text Parker and see if he can get a bottle chilling to share before dinner," Cade said.

"Great idea. Oh, and some of those chocolate-covered strawberries."

As Isabel's fingers flew over her phone keyboard, Darcy's heart rate slowed from complete panic to mere anxiety. "I…um, well, I have a friend who owns a catering company. She can get Belgian chocolate at cost."

Isabel turned in her seat again. "You can *make* chocolate-covered strawberries?"

"Sure."

"Very cool. Can you teach me?"

"Aye." She pressed her lips together. Why did the Irish always pop out when she was nervous? "Yes. It's easy."

"How about cooking lessons?"

"Anytime." She glanced at Bryan, who faced front, his profile giving away nothing of his mood. His hands were lying calmly along the armrests. "As long as I can manage my training schedule, too."

"You're on." Isabel faced front again. "That Parker, he's a freakin' genius at personnel."

So maybe she wasn't going to be fired. But she'd insulted an extremely powerful man in racing circles. There was no way she wouldn't face consequences for that impulse. "I'm still sorry for what I said to Mr. Baker. I—"

"Please don't show him any respect when he showed none for you," Isabel said, her voice somehow even-toned but hinting annoyance at the same time. "Or any of us."

"But I shouldn't have jumped in. It was impulsive and rude, but he was such a neddy that I—"

Cade's gaze again flicked to the rearview mirror. "Neddy?"

"A fool." Her face heated again. "It's an Irish thing. Basically somebody annoying."

"That's the Bakers," Cade and Isabel said together.

"You did good," Isabel added. "Our eye's on the championship prize, but if we get a few good digs in to people who've made it hard for us along the way, all the better."

Not fired but praised?

Too strange.

She was living inside the NASCAR world, so maybe she should get used to surprises. They were bound to happen at 180 miles an hour.

"You're one of us now," Cade said.

Isabel laid her hand over her husband's. As their fingers entwined on the console, Darcy's heart contracted. She *used* to be part of a team. A pair who had love and stability and hope for the future and happy contentment for the present.

Yet she knew, just as Bryan Garrison knew, that sometimes the ground shifted beneath your feet. Sometimes the future didn't even closely resemble your dreams. Maybe dealing with that realization was part of the reason they were suited to each other.

"Defending your team is part of your job," Isabel said. "It won't be the last time. I'm glad to have you—"

Cade shook their joined hands. "*We're* glad."

Isabel slid her fingers along the back of Cade's hand, then linked their fingers again. "*We're* glad to have you with us."

Though she was glad she wasn't about to be fired, she felt an element of despair when she looked at Cade and Isabel. It lingered like the resentment between the Bakers and the Garrisons. They had what had once belonged to her, and she was ashamed to find herself jealous.

She had no doubt they appreciated the rarity of their relationship. And instead of wishing her circumstances were different, she had to be happy for them. Otherwise, she'd wind up cold and bitter.

Thinking of the man next to her, she turned to see him staring out the window. The scene with his ex-wife left little doubt that his issues weren't entirely wrapped up in the end of his driving career and the pains of his injury. He had unsolved emotional pain.

Like her.

She said nothing during the drive to the hotel. Neither did Bryan. Cade and Isabel talked quietly about sponsor meetings and functions that were going on during the weekend.

As Cade pulled into the front drive at the Huntington, she could see Parker standing beside the other SUV, talking to a group of valets and bellmen along with a man in a dark suit, who was probably the manager. Luggage was being loaded onto brass-rimmed carts. In their red-and-gold uniforms, the hotel personnel looked polished and professional. First class. Parker expected nothing less.

She was still concerned she'd embarrassed him and vowed to speak to him privately at the first opportunity.

When the car stopped, she reached down for her soft-sided cooler, which she'd filled with her usual collection of fresh fruit, nuts, water and organic juice. She was hesitant to suggest a yoga session before dinner. Her client sorely needed the focus, but she—

He turned suddenly and met her gaze. "Joe Baker is an undisputed jerk. But you guys are conveniently leaving out the fact that *she* dumped *me*."

He'd opened the door and stepped out toward the waiting smile of the bellhop before Darcy could begin to think of a response.

CHAPTER FIVE

"You and Bryan are on the same floor," Parker said as they boarded the elevator. "I thought it would make the training sessions simpler to schedule."

Darcy nodded. He always thought of everything. "I'm sure it will. I bet race weekends are hectic."

"They are," Bryan said, looking more annoyed than ever. "Wouldn't it be easier to do the training at the beginning of the week? At home?"

"Sure it would," Rachel said, glaring at her brother. "But you claim to be too busy then, too."

"She's right, Bryan." Parker smiled. "Don't look so concerned. Darcy wouldn't hurt you."

"Can she hurt him a little?" Rachel asked, hopeful. "He's been a complete bear the last few weeks."

"Then a spot of yoga will be just the thing," Darcy said, trying to sound optimistic.

Rachel nudged her husband. "Isn't the Irish adorable?"

"Absolutely," Parker said.

Darcy cast a furtive look at Bryan. She needed to be tough with her client, not adorable. "I doubt you'd think so after one of my training sessions on the treadmill."

Bryan crossed his arms over his chest. "I'm not getting on the treadmill or doing any yoga. I'm starving. Maybe after dinner."

Darcy chose to ignore his protest. "I'm not opposed to a before-yoga snack. I have some apples and organic, no-sugar-added peanut butter in my bag. It'll be just the thing to get your blood sugar level again."

The elevator door dinged, and she stepped through the opening. Bryan remained in the car, his expression set in stubborn lines. Behind him, Parker and Rachel looked positively gleeful. They were no doubt going to indulge in champagne and chocolate-covered strawberries like Cade and Isabel. She'd allow her client a similar indulgence…eventually.

"Come on, mate," she said to Bryan when he still hadn't moved. "I can't wait to get you into Cobra."

The expression on his face was certainly mood-boosting for her. Somewhere between confusion, disbelief and a hint of sensual interest. "Into—what?"

She angled her head. "You'll see."

He stepped out.

"I'll change into my workout gear then meet you at your room in ten minutes." She looked him over from head to toe. "You need to put on something a little less restrictive. Sweats, shorts, pajama pants—any of those will work." Walking down the hall toward her room, she thought of one last thing and turned back. "And no shoes."

The aggravated expression was gone, and she couldn't say she wasn't loving the confusion. "Pajama pants? No shoes? What kind of workout is this?"

"The relaxed kind." She was several steps away when he spoke to her back.

"I don't have pajamas."

Though her steps stuttered, she managed to continue to her room, eyes closed and *not* imagining what he slept in.

None of my business. He's just a client.

Workouts were professional—at least to her. But him being…intrigued by her methods wasn't a bad thing. Anything that could jolt him out of his negative head space was warranted. And, if all else failed, she was pretty sure she'd figured out a way to throw a trump card.

But she wasn't going to fight dirty.

Smiling to herself, she opened her door. At least not yet.

"You hired me to do a job. Are you going to let me do it or not?"

Bryan had reluctantly hired a trainer who acted more like a drill sergeant. In fact, the guy he'd *wanted* to hire had, in fact, *been* a drill sergeant, and he didn't think that guy would be as demanding. "Yeah, sure. Whatever."

Though he was still knocked way off balance by the barefoot woman wearing a fitted black tank top and matching pants who was currently standing in his hotel room.

She set a plate of cut apples, smeared with peanut butter, then her cell phone on the coffee table. "Here's your snack. I've already called room service and ordered your dinner. It'll be here in less than an hour. So we have twenty minutes to—"

"You ordered dinner?"

"Of course. A low-fat, high-protein regimen is essential to—"

"What did you order?"

"Steamed fish, green beans and fresh fruit."

"Are you cra—" He stopped. Evidently, she *was* crazy. And he could always change the order after he got rid of her. "Sounds great," he managed to say.

"No, it doesn't. At least not to you." She held out her hand. "Before you eat your snack, hand me your phone."

"You're taking my phone?"

"I'm turning off the ringer. This won't do you any good if we're interrupted."

In the hopes of getting the whole thing over with as soon as possible, he gave her the phone and forced himself to eat the snack. His evaluation? Organic, no-sugar-added peanut butter sucked. He'd kill for some fries and a cheeseburger. And plenty of salt.

Later, that's just what he'd have.

"Shall we begin?" she asked when he pushed the empty plate aside.

They started off with their legs crossed, while she taught him how to breathe. Since he had nearly thirty-four years of experience at that, he figured he wouldn't have any problems. But, oh no, he'd been breathing wrong all this time. Not deep enough or in the right rhythm or position.

Plus, he usually had his eyes open while breathing. *How backward can you be?*

When he grumbled, she got frustrated, told him his energy was misplaced and he was missing the point.

No kidding.

Cobra turned out to be a position where he had to lie on his stomach, straighten his arms and bend his back in a way it couldn't possibly be meant to bend.

She encouraged, coaxed and eventually pushed his body into so many odd positions, he didn't think he'd ever stand erect again. He didn't see how any of it could help his knee.

"One last cleansing breath," she said—finally. Then, moments later, she commented, "Now, don't you feel better?"

He opened his eyes to see her standing in front of him, a pleased smile on her face. "I don't think I can get up."

"Try."

With minimal pain and only a slight grimace, he managed to uncross his legs, then wobble to his feet.

His muscles twinged in protest as he straightened. Maybe she planned to make every other part of his body ache so his knee would be the least of his problems.

As if satisfied, she nodded. "In a few weeks, you won't be able to sleep without going through that routine."

So much for positive thoughts.

He focused instead on his new yogi—a yoga master, he'd learned—and her compact, subtle curves, shown off by her clinging outfit. Her regimen of torture certainly kept her fit.

Maybe he *had* put on weight since the accident. He hadn't stepped on a scale in years. What was the point? His mass didn't have to be figured into the weight of the race car anymore. So if he wasn't driving and sweating off nearly four pounds every week, if his limited mobility had added a few pounds, who really cared? If his stomach wasn't as solid as it used to be, who saw his body anyway?

He'd been mostly celibate for months, which was mostly lousy, but he didn't want to get involved with anybody. He was busy running a race team and didn't have time for the drama of a relationship.

But if he did have desire to get into better shape, if doing so would alleviate the pain in his knee, were steamed fish and strange body positions the only way to go? Couldn't he box or jog or do push-ups?

Remembering the last time he'd done push-ups, he

struck those off the list. And he couldn't run anymore because his knee wouldn't let him jog more than half a dozen steps without collapsing beneath him.

It was possible his trainer's lifestyle had merit.

"You don't have any problem sticking to this fish and yoga stuff?" he asked her.

She smiled serenely. "Not at all. You won't, either. You'll see. It'll change your life."

"You don't ever crave cheeseburgers or brownies?"

She wrinkled her nose. "Definitely not."

"You don't have any vices? No bad habits at all?"

"Nope." She crossed the room and picked up her cell phone. "Have a nice dinner, Mr.—" She stopped briefly, then corrected herself, "Bryan."

As she headed toward the door, he nearly asked her to stay. Only the prospect of a tasteless dinner kept his lips together. Maybe tomorrow he could eat before she arrived for round two of the torture, then he could stomach the healthy stuff. It would be nice not to eat alone for a change.

"I'll see you in the morning," she said.

He leaned against the door frame. "Okay."

She *was* ridiculously cute. Her warm brown eyes were so clear and direct. Her accent and pert nose adorable. Staring at her across the dinner table wouldn't be a hardship at all.

Those spectacular eyes narrowed briefly. "Are you okay? You look strange."

He was relaxed, he realized. He felt…well, good.

Of course, he wouldn't admit that even under the threat of more yoga torture. "I feel fine."

"Glad to hear it," she said cheerfully, then she turned and walked down the hall toward her room.

He watched her go. Her hips swayed in an inviting way he was sure she wasn't aware of. Or maybe all those months of celibacy were affecting him too strongly around a woman he was attracted to. He hadn't been—

Hold everything. He was *relaxed?* She was cute and adorable?

It would be nice not to eat alone?

He slammed the door and leaned back against it, his heart racing. He *liked* being alone. What had the woman done to him? He was going soft. Falling into that dazy, silly state his brother and sister fell into when exchanging glances with their spouses. No way was he going down that road again.

Surely his condition wasn't anything a bacon cheeseburger couldn't fix.

He dived for the phone.

MITCH GARRISON PUSHED ASIDE the rest of his steak, cooked medium rare, just the way he liked it. He wished he could appreciate his son-in-law's excellent chef, and his garlic/wine/something-or-other sauce, but he wasn't very hungry.

"You okay?" Leanne asked from across the candlelit table. "You're pretty quiet."

He didn't think *I've been thinking about my ex-wife* would be a good way to break the silence. Why had Barb looked so pretty in Daytona? So happy with that idiot florist?

"Just thinking about the weekend," he said finally to Leanne. "Without the normal testing schedule, we only have last year's data to rely on."

She laid her hand over his and squeezed. "You'll figure things out."

Smiling, he pushed Barb out of his mind. Leanne McCrary Tew had a doctorate from a prestigious university. She was a community volunteer and a successful dermatologist. She was divorced, like him, and had raised a son practically on her own since her husband had liked cocktail waitresses more than home life. She was easy to talk to, beautiful and a big race fan. She was thrilled to come to the track, and whenever he talked about tire compounds or air pressure, she not only knew what he was talking about, she wanted to know more.

He was lucky to be with her.

So why didn't he *feel* fortunate anymore? Why did he wonder what it would be like to reminisce? To talk about something that hadn't happened in the last three months?

It wasn't like Barb didn't have a career. Hers was just a nonprofit thing related to motorsports. She was a vital part of the group, and they were always organizing charity fund-raisers that assisted women, children and families who needed medical or financial help. They worked behind the scenes of the sport, and everybody who lived and worked in the business was aware of their quiet, but effective contributions. Their fall fund-raiser was a big-time arena concert with some high-profile entertainers already on board.

Or so he'd heard from Rachel and Isabel. Barb made sure her daughter and new daughter-in-law were also included in the nonprofit's projects.

When he'd been racing, Mitch had always been proud of his wife's accomplishments and support. When had he stopped appreciating her? *Why* had he?

"Mitch?" Leanne asked, raising her eyebrows at his continued silence.

He forced himself to smile. Regrets were for old men, and he had plenty of life in him yet. Maybe he'd even visit the dang florist and order some flowers for Leanne.

AT SIX-THIRTY THE NEXT MORNING, Darcy knocked on Bryan's door.

And knocked. And knocked.

Finally, she heard pounding footsteps. "What the hell are you doing here?" he demanded as he flung open the door.

With all six foot two inches of him standing before her, hair rumpled, wearing nothing but faded, low-slung jeans, she tried to swallow around her dry throat and wound up coughing. She managed to gesture to the room service waiter behind her. "Feeding you."

"At six-freakin'-o'clock in the morning?"

"You have to be at the track in little more than two hours, don't you? You need a healthy breakfast before we go."

He started to close the door. "I can grab a doughnut at the track."

She stepped forward to block the opening and waggled her finger in front of him. "Oh, no. There will be no eating from the doughnut family today. There will also be no cheeseburgers, fries or soda."

A spasm of guilt crossed his face before he settled on disbelief. "How'd you find out?"

"After last night's menu changing, the hotel kitchen has been directed to inform me of everything you order."

He sighed. "Parker."

Unconcerned with his anger and frustration, Darcy studied her fingernails. "You could always transfer out of this palace to the local fleabag motel. Then you could have whatever you want. Since it's race weekend, I'm sure they wouldn't charge you more than three hundred dollars a night."

He said nothing, and she found herself disappointed. His spirit was broken in so many ways.

Summoning every professional instinct she possessed, she hardened her gaze. "So, because you chose not to eat healthy last night, we will start again this morning." She paused significantly. "With oatmeal."

Glaring at her, he shook his head. "No way, sister."

"Come along, Ming," she said to the waiter. She stood against the open door, so the waiter could push his white-linen-covered cart into the room.

Bryan leaned against the wall, his arms crossed over his bare chest. The sharpness in his eyes had turned them pewter-gray and spoke of a restful night, even though his expression was pure, raging thunder.

Truth be told, he was incredibly sexy when he was angry. Maybe it was all that energy and power so tenuously held behind a crumbling dam. Maybe it was simply a chemical thing between the two of them. Regardless, Darcy thanked all the saints for Ming's presence.

"How'd you sleep?" she asked, hoping to diffuse the tension.

"Fine."

"Better than usual?"

"I guess."

Mr. Communicative. Good grief, he tried her patience. "How's your knee?"

"Fine."

"No pain?"

"No."

"Does it usually hurt in the morning?"

She watched him struggle between the truth and his pride. Thankfully, he chose honesty. "Yes."

"I wonder what you've done recently to cause the change?"

Not waiting for the answer, she crossed to Ming and signed his check so that he could get on with his day.

She glanced around the room, which was decorated in steel, wood and neutral colors. The clean-lined furniture, skillful lighting and interesting shapes in art and other accessories fit the progressive California lifestyle. With little effort, she imagined the same furnishings in a 1930s art-deco apartment and had little doubt that Parker had approved of the design personally.

Bryan, by contrast, had probably taken no notice of his surroundings. He was a single-minded man. Her husband, Tom, had been that way about his job, about protecting the lives and property of people in their community.

He wouldn't have given a hang about the room decoration, either.

Startled by the direction of her thoughts, she waited for regret to wash over her. For shame, at comparing her deceased husband to another man, to overwhelm her.

Both did, with aching swiftness. Her heart and stomach clenched. She braced her hand against the table to keep herself upright.

Thankfully, Bryan either didn't notice or didn't care, and the weakness passed quickly. As she shoved her personal issues aside, she pulled a steel-framed chair over to the room service table Ming had set up. "Have a seat," she said to her client.

His arms still crossed over his chest, he shook his head. "No."

"No?"

"No. I'm not a kid. You're here to train, let's train. But I'm not eating mush."

"I'm here to *rehabilitate* you," she felt compelled to point out, and she was getting tired of arguing, defending and persuading him to get with the program. "You're not ready for training."

He leaned toward her, fury suffusing his face. "I'm a professional athlete."

The moment the words were out of his mouth, he leaned back. Realization of just how wrong he was turned his face pale.

He moved away. As oddly embarrassed as she felt having this conversation with a half-dressed man, a man who'd lost everything and had no idea how to get his life back, she sensed opportunity. She needed something from Bryan she hadn't yet received but absolutely had to have.

Commitment.

"Obviously, I'm not an athlete anymore," he began in a slow, measured voice. "But I was for a long time."

Now wasn't the time to mention she'd also ordered scrambled eggs, Canadian bacon and mixed fresh fruit. Frankly, she wasn't a big fan of oatmeal herself. She'd ordered the dish mostly out of spite.

She should probably feel guilty, but with a take-charge man like Bryan Garrison as her client, she needed all the advantages she could get.

"Sit," she said to the stubborn, annoyingly aggravating, attractive…seriously hurting man beside her.

His eyebrows raised with the practiced effort of the blue-blood set. "Excuse me?"

Since she knew he wasn't high society, she decided Parker had been an influence on the Garrison family. Change was inevitable. Good, even.

She tapped the back of the chair. "This will go over better if you sit."

"More yoga torture?" he asked as he walked slowly toward her.

No. Much worse.

When he was seated, she stood facing him. "If we're going to work together, we're going to have to be honest with each other."

"You haven't been honest so far?"

"I have. Maybe honest is the wrong word. Let's call this getting real with ourselves." She paused, considering the lingering ache in her heart. "Well, getting real with you."

He said nothing, just looked wary.

"I know you're angry and embarrassed about your ex-wife leaving you. I know what it's like to have someone you love stripped away. Everything you once had seems like an illusion."

"I'm fine being divorced," he said, his jaw clenched so tightly she wasn't sure how he spoke. "I like being alone. My feelings about it are none of your business."

"They certainly are when they affect my training program. You need a motivation to get better, so I'm giving you one." She met his gaze. "Revenge."

Something flashed through his eyes, and she pounced on the opportunity.

"You know the best way to get your confidence and pride back?" she asked him. "Looking and feeling amazing. Letting her know you've moved on, and you're happy about it."

"My pride is—"

She ignored his protest and rolled on. "Maybe you don't want to subscribe to my theories or do the work required for my program, but you understand revenge, don't you? That's angry and forceful, and you can get behind an idea like that." She paused and leaned close. "Can't you?"

CHAPTER SIX

SHE WAS A FAIRY ONE MINUTE and a bloodthirsty warrior the next.

Part of him was humiliated by the personal details she knew. Another part of him was intrigued by her reaction and impressed by her strategy.

Yes, revenge was an idea he could embrace. And for the first time since his accident, he was energized by a proposition. A goal that had nothing to do with racing.

Nicole had married him because of what he did, what he offered, not who he was. She'd used him ruthlessly, and he still felt as if he'd done something wrong, that he should have been able to hold on to her and his life—even if both were an illusion.

A wife was supposed to support her husband through good and bad, and she hadn't. Marriage wasn't easy. He certainly wasn't easy to deal with most of the time. But she'd left when he'd needed her most.

At some point, he ought to stop blaming himself.

Hell, even his stable parents hadn't been able to hold things together after his accident. For some unknown reason, the end of his career had caused irreparable harm in their relationship. Again, he couldn't control that. Much as he'd like to.

He couldn't alter the past, but he could adjust his present and his future. That was what Darcy was offering—a chance to change. A challenge to accept what was, not wish for what had been. To quit wallowing and start moving forward.

Maybe he'd never drive again, or trust another woman again. But he could be whole. At least in his own way.

He stood and walked toward the sliding-glass doors to the balcony and thought about what Darcy had said. He *did* need a motivation. Something to jolt him from this rut. Workwise, he had drive and focus. He gave everything to GRI. Why couldn't he share that commitment with himself?

And if he could show up his traitorous ex or that jerk Chance Baker, all the better.

"Aye," he said finally, turning to face Darcy. "I understand revenge."

She smiled as he'd hoped she would. "Good." She waggled her finger back and forth. "But we're not drinking beer and singing songs about war and lost love in the pub."

He blinked. "Do what?"

"That's what the Irish do before, after and sometimes during revenge quests."

He recalled that movie from years ago. "Is that where the blue body paint comes in?"

She wrinkled her nose. "That's the Scots. We ought not get started on them. Instead, we'll start on the treadmill." She extended her hand toward the table. "Right after breakfast."

He groaned.

"Change is sometimes painful," she said, grabbing his hand and tugging him into the chair. "But rewarding."

He was sorry when he was seated and no longer touching her. The faint scent of vanilla and something citrusy drifted over him whenever they were close. He wished he could put his finger on just what the smell reminded him of, but the thought was yanked away as she pulled the silver cover off the breakfast plate.

Amazingly, there was more than oatmeal—he'd have to remember his trainer had a sneaky, as well as demanding, streak. There were scrambled eggs, something round that wasn't exactly ham and fruit. As they were in SoCal, this meant exotic stuff like mango, pineapple and something star-shaped that tasted great even if it looked a little weird.

In the gym, she urged him on the scale, where he was embarrassed to discover he'd put on twenty pounds since the last time he'd weighed himself. Though his instinct—besides crawling under a rock—was to run until he fell down, ridiculously hopeful he could run off all those pounds in one morning, Darcy directed him to walk briskly for thirty minutes, then do a short yoga stretch. She assured him weight loss and injury rehab were measured in millimeters, not miles.

By the time he'd shaved, showered and dressed, he felt energized and ready to head to the track.

"Morning," he said, peeking over his newspaper when Cade and Isabel found him and Darcy at the appointed meeting spot in the lobby at seven.

Eyes wide, their hands wrapped tightly around travel coffee mugs, they stared at him.

"Huh?" Isabel asked after a long, silent delay, her forehead wrinkled suspiciously.

"Morning," he repeated.

Isabel looked at Cade. "He spoke to me."

"He even said it…cheerfully." Cade angled his head, staring at Bryan. "Are you okay?"

"Of course I'm okay. What's with you two?"

Cade pointed, his finger trembling. "I think he smiled. Izzy, quick, get the camera."

Bryan grabbed his brother's finger and shoved it away. "Cut it out. I smile."

Simultaneously, Cade and Isabel looked at each other, then shook their heads.

What's with people in this family? His playboy brother could fall like a brick for a hot-tempered half-Italian; his business-minded sister could coo—and he meant that literally—at a blue-blooded hotel chain owner, but he was, well…pleasant, and they all looked as if they were going to faint or call the media.

Bryan ground his teeth and glared at them. "I'm not smiling anymore."

"Come on, guys," Darcy said, stepping between them. "A good night's sleep and a healthy breakfast does wonders." She raised her eyebrows. "Which I can tell neither one of you have had much of in the last twenty-four hours."

While Cade and Isabel huddled over their coffee and mumbled something about champagne and needing a bagel, Bryan felt positively righteous. He was the one always getting the speech about more rest and taking better care of himself.

Oh, how the worm has turned.

After a brief nod at his trainer, he went back to reading his newspaper, and when Dad, Leanne, Parker and Rachel showed up a few minutes later, he gleefully gave them all a big, wide smile.

They, in turn, all looked on the verge of passing out face-first on the floor, so he whistled as he walked out to the valet stand to call for their SUVs.

On the way to the track, he wound up in a car with his dad—who, thankfully, didn't bring up the smiling—and they got down to business, discussing the day ahead. There was practicing, a sponsor hospitality event and qualifying to handle. They went over all the technical aspects of the cars' setups and called all the crew chiefs to confirm a meeting at Cade's hauler before qualifying that afternoon.

Between now and then there were a million things

to do—sign in at the NASCAR hauler, check with the mechanics and engineers to be sure they were ready to go, meet with each driver and verify they were comfortable with the setups, visit with the over-the-wall crew and give them a pep talk.

Though he rarely saw his trainer—except when she showed up to supervise lunch—he thought about her, the revenge mission she'd inspired…and the faint mix of fruit-laden vanilla he couldn't seem to forget.

"HE WAS SMILING," Rachel Garrison Huntington said, tapping a pen against the notebook on the desk in front of her.

Nodding, and trying not to act smug, Darcy sipped her tea and propped her elbow on the red leather sofa's arm. "I saw."

"What my wife is trying to say is *thank you*," Parker said, leaning back into the opposite end of the sofa with his cup of coffee.

They were in the back room of Cade's hauler, which was used as a combination office, meeting room and locker room. Especially at a track where the drivers didn't have their motor homes, they relied on the transporters—which hauled the cars and equipment from race to race every week—as a refuge from the chaos of press, fans and other competitors in the garage area.

With qualifying underway, the teams were occupied, so she'd finally had an opportunity to talk to

Parker and Rachel and apologize for her outburst with Joe Baker the day before. They had no problem with her unprofessional comments, and, thankfully, didn't even see them as unprofessional. Like Cade and Isabel, they seemed to consider her defense of GRI as a test of loyalty she'd passed. They were thrilled to have her on their side.

And, for the first time in a long time, she also felt like part of a team. The firefighters her husband worked with always had family cookouts and camping trips, and they had bonded in the joys and dangers of the profession. She'd never expected to find that comradery again.

"He was *smiling,*" Rachel repeated.

"I admit we were concerned about your ability to deal with Bryan," Parker added, wordily translating Rachel's disbelief. "He can be temperamental at times."

Darcy was all too familiar with Bryan's irritability. His "Steel" nickname was well-earned. "It's understandable. He's been through a lot."

"Sure," Rachel said. "But shouldn't he be over all that stuff by now? It's been four years."

Dousing her own surge of temper, Darcy carefully set her cup back in her saucer—the china was fine and no doubt expensive. "No. In fact, he may never get over *all that stuff.*"

Rachel's face flushed. "Sorry. That was pretty insensitive. I'm just—"

"You're happy and impatient for him to be, too."

Darcy knew Rachel wanted the best for her brother; she was simply unsure how to help him.

It was this kind of conflict that made Darcy think remaining an outsider would be best for her client. She could be loyal to the Garrisons and cheer for them above every other NASCAR team, but it was essential she maintain a bit of distance.

Though she was failing at that goal miserably.

"Losing your wife and your life's ambition in one sweep is pretty traumatic," Parker said quietly.

Rachel's gaze darted to her husband's. "What would you do if I left you?"

"Pine remorsefully the rest of my miserable life."

Rachel grinned. "You bet your ass you would."

As cute as these two were, Darcy had her own agenda to push. "About Bryan…"

"This is why she's good," Parker said, lifting his coffee cup in a toast. "She relentlessly keeps you on task."

"He's making progress," Darcy continued, accepting Parker's compliment with a nod. "But there's a long way to go. I've convinced him to get on board with my program somewhat, but he has no idea what's coming."

Her expression gleeful, Rachel leaned forward. "Can I please, *please* watch when he does realize what he's in for?"

Darcy couldn't think of a single response to that zealous idea.

"Darling, please," Parker managed with a wince.

Rachel shrugged. "Hey, you guys weren't around when big brother was building firecrackers and putting them under my bed in the middle of the night."

Darcy reminded herself they were a family, not just a business. They were supposed to be both, of course, but she'd bet ninety-five percent of their conflicts came from merging those two opposing goals. "Bryan's making progress," she repeated, "but I think he could benefit from some emotional counseling."

Both Rachel and Parker shook their heads. "He won't go," Rachel said. "We've tried for years."

Darcy had anticipated this response, though she'd still felt compelled to make sure Bryan's family understood the scope of his recovery. "Then the best I can offer is physical strength and confidence. For a man like him, that's most of the battle."

Rachel and Parker exchanged a look. "We have full confidence in you," Parker said. "And, frankly, we're not all that concerned about him at the moment," Parker began.

"We know it'll take time with Bryan," Rachel said.

Parker leaned forward. "But we wanted to meet today to find out not only how he was doing, but how *you* were handling everything."

"I'm handling everything just fine," Darcy said automatically. It was a defensive response to the panicked idea that she wasn't fine at all, the reply she gave to everybody who had been concerned about her emotional state over the last year. But Rachel and Parker weren't talking about her grieving process, they were simply being kind. "You really don't need to worry about me. I've handled difficult clients before."

Rachel scowled. "So, he's difficult."

"He's…" Darcy could hardly say he hadn't been difficult, but neither could she deny the encouraging moments. She and Bryan had turned a corner this morning. They'd drawn closer, become a team. That bond was as essential in her business as it was in racing.

And just as precarious.

"I think we've come to an understanding," she said finally, meeting both Parker's and Rachel's gazes in turn, hoping they'd drop the subject and let her handle Bryan on her own terms for the next few weeks. As much as the growing bond between her and her client made her uncomfortable on a personal level, they had to work out their issues one-on-one. Interference by his family would only strengthen Bryan's defensive walls.

"As Rachel pointed out, it will take some time," Parker said, rising. He'd apparently picked up on Darcy's reticence. "In the meantime, there are sponsors to be coddled."

Rachel sent him an amused look. "Does that include you?"

"Naturally."

The door swung open, and a male voice filled the small room. "We need to make sure—" A man with sandy hair sprinkled with gray stopped just over the threshold. "Sorry. We didn't know anybody was in here."

Bryan Garrison walked into the room a moment later.

Though she'd seen him that morning, then at lunchtime, Darcy's breath caught. He'd changed into black pants and a pressed white shirt with the GRI logo stitched over the pocket. He'd shifted from just-one-of-the-guys into big-time-team-owner mode.

Embarrassingly, big-time-hottie mode for her.

She wished she could tell him how he dominated a room. Whether he was a driver, ex-driver, owner... whatever. Even if he pushed a broom, he'd command attention. In a T-shirt and worn jeans, he was danger-ous and sexy. In more polished clothes, he made her head spin.

"Darcy?" Parker asked, stepping in front of her, making her realize he'd probably called her name more than once.

She resisted the urge to lean around him and look at Bryan a little longer. "Hmm?"

Parker laid his hand in the center of her back and urged her toward the sandy-haired man who'd walked in ahead of Bryan. "I wanted to introduce you to Cade's crew chief, Sam Benefield."

"Hi, Sam," Darcy echoed automatically, shaking his hand. "I hear you guys are on track to win a cham-pionship this year."

Sam shook her hand, then scowled at Parker. "What've you been tellin' people? It's race *two* of thirty-six, and you're talking championships? You tryin' to jinx us?"

"Sam's pleased to meet you, as well," Parker said to her. "He's just a bit superstitious."

Sam's already lined brow furrowed deeper. "And with good reason."

"Oh, good grief, Sam," Rachel said, crossing her arms over her chest.

Sam's gaze flew to Parker. "You still have the lucky penny, don't you?"

Parker rolled his eyes, but he reached into his pants pocket, then opened his palm so everybody could see the shiny penny lying in his palm. "It's getting a bit silly, don't you think?"

"No," Sam, Rachel and Bryan said at the same time.

"I've been carrying around this penny since last year," Parker explained to Darcy. "Everybody thinks it's good luck for Cade."

Her gaze slid to each person's in turn. All of them looked resolute except Parker, who seemed embarrassed. "Has Cade done well since then?" she asked.

"Yes, but—"

Darcy quickly grabbed Parker's hand, curling his fingers around the penny. "Then hold it tight. Karma's a serious deal. Don't mess with universal balance."

"Ha!" Sam bobbed his head in a decisive nod. "*Universal balance*, no less. I told ya'll."

"Would it be all right with you guys if Sam and I actually had our meeting now?" Bryan asked, glancing at his watch. "Our schedule's a bit tight." He raised his eyebrows. "Unless you're planning to balance the universe at this moment, of course."

To Darcy's surprise, Parker and Rachel immediately hustled out. She followed more slowly, still intrigued by the concept of the lucky penny, still a bit dazzled by Bryan and his crisp, white shirt.

She turned at the doorway, unable to resist the urge to comment, "You guys are pretty cute."

As she walked out of the hauler, she nodded to crew members she passed and reflected on a memory, one where she smiled as her husband walked out the door in his white uniform shirt.

Unbidden, tears filled her eyes. Guilt and a sharp stab of betrayal followed. She ruthlessly swallowed all the unwanted emotions in one gulp.

Would she ever be able to enjoy being attracted to an interesting, compelling man—even if the desire was for a client and could go nowhere?

Would she ever heal? Was her work with Bryan helping him but hurting her?

All her friends told her things would get better. Hour by hour, then day by day, everybody—friends, family, experts—told her she'd eventually be able to move on.

When? she wanted to scream. When would that happen?

Just as she stepped outside, someone grabbed her

arm. Even before he'd briskly urged her to the tiny area between the GRI hauler and the one next to it, she'd sensed Bryan.

"Cute, huh?" he asked, scowling down at her.

Even as her attraction to him flared to life, the guilt remained. She forced herself to smile. "I had no idea you were so superstitious."

The scowl turned dangerous. "I'm not. Sam is."

"It's not anything to be embarrassed about."

"I'm not embarrassed."

Her smile widened. "Sure you are." She tapped his cheek. "Your face is red."

He stepped back. The flush deepened. "No, it isn't."

"The great Bryan Garrison isn't susceptible to normal human emotions?"

"No."

Though she felt silly, touching him only to have him step back, she nodded. "Oh, right. *Steel.*"

"Look…" He glanced away and shoved his hands into his pants pockets. "I know we're doing all this yoga and deep breathing stuff, and it's working fine. I'm on board. Treadmill walking, Downward Dog and revenge."

"You remembered a pose. I'm so proud."

His gaze, dark gray and seemingly impenetrable, slid to hers. "You're not telling anybody, are you?"

"About walking, posing or vengeance?"

"*Any* of it."

"None of it." She wanted to touch him again,

maybe even hold his hand and hopefully watch some of the anxiety drain from his expression. But having already experienced his retreat, she wasn't about to push herself forward again, even in a friendly, trying-to-forget-her-dead-husband way. "We're bonded like a doctor and patient," she said to assure him of her discretion. "What we do together is private."

The moment the words were out of her mouth, she realized how provocative they sounded. "I mean, personal." *Good grief, that doesn't sound much better.* "Not anybody's business but yours."

"I got what you meant." He cocked his head. "You wanna keep digging?"

She imagined the hole where she was standing— representing the muddy area between client and friend—was already pretty deep and thick. "No, thanks."

"I just don't want you to talk in too much detail about the…unconventional aspects of our training."

She nodded. "You have to protect your tough-guy rep."

"Exactly."

"Your secret is safe with me. You were pretty great this morning, by the way. The glowing smile was a nice touch. It totally threw your family off balance. Unlike your business, there's not a lot of entertaining moments in mine. But that was one for the books."

The satisfaction was plain on Bryan's face. "Did

you see how Isabel couldn't even drink her coffee? The woman *lives* on caffeine."

"Speechless Cade was my personal favorite."

"Even Parker seemed surprised. Believe me, it's hard to throw him for a loop."

"I bet."

"Bryan, let's go!" someone called from the hauler.

"Be right there," Bryan called back, never budging his gaze from Darcy's. "What's for dinner?"

"Tofu surprise," she said as she backed away.

His pleasant expression vanished. "You're not serious."

"Probably not. Maybe you'll be surprised when it *isn't* tofu."

"You're not so bad after all, Darcy Butler."

CHAPTER SEVEN

"I'M GONNA KILL HER."

Staring at the contents of his refrigerator in disbelief, Bryan vowed a new vengeance—on Darcy's head.

He saw skim milk, water bottles, eggs, sliced turkey, low-fat cheese—what was the point of cheese without plenty of fat?—fresh fruit and vegetables, lettuce, tomatoes, alfalfa sprouts and something called hummus. No bacon. No premade hamburger patties. No salami. No beer. No Go! The energy drink was one of Cade's primary sponsors. How could Bryan invite their business executives to his motor home and not offer them their own product?

It was humiliating. It was crazy.

It was unacceptable.

He scoured the cabinets and found the same drastic change. No chips. No boxes of macaroni and cheese or instant, flavored rice. In fact, there was nothing but whole-wheat pasta, almonds and rice cakes.

Rice cakes, for pity's sake.

He paced his motor home, trying to figure out where he'd gone wrong, where he'd failed to explain to Darcy that his rehab wasn't prison. That he needed *real* food, not rabbit nibbles. Plus, with all the freakin' exercise—and the torturous stretching—she had him doing, he'd already lost six pounds. He'd drop the last fourteen in no time. There was no need for drastic measures.

Rice cakes and alfalfa.

No damn way.

They'd cruised along the last several weeks, from California and Las Vegas to Atlanta and Bristol, with all the GRI teams doing well. Arriving in Martinsville, VA, Cade was third in points, Shawn tenth, and the combination of last year's champion Kevin Reiner and their new driver, Lars Heiman, were twelfth.

He and Darcy had found a rhythm to their exercise and meal routine. She dragged him to the treadmill in the morning. She grilled food at lunch, provided snacks during the day, then consulted with the chef at the hotels or made him simple meals at night that met her nutrition requirements. It hadn't all been steamed fish and tasteless vegetables. Either just before or after dinner, they went through the yoga, at which he was improving.

His knee felt better. He slept easier. He was stronger. With this being an East Coast race and his motor home kitchen readily available, he'd been looking forward to finding out just how good a cook Darcy really was.

Parker had been bragging about her fettuccine Bolognese and shrimp with pesto sauce. Isabel went on and on about Darcy's advice and tips, which had given Isabel's Quest for Cooking Perfect Italian an extra kick. Even the office manager at GRI—whose Latino roots ran as deep as the racing tradition of red hot dogs at the Martinsville snack booths—bragged about Darcy's fresh salsa and chicken with yellow rice and black beans.

Where was *his* Bolognese? Where was *his* chicken and rice?

A knock at the door jolted him from his vengeful thoughts. Whoever was unlucky enough to need to see him now wasn't going to go away happy.

It was Darcy.

Dressed in the now-familiar fitted yoga clothes—this time in pale pink—she held a covered platter high in one hand. "I brought—" She stopped, her gaze roving his face. "The rice cakes were a joke. They taste a little like cardboard, don't you think?"

He was so pleased she didn't pretend the fridge and cabinet ambush wasn't traumatic and unwarranted, he nearly smiled.

But stopped himself just in time.

He crossed his arms over his chest. "I have no idea. I've never eaten them and never will."

She shrugged, then scooted past him, setting her platter on the counter before ducking into the fridge. "Some of my clients like them. But I think you'll prefer the hummus and veggies."

"What about the alfalfa sprouts?"

She glanced back at him. "I don't see how you can dip those in hummus."

"I mean, what are they doing in my fridge?"

"I'll add them to salads. They're very good for—"

"No."

She straightened. Her eyes narrowed. "What do you mean *no?*"

"I mean, *no alfalfa sprouts.* No rice cakes. I have a line, and you've crossed it. Get rid of them."

She said nothing. Instead, she pulled a bunch of broccoli and a yellow pepper from the fridge. Setting both on the counter, she began to chop. "Exercise has only a minor role in weight loss."

"Then what the hell am I doing it for?"

As if she hadn't heard him, she continued, "You need to control your caloric intake. You also need to lower your cholesterol."

"You're supposed to be treating my *knee injury,*" he returned just as sharply. "The weight loss thing somehow got added."

"Part of the revenge, right? To get your ex-wife's attention?"

"Well…" He didn't want to get her attention all that much—except for her to briefly notice that she'd made a huge mistake by dumping him. It's not like he wanted her back. He wouldn't ever take her back. All the great times they'd shared had been obliterated by divorce papers arriving a week after she'd moved in with Chance Baker.

"You need to get the extra weight off your knee," Darcy continued matter-of-factly.

Like he was an overweight blob. "Fine. I am. I've already lost six pounds."

"Yay for you."

"I've worked hard for those pounds."

"Some. Mostly, you go through the motions."

"Aren't you supposed to be *encouraging* me?"

She ceased her chopping and glared at him. "I'm trying. Up until today I thought you'd stopped grumbling, arguing and complaining every five minutes. But, oh, apparently not. You'll continue to lose weight and get better if you do as I say. Eat what I tell you to eat, and move when I tell you to move."

Had her eyes always had those pale golden stars in the center? Did they only come out when she was angry? No matter how hard he tried to focus on his fury at having his life disrupted and taken over, he couldn't look away from those stars. "I don't like being told what to do."

"News flash—that's exactly what you hired me for."

What had started as a heated argument had become intense in another way. The tips of his fingers tingled with the need to touch her. He willed the urge away. He wanted to be pain free. He wanted to make what he could of the cards he'd been dealt. And, yes, he wanted to prove to his ex-wife that he'd moved on.

Reminding himself of his goals *should* have calmed him.

Her eyes flashed with challenge. "Do you want to change or not?"

He wanted a great deal out of life. She'd helped him to see how much was really possible, how far he could go. She'd made him wonder about the future. Not just the team's future, but his own.

But, mostly, just then, he wanted to kiss her.

He flung his arm around her waist and pulled her toward him, laying his hand against the side of her face to angle her head. He didn't think or wonder or even breathe, he simply drew her close. He absorbed her energy and fire.

She responded for a moment. He forgot his goals and responsibilities for the same moment.

Then she jerked back out of his reach.

Breathing hard, her eyes wide, she laid the back of her hand over her lips, as if she was shocked or ashamed or both. "What are we—"

She turned away.

He leaned back against the kitchen counter. What had happened to him? She was an *employee*. She wasn't to be handled. Maybe there was some chemical attraction between the two of them. No doubt they were both lonely. But his actions were inexcusable.

So why had he felt better during those few seconds than he had in four years?

Still, he couldn't look at her. "I'm sorry. I—" He scraped his hand through his hair. "Talk about crossing a line."

"We shouldn't be—"

"I know."

"We're supposed to be—"

"Professionals."

"I don't want—"

Now there he couldn't honestly stop her. Because he did want. He wanted *her.*

Very much.

"We need to run," he said abruptly. Exercise released endorphins, right? Any feeling was better than the regretful, but still needy one zipping through him at the moment.

"Run?" Her gaze zoomed to his. "You can't run."

"Sure I can." *I can run away from these feelings. From you and...everything else.* "Let me throw on some shorts." He headed toward his bedroom in the back.

"Get sweats or a jacket," she called. "It's cold out."

The fact that she'd argued so little told him that either she was knocked as off balance as he was, or she was so pissed she simply didn't care if he collapsed at her feet.

When he came out, she was pulling on a hooded sweatshirt. The GRI logo was stitched across the front in bold red letters. Parker's or Cade's generosity, no doubt. Why didn't he ever think about giving her anything? Was their relationship—their *professional* relationship—so all about him that he never thought of her beyond the moments they trained together?

The problem, he decided as they walked silently out of the motor home and into the dark, chilly night, was that he thought way too much about her. Her honesty and genuine caring for others, the shadows behind her bright smile. She was a woman determined to be positive, even when she lived with so much pain.

He understood pain, even if he didn't know how she kept her positive attitude.

"We shouldn't be doing this," she said as they stepped onto the track after walking from the motor home parking lot.

Being Thursday night, the track itself was quiet, the grandstands dark and deserted. There were flood-lights on around the motor homes and parking lots. Night-lights of sorts to all the fans, drivers, owners and media people who would be flooding into the track over the next several days, preparing for the weekend of racing.

Bryan glanced from Turn One, across Start/Finish, then back to Turn Four. There was no one around. "It's fine. Several drivers are dedicated runners, though. I'm surprised they're not out here."

Her gaze connected with his. The gold stars were visible again. Somehow, both haunting and sexy. "That's not what I meant." Then, she pumped her arms and took off in a brisk, but controlled jog, straight toward the first turn.

Other than giving him tips on his pace, warning

him to slow down and walk at certain intervals, she said nothing during the run. He'd been so busy feeling guilty himself, he hadn't realized that she probably had guilt of her own.

According to Parker, Darcy had been devoted to her husband. Had his death, like Bryan's injury, caused a shift in her world that had changed her entire outlook? She seemed like a woman who gave her whole heart to everything and everyone, so he didn't doubt her concern.

We shouldn't be doing this.

She meant him. Them. Whatever craziness had brought them to the point of him grabbing her and kissing her.

Then being unable to forget those amazing moments. Even when he knew he should.

When she called a halt to the run, he followed her lead, walking back to the motor home to cool down. She retrieved bottles of water, then took off her tennis shoes and sat cross-legged on the floor.

Yoga.

He joined her, and in a few moments, in a quiet voice, she began calling out the now-familiar names of poses. He kept his eyes shut. The routine that had been a trial a few weeks ago had somehow become sensuous. If he watched her slim body move through the asanas in his current state, he'd never get his mind off the idea of touching her.

Though he normally felt calmer after yoga, he

opened his eyes to find her watching him. And his heart pounded again.

"Do you mind if I take a shower?" she asked.

"No, I—" He resisted the urge to ask to join her. He needed cold water and lots of it. "I'll get you some clean clothes to change into."

Out of breath—and not just from the exercise— sweaty, his thoughts racing, he sat on his bed and listened to the water run. He fought to dismiss the visual his imagination provided. He closed his eyes, which didn't help.

This whole…whatever between them wasn't viable.

They were working together on a project. The same as his engineers worked on chassis and engines. The same as the marketing team produced logos and promos. The same as the office staff answered the phones, sent faxes and e-mails.

And all those, lofty, professional thoughts went out of his mind the moment she stepped out of the bathroom, wearing his clothes.

THEY SMELLED LIKE HIM. Spicy and enticing.

His clothes should have smelled like laundry detergent. Instead, she imagined Bryan sliding them on after a long day at the office, or collapsing in front of the TV to watch whatever sports event or news happened to be on at the time.

She couldn't dismiss the intimate connection, no matter how many times she reminded herself that she'd loved and married another man. That *he* should be the one she fantasized about. She should be kissing *him.*

Instead, she'd attended her husband's funeral. She'd watched them lower him into the cold, hard ground. She'd watched her dreams and her future die along with him. And for two seemingly endless years she'd walked through life in a daze.

Suddenly, she was wide-awake.

She glanced down the hall and saw Bryan sitting on his bed. She clenched her hands around the exercise clothes she'd taken off and fought the urge to sit beside him, to rub the frown lines from his forehead. "All finished," she said with forced brightness. "I'll start dinner."

He nodded, and she fled toward the kitchen.

She set the oven to preheat, then retrieved an onion from the pantry and began chopping. Unfortunately, it was mindless work she'd done a million times before, so her thoughts were free to roam.

Bryan had been right. Their kiss had crossed a line. She wished she could be angry at him for touching her, but the recollection of his mouth on hers, his heart hammering beneath her palm, was too powerful and amazing to deny. She searched her conscience desperately for shame—at her unprofessional behavior, at not honoring her husband's memory—and, for once, found none.

She hadn't touched a man in anything more than friendship in so long, it was probably natural that she would eventually have those feelings again. Mere weeks ago, she'd been resentful that the *when* of her healing was still in question.

Had it now begun?

There was nothing shameful about sex, thinking about it or doing it. If her face wasn't hot and flushed, of course, that argument might be more effective.

It was silly to feel all goofy and teenagelike. But she did. She felt kind of giddy, like she was in the throes of her first crush. Then again, maybe it was the endorphins.

"Can I help?"

She jumped, not having heard Bryan's approach. He'd dressed in jeans and a white T-shirt, his hair was still damp, and she could smell a hint of the soap from his shower. She'd never been this light-headed because of endorphins. No, this crazy feeling was all him. "You can get the pot out of the fridge and set it on the stove, on low heat."

"I didn't see this earlier," he said as he lifted the pot.

"You mean, when you went into a rage about the lack of Go!"

"Yeah, then." With the pot started, he turned to face her. "We have to have Go! in the fridge. They're a sponsor."

"Have you looked at the sugar content of that stuff? No way."

"We have to have Go! in the fridge. They're a sponsor."

She stopped chopping and looked at him. The man could give a mule lessons in being stubborn.

"I won't drink it," he said.

"Deal."

"What's in the pot?"

"Black beans. I'm making a Cuban specialty."

"Chicken and yellow rice?" At her surprised look, he added, "Carmen's been bragging."

"It's really pretty easy." She retrieved the platter of chicken from the fridge, then slid it in the oven. "It's all in the marinade."

"You actually *like* to cook, don't you?"

"Sure. Who doesn't?" When he shrugged, she guessed, "Your ex."

"She liked going out."

"With a champion race car driver decorating her arm?"

His face tightened in anger. "I guess so."

After wiping her hands on a towel, she started water to boil for the rice. "That's her flaw, not yours, you know."

"But I picked her, didn't I? I fell for her beauty, her fake sincerity."

"Her body," she added lightly.

"That, too." He shook his head ruefully. "You may not believe this, but I used to be a pretty hot commodity on the racing circuit. Among women, I mean."

She swallowed. "I believe it."

"So, I had all these women after me, right? I pick Nicole. Some judge of character I am."

"I can see how a man could be dazzled by her. Look at Chance. All he does is stare at her."

He gazed at Darcy in disbelief. "You did not just compare me to Chance Baker."

"Hey, you guys are the ones who fell for the same woman."

"So we did."

"On the bright side, the accident was kind of a blessing. It showed you who she really was."

"Sorry to disagree, but I'd rather be married to a hot blonde and be racing for a championship."

"Even a disloyal hot blonde?" she asked. Surely she hadn't so badly misjudged his character.

He frowned. "I guess not."

"And you are racing for a championship. You're just not the one driving for it."

"You always manage to put a positive spin on everything—even divorce and career-ending injuries."

"What good does it do to want to change what's already happened?"

"This is why I'm in therapy, and you've moved on with your life. I imagine the death of a spouse is much more traumatic, and here you are, handling things with much better grace."

She thought of the light-headed panic she felt whenever she heard emergency sirens, the stashes of chocolate bars she hid everywhere, how she turned to them when she couldn't find a way to make it through the day. Even though she knew emotional eating was a big no-no, she couldn't stop. She'd lied in a huge way when she'd told Bryan she didn't have any vices.

"I have my troubled moments, too," she said, not willing to admit how crazy she was.

"You still miss him?" he asked after a moment.

The lump in her throat seemed insurmountable, but she managed to nod, then speak around it. "I do."

"I miss her, too, sometimes. Well, not *her* exactly. Just someone being there."

She moved her gaze to his. "Yeah, me, too."

"I like having someone to eat with at night, like we've been doing. I know it's your job to cook, but I like it when you stay and have dinner with me."

If he'd said those words to her yesterday, she wouldn't have thought much about them. Tonight, though, after that kiss, his comments were more personal, intimate even. "I'm flatter—"

"Who else would I complain to about steamed fish and vegetables?"

She swatted him with the towel. "Sometimes, Bryan Garrison, you are not a nice man."

He grinned, and she knew he'd been teasing about dinner. He did like her company. Apparently, he also had a thing for her lips. "Speaking of nice…I'm sorry. About earlier."

"That wasn't nice?"

His eyes lit like blue flames. "It was…" He couldn't seem to find the words. "You work for me."

"I know. You're a client, and I don't kiss clients." Truthfully, she didn't kiss anybody. "But we seem to have this chemistry between us."

His gaze remained locked on hers. "Yes, we do."

"What are we going to do about it?"

"I don't know."

He walked a few feet away, and she wondered if he was as confused, intrigued, nervous, yet excited, as she was. It shouldn't be possible to feel all those emotions at once, but meeting Bryan had brought parts of her back to life that she thought had died with Tom. She couldn't deny she felt something for Bryan that she hadn't felt for anyone in a long, long time.

But he was in pain and lonely; she was in pain and lonely. Could anything come of them turning to each other? Or could it be just that simple?

"Do you want to know what we *should* do, or what I *want* to do?" he asked her finally.

"Want," she whispered.

"I want to kiss you again." He shoved his hands in the back pockets of his jeans. "Actually, I want to do much more than kiss you."

Oh, boy. She pressed her lips together. "Okay, well…"

He was not only a client, he was still hung up on his ex-wife. Was she crazy to risk involvement in his tangled emotions? Had she been alone for so long that any man's desire was a compliment? Or was this whole business a problem she wasn't prepared to deal with?

"These…*wants* will complicate things between us," she said.

"Only if you don't feel the same way."

She could hardly believe they were having this conversation. They were barely getting along a few weeks ago. That kiss had catapulted them into a new arena, though she could hardly deny she'd been attracted to him from the first moment they'd met.

"Darcy?"

She jerked her gaze to his. "I do feel the same way. I just—" She wanted to laugh at herself, and them, for being so serious about a single kiss. "We have to be the two most romantically wary people on the planet. Maybe we're just lonely."

"I wasn't lonely before you showed up."

"But earlier you said you missed having dinner with someone."

"I did. I do—but that only started a few weeks ago. After you showed up and starting feeding me every weekend."

How he could look annoyed about something he enjoyed, she had no idea. But then they'd promised each other honesty. She supposed they were getting it. "I was perfectly content, too, you know."

"Super. What're we going to do about all this?"

The timer on the oven saved her from deciding or replying.

She served the plates of tender, baked chicken over the black beans and yellow rice, adding chopped, raw onions on top. They ate for a while in silence, other than Bryan's compliments about the dinner. Darcy always enjoyed the hearty dish, but she was too distracted tonight to fully appreciate her efforts.

As Bryan rose to clear the plates, she remembered something that had her choking on her water. "You have a massage scheduled tomorrow."

"Massage?"

"It'll help relieve the stiffness in your knee."

"I figured. There's a massage therapist at the track?"

"Sure there is." Her heart rate zipped into overdrive, even as the practical parts of her went into panic mode. "Me."

CHAPTER EIGHT

"ARE YOU SURE you're comfortable with this?"

Bryan, lying on his back, on a portable massage table, wearing nothing but a pair of gym shorts, clenched his hands at his sides. "Oh, sure."

"I don't want this to be awkward."

"It'll be fine."

She didn't move, and though his eyes were shut tight, he could feel her hands hovering over him.

Truthfully, he'd both dreaded and craved this moment since she'd said it was coming the night before. And he wasn't comfortable in any way.

"Okay, so I'm going to, ah…touch you now."

Bracing himself, he clenched his jaw. "Go."

She laid her hand on his thigh; he jolted and sat up.

Eye-to-eye, his hands curled into fists, her hand jerked behind her back, and they stared at each other.

Then her hand cupped his jaw, her other hand slipped around his waist, and her lips were on his.

He pulled her tight against him, realizing he'd accomplished a great feat—he'd kept his hands off her for nearly twenty-four hours. The kiss went on as if they didn't have to be on pit road in less than an hour. As if qualifying wasn't about to take place, or there wasn't the possibility of anybody in his family or on the team walking into his motor home any minute and finding them—

He turned his head. But he didn't let go of her. He panted to get his breath back. "So it was a little awkward having you touch me."

She took a step back; he pulled her close again.

"We have to stop doing this," she said, breathless and looking appalled.

"I don't see why."

"I don't kiss clients."

"Gotta argue with you there, babe."

"Babe?" She worked her way out of his arms and planted her hands on her hips. "Seriously, *babe?* I'm a professional. You don't call me names like that."

He made an effort to control his amusement. Because he suddenly felt really happy. "I apologize for my unprofessional comments." He leaned back on his elbows. "You want to try that massage thing again?"

Her gaze raked him—from head to toe—then her face turned bright red. "I'm— We're not—"

At least her frustration had calmed him. He was through pretending—to her or himself—he didn't want her. Even though he'd been honest with her the night before, he'd wanted to reject those feelings. Today, he was ready to embrace them. Maybe they *were* both just lonely.

But they didn't have to be.

Her working for him made things a bit awkward and unconventional, but it wouldn't be the first time in the small community of racing that a relationship had sprung from professional ties.

Oh, so now you're thinking about a relationship with her, are you?

He ignored his conscience and his gut telling him neither of them were ready for that. "Come on. I won't touch you." Raising his hands to promise innocence, he also forced his expression into seriousness. "I've got to go to qualifying. We need to get on with this."

She glared at him suspiciously. "On with what?"

She was the one who'd grabbed *him*. But pointing that out at the moment didn't seem wise. "The massage." He smiled. "That's it, I promise."

"Put on your shirt."

"But I'm a little tight right…" He slid his fingers across his shoulder. "Oh, about here."

Her eyes widened. "Oh, no way." She shook her head, then visibly drew a deep breath. She paced, glared at him, then stopped in front of him. "Let's do the knee thing."

He'd love to know the thoughts jumping around in her head, the reasons she was moving on with the therapy session, but he wasn't stupid enough to question his bounty.

Obligingly, he grabbed his T-shirt and slipped it on

before lying down. Was his bare chest that distracting? The working out had given him a bit more definition, but he was a long way from what he used to be. He barely had a two-pack in the abs department.

He anticipated his physique changing with Darcy's military-like diet and exercise regimen, but that was a future goal so—

Her fingers probed his thigh, and he sucked in a breath.

Eyes closed, fighting to remember they had to work together to make anything else remotely possible, he let her rub down the muscles in his legs. At some point, his mind went blank and he relaxed. Though a sensual thread certainly lingered, he gave himself over to the clinical aspect of her touch, realizing, for possibly the first time, that Darcy and her program could enable him to walk without a limp, to move easily, to recover some of the man he used to be.

Low music filled the room, and he realized she'd snapped her MP3 player into his stereo system. He'd heard the rhythmic guitar and dancing flutes many times during their yoga sessions. The sounds were familiar and comforting.

How did she always think of details like that?

She knew the right note, the right key, to get to him. And he didn't believe that was all professional instinct. There was an extra bond between them, something that gleamed in her tawny eyes only occasionally, but that was all the more powerful for its brevity.

"Be still for a minute," she said, her voice seeming to float over him. She laid her hand on his shoulder. "Let go of the negative energy. Push it away."

Amazingly, he already had. Maybe even from the moment she'd walked into his life.

Her fingertips drifted across his cheek, and he was fairly certain that wasn't part of her normal routine. "I'm going outside. When you're ready we can—"

He snagged her hand.

She stilled beside him, though he held only her fingertips. He could hear her breathing and only a hint of the background music. So much of him centered on her. Maybe he had from the first. Maybe being drawn to each other wasn't sensible, or the path they should have taken, but he'd somehow committed to that fork in the road.

And he had no intention of turning around.

He opened his eyes and found her staring down at him. Her golden eyes held curiosity and wariness. He wanted to know what else she hid. What other secrets and pleasures might be revealed?

"Will there be more kissing?" He threaded his fingers through hers and added, "Just wondering if I should be prepared to have you grab me again."

She glared at him. "Hey, you grabbed me, too. The grabbing is, in fact, tied—one each."

"Who do you think will be the first one to break the tie?"

"Not me."

"Then I will."

"No."

"Why?" It was a reasonable question, though she looked even more annoyed. He liked that she was flustered. It was cute, and she could hardly find too much fault with his honesty. That was her credo, right?

"Don't smile at me like that," she said with that guarded look still in her eyes. "You're supposed to be bitter and brooding."

"I don't feel like doing that today." In fact, he could almost call what he was doing *flirting*. Very weird. And though he was seriously out of practice, the instinct seemed to come naturally when he was with Darcy.

"You didn't seem to think the kissing was so hot last night," she said.

"Oh, it was hot. I just didn't think it was smart." He'd also been embarrassed by his impulsiveness. These days he thought through his actions very carefully before he made them. "But knowing you have as little self-control as I do has changed my attitude. I'm all for more kissing." Keeping a hold on her hand, he sat up. "Wanna try again?"

"You're a client."

He scooted off the massage table. "Not anymore." He shifted his weight from one leg to the other. "Nice work on the knee, by the way. It feels better."

"You're welcome, but you're changing the subject. I don't go around kissing clients."

"Good." He tucked her arms around his neck. "I'm possessive."

She squirmed, but he held her by her waist. "Bryan, I really need to—"

"Kiss me. Let's try again. On purpose this time."

While he puckered, she searched his gaze. He had no idea what she was looking for and was reluctant to say anything more and screw up his chances.

"Okay," she said quietly a moment later.

Her eyes were still full of anxiety.

It wasn't a promising start.

Before he could question their decision, or she decided to back out, he leaned toward her, cupping her face in his palm. He stroked his thumb across her jaw, then laid his mouth over hers.

His memory hadn't exaggerated the wild, swooping feeling in his stomach, or the taste and smell of vanilla, plus something fruity, spicy, unique to Darcy.

Her lips trembled, and his heart lurched in response. What had started out as teasing had become something else. Serious. Meaningful. It had been a long time since anything in his life but the race team and his family meant something. Concern crawled over him like a rash.

But neither did he want to let go of her.

He wasn't sure why she made him feel this way— good, excited and worried all at the same time. Having her around was simply better than not. He wasn't sure he was capable of deeper thought than that at the moment, even though the admission that he wanted and needed someone else was a fairly revolutionary idea.

When he finally pulled back, she looked as dazed as he felt.

He slid his thumb across her velvety skin. "Yeah. I'm all for more kissing."

"We, um…seem to be pretty good at it."

He smiled. "We certainly do. Why don't—"

A knock at the door prevented him from suggesting that she come with him to qualifying. If she was going to hang around and be part of the team—and he sincerely hoped she was—she might as well learn how everything worked.

Reluctantly, he stepped back and dropped his hands to his sides. "Come in!"

Cade stuck his head around the edge of the door. "You ready?"

"Sure." Bryan glanced at Darcy. "Come with us."

"No, I—" Her face flushed, and she cleared her throat. "I need to start dinner."

"Cade goes out fifth. You'll be back in no time." He gave his brother a meaningful look. "Won't she?"

It might have been a while since they'd worked in tandem to accomplish more than winning races, but Cade apparently got the vibe that Bryan wanted to be with Darcy. Helpfully, he turned on the super charm that had dazzled women all over the country before he'd fallen hard and fast for his wife.

Walking inside, he approached Darcy, sliding his arm around her waist. "You work too much, slaving over a hot stove to feed this guy." He lowered his voice as if sharing a secret. "Which everyone in the family appreciates, by the way. He would live off burgers and fries if it was left up to him."

Darcy sent Bryan a superior look. "Don't I know it."

"You've been such a great influence on him," Cade added.

"Well, I was hired—" Darcy stopped, her gaze jumping to Bryan's. The subject of employee/boss was one she obviously didn't want to go into. "We're making progress, and I'm not slaving. I like cooking."

Cade nodded, but steered her toward the door. "Still, everybody needs a break."

"I did do a lot of the prep work earlier," she said. "But I can watch qualifying from here."

"TV's great, but you're part of the team now. You need to watch the action from our perspective."

The guy was a master. If Bryan had had to convince her to come with them, she'd have refused on principle. Since his brother already had the door open and was in the process of escorting Darcy out, Bryan figured he needed to move fast. "I need to put on some jeans. Will you two try not to bond too solidly against me while I'm gone?"

Darcy turned to Cade. "Has he always had an aversion to fish, or is it just the way I'm preparing it?"

Bryan rushed back to his bedroom as he heard

Cade begin an explanation of family fish fries back when they were kids. With her mind on food, Darcy had probably dismissed the massaging and kissing completely. He'd have to work later to get her thoughts back where he wanted them.

He changed quickly, not wanting Darcy to spend too much time with Cade. He'd rather her not compare his brother's lighthearted charisma and compliments with Bryan's own tendency toward moodiness.

He'd always been the more serious of his siblings. There was a time he'd thought that was simply because he was the oldest, but the accident and his retirement from racing had brought out a cynical edge that seemed natural and yet sometimes scared him with its intensity. He didn't want to be angry, resentful and demanding all the time. He just was.

And he didn't do compliments well. Maybe because his ex had expected them constantly and never seemed to think he appreciated her enough. Or gave her enough jewelry to show his devotion.

Stop thinking about her.

He smoothed his hands over his black T-shirt and considered changing into something more polished, which he did rarely these days. Most owners dressed more formally—button-down shirts and khaki or black slacks. He wore his jeans, T-shirts and stubble-covered jaw like a badge of honor. Silly, in a way.

He met Darcy and Cade outside the motor home, and she walked between them toward the garage, head high, the awkwardness over their kiss apparently forgotten.

Bryan decided they could overcome her unease with a little more practice. And he was more than willing to go through that particular routine, over and over, even though it was already just right.

DARCY WALKED TO PIT ROAD with Bryan and Cade, moving through groups of other teams, media and a few fans. Despite the rather intimate job she had with Bryan, she hadn't seen much of the public side of the Garrisons. She only knew that when Bryan left the motor home he was headed into a very visible and competitive arena.

As she prepped Friday night's dinner, she always watched qualifying on TV. Now, as she looked around, gazed into the grandstands and at the cars being pushed through inspection or toward pit road, she realized she was part of the show. She felt a rush of pride and adrenaline. She was a cast member in this traveling circus. Maybe not as vital as a driver, crew chief or spotter, but still part of something larger and greater than she had on her own.

Watching the behind-the-scenes process of putting on a spectacle as large as a NASCAR Sprint Cup Series event was surreal and amazing.

For one thing, people swarmed Cade like bees on a honey hive. Reporters stopped him for quotes or on-camera interviews. Fans, though there were significantly less of them on qualifying day than race day, hopped around with hats, die-cast cars and programs to sign. Other drivers nearby received the same treatment.

The members of other teams they passed and greeted were serious, but there was an element of good-natured anticipation in the air. Uniformed officials walked or stood nearby, supervising every aspect of the event. Bryan told her that around seventy-five officials traveled to all the races and supervised the proceedings, As opposed to sports like football and baseball, where only two teams competed per venue per event, NASCAR racing hosted at least forty-three teams, thirty-six weeks a year. It made for a massive undertaking in staffing.

And that was just the stats for the officials—which she was at least somewhat familiar with, seeing as her uncle had been part of the show for many years. Everywhere, there were both uniformed and non-uniformed members of individual teams. She saw and met people like the guy who changed the tires during pit stops, the engineer who helped with race strategy and technical issues with the engines, and the public relations reps who represented various sponsors and drivers.

She probably looked like a wide-eyed child, staring and gawking, pestering Cade and Bryan for more information and explanations. They knew all the answers, though, and she realized this brand-new world to her was second nature to them.

They approached the garage stall assigned to

Cade's No. 56 red-and-white car with the Huntington Hotels logo plastered on the hood along with various other sponsors—one of them being Go!, Darcy noted—filling up the sides and back.

Having been through inspection already, the team was apparently getting ready to roll the car out to the track, so Cade could take his qualifying laps. Here, she finally found some familiar people, since she'd been helping the GRI hauler drivers—who, oddly enough, also served as team chefs—make breakfast and lunch for the team members over the last few weeks.

"Hey, Darcy." Allen, the team safety coordinator, grinned at her. "The boss man's lookin' pretty good. You need to put Rex on your diet now."

Rex, the jack man, who was six feet four inches of solid, bulky muscle, shook his head. "You wish you had this body, man."

"Lean and mean is the way to be," Allen said. "Right, Darcy?"

She glanced from Allen to Rex, who looked as though he could body slam her with his pinkie. "Rex looks fine to me."

Before Allen could reply, one of the other guys caught the eye of a trio of young, attractive women as they walked by.

The guys around the garage worked with noise, confusion, fans and media wandering in and around their pit box "offices" without pausing. They paused for exactly two things—attractive females and military flyovers. Otherwise, you couldn't budge their attention with a crowbar.

The trio of women flipped their hair, giggled and waved.

"Rex, I believe those young ladies are trying to get your attention," Darcy said with mock surprise.

Rex snorted. "Right." He elbowed Cade, who was standing beside him. "Your fan club's here."

Cade, whose girl-watching days were behind him, nonetheless sent his team a smug smile. "It's a tough job." Then, to the ladies' great surprise and delight, he walked over to them.

After signing autographs, he brought them back with him, introducing them to the guys.

Darcy smiled over his generosity. The guys worked from sunup until way past sundown and were entitled to a break. Talking to a group of pretty women probably ranked high. And though Bryan stepped away from the flirting and did little more than nod politely, he was a big distraction anyway. The fans watched him out of the corners of their eyes with a mixture of awe, curiosity and thinly disguised desire.

And, oh, could Darcy ever relate to those feelings.

She worked with him on a daily basis, practically lived with him on the weekends and was now involved with him on a personal level, and she still had trouble believing he was standing beside her.

But then was she *involved* with Bryan Garrison?

Was she his trainer, personal chef, masseuse and… kissing partner?

She waved away her concern. Defining the scope of their attraction seemed impossible. She was going with the moment, since that seemed the only decision she was capable of making. She was grateful she wasn't completely numb after all.

"At least we can be glad Isabel's not here," Bryan said in a low voice next to her ear. "She gets impatient with the female fans."

Watching the women fawn over Cade, Darcy could see why.

"She's very possessive," Bryan added.

Darcy turned her head and found him extremely close. Her heart picked up speed in response. He'd said the same thing to her earlier when she'd commented that she didn't kiss clients. So they were *exclusive* kissing partners?

And what about his revenge mission? His desire to prove to his ex-wife that she'd made a mistake by leaving him? What if she started to care too much about a man who might never completely get over the end of his marriage? Or was it worse to wonder if she might never get over her own past to care that much for anyone?

With effort, Darcy focused on their conversation instead of on her confusing feelings. "Isn't being fanfriendly part of his job?"

He shrugged. "Sponsors like popular drivers, and

we can't race without sponsors, so I guess so. Cade is certainly better at it than I ever was."

"I have a hard time picturing you in a driving suit, multicolored logos and patches all over your chest, smiling for the cameras."

"I didn't do a lot of smiling, even back then."

"That's a shame."

He angled his head. "Why?"

"Because you have a really nice smile."

Good grief, she was *flirting* with the man. At the acknowledgment of her actions, a flutter of panic settled in her stomach.

His tone deepened. "And my lips? How do you feel about those?"

She laid her palm over her stomach, hoping to stem her anxiety, and studied Bryan's lips. They looked pretty appealing.

He groaned. "Okay, stop," he said, leaning back. "I should know better than to talk to you in public."

"Why?"

"You're too distracting." He turned to the team. "If you guys are waiting for Darcy to push the car onto the grid, I can assure you that isn't going to happen."

Steel was back. Tough, uncompromising and in charge.

The abrupt change in his personality wasn't as disconcerting as it once was. Maybe because she felt she got to see a side of him that few people were privy to.

The fans moved away reluctantly, and the team got back to work. They pushed the car around equipment carts, stacks of tires and groups of people. As they neared pit road, she saw her uncle standing in one of the pit boxes, having what seemed to be a serious conversation with some other man. She simply waved and kept moving beside Cade and Bryan.

When they *moved* past the opening in the pit wall, she noticed something that had her heart jumping to her throat.

A firefighter was pulling a flame retardant jumpsuit over his uniform.

Much like she'd felt earlier in Bryan's arms, her knees went weak. The feeling wasn't at all welcome this time, though. She was dazed, sick and embarrassed.

Was this the payback for her desire?

In a haze, she felt Bryan grab her elbow. "Darcy?"

"I—" She'd started to say *I'm fine,* but she wasn't. Not at all.

To her further embarrassment, she sensed Cade stopping along with Bryan and looking at her with concern. "I—I was just dizzy for a second." With every ounce of strength she possessed, she forced herself to smile and start walking again. "I think my blood sugar's a little low."

Though Cade seemed relieved, annoyance flickered across Bryan's face. "You spend most of your waking hours making sure I'm fed and cared for, have you tried your own program?"

The friendly jab only made her feel worse. He cared, and she was pleased he cared.

And Tom was dead.

Reaching into the back pocket of his jeans, Bryan pulled out a twenty-dollar bill, which he pressed into the hand of the GRI team member nearest him. "Go get Darcy a soda."

"I don't want—"

"Don't you dare argue with me," Bryan said, rolling over her protest. "Or tell me the caloric, sugar or caffeine content of the soda."

"That's our Bryan," Cade said. "Strong and silent."

Darcy was grateful for Cade's well-placed humor. "He usually is."

Still supporting her arm, Bryan shot his brother a glare. "Why doesn't she get the speech about taking better care of herself?"

Cade patted Bryan's shoulder. "You know what, bro? I think you've got that covered."

The awkward moment faded, and a couple of team members ragged Darcy about eating too much salad, then they got in line behind the other competitors as if nothing odd had ever happened.

When a TV crew hustled over to interview Cade, Darcy stepped carefully out of the camera shot and recovered her composure.

Moments later, one of the crew handed her the soda she didn't want, but she sipped it anyway, barely wincing at the overly sweet taste. She wanted no questions asked about her panic attack—because that's exactly what it had been—or its true cause.

After Cade, the reporter asked Bryan a few, brief questions. *Brief* being the operative word. True to his earlier confession, he didn't smile and kept his answers professional and concise.

Clearly, she'd been right. The people who saw his charming side were extremely limited. She wondered if that made her special, and not simply convenient.

But the hope and promise of that idea was crushed by the lingering uneasiness churning inside her, the doubts that reminded her she might never be whole and free from the past again.

CHAPTER NINE

WHEN THEY REACHED Texas the next weekend, Darcy paced the motor home while she waited for Bryan to get out of a meeting.

After watching all the action from the pit box at Martinsville, she couldn't wait to do it all over again. The rumble of engines, the roar of the crowd, the heat from the track, and the breath-holding awe of speed had turned her into a fan seemingly overnight.

Racing, it seemed, was one of those events you just had to experience live before gaining a full appreciation of the sport. The fact that she knew and liked Cade and the other drivers and team members made everything even more special.

As for her and her kissing partner…

At home this week there'd been training sessions, massage therapy, and one dinner and a movie. Just as she had since the beginning of the season, she dropped his meals off at his house during the day and let him police himself in the cardio training and yoga except on Tuesday when they worked together for two hours. That night he'd invited her to stay for dinner, after which they watched a DVD.

But there were no actual *dates,* where he asked her out, picked her up, took her somewhere, then brought her home and kissed her good-night at the door.

There were kisses—some pretty hot ones in fact—but nothing beyond that.

Since her emotions ranged from giddy excitement to nearly overwhelming guilt, she knew that little physical contact was all she was capable of handling.

And while there were times he looked at her with a hungry gleam in his eyes, he always doused it quickly. So either his self-control was impressive, or he, too, had demons from the past he'd yet to conquer.

She knew only that at some point, they'd have to have one of their getting-real-with-each-other sessions and figure out what, exactly, they were doing together.

In the meantime, she was pretending she was fine.

"There you are," she said when the door swung open a few moments later and Bryan appeared in the opening. "Finally." She handed him a plate of almonds, grapes and cheese. "Here's your snack. Eat it, then let's go."

Bryan glanced from her to the plate. "Should I chew or swallow it all whole?"

"Of course you can chew. But do it quickly." She flung her hand toward the TV screen on the wall. "Qualifying started twenty minutes ago."

Looking amused by her impatience, Bryan walked over to the sofa, then sank down and took his time choosing the grape he wanted, which he popped into his mouth. "Cade, Shawn and Kevin all qualify near the end of the session," he said after he swallowed. "We have plenty of time."

"We're not watching the whole thing?" she asked, unable to hide her disappointment.

"The only reason we stayed for it all last week was because I couldn't drag you away. I'm beginning to think we've turned you into a race fan, Darcy Butler."

"Well…yeah." And she'd been doing her home-work on the upcoming races, so she knew that here at the big, wide, high-banked Texas track, the speeds would be some of the fastest of the year. She'd really been looking forward to watching all the action.

Bryan patted the space on the sofa beside him. "Come convince me why I should go out there and get ambushed by more reporters."

She settled beside him, tucking her legs beneath her. "Ambushed because of Lars?"

Bryan sighed. "The punk idiot kid. I've been in sponsor damage control meetings all day."

Lars, who'd been given a chance to prove his readiness for NASCAR's big leagues by sharing the No. 53 car with GRI's champion driver Kevin Reiner, had told a reporter after the race last Sunday that he had a chance to make the Chase for the NASCAR Sprint Cup. Since the championship standings were based on driver points, neither he nor Kevin would be able to make the Chase as things stood now. Lars had called for the Garrisons to take Kevin out and keep him in permanently.

He had all this confidence/arrogance after completing all of three races, mind you.

On the flight home last week, Bryan had paced, Cade had raged and Parker fumed. There was talk of immediately pulling Lars from the car. There was talk of meetings with sponsors, the team, the other drivers. There was talk of tar and feathers.

The *punk idiot kid* for all his smart mouth and premature bragging apparently had some brains, though. First, he'd caught a flight home with another driver, then he'd realized quickly that the press and fans were appalled by his self-importance and he'd appeared in Bryan's office first thing Monday morning with a ready apology.

Still, the public damage had been done. Was there trouble at GRI? Were the drivers not getting along? Were they really going to boot a beloved veteran like Kevin out of his seat for a younger guy?

"Qualifying will take your mind off your troubles," she said in her efforts to convince Bryan they should go. "And we'll sneak out to the pits. We can get beside the hauler, then—"

"Darcy?" He captured her hand and threaded his fingers through hers. "You don't have to talk to convince me."

"Oh." With a slight smile and a happy sigh, she leaned into him, angling her face for his kiss.

Offering him comfort after the stressful day he'd had was lovely. It was this kind of bond, this kind of closeness that had given her the strength to beat back the guilt time after time.

He needed her.

It had been a long time since somebody had needed her for something besides her job. Professionally, she took care of her clients, but personally, everybody wanted to comfort her, believing her emotions weren't as strong as she'd made her body.

Which they weren't, but nobody had to know that besides her. As long as she kept moving forward, the past would have no choice but to stay behind her.

She rested her palm against Bryan's chest, feeling his heart thrum rhythmically. As his mouth glided over hers, his hand slid behind her back, pulling her closer. The spicy, woodsy scent from his cologne teased her senses, and she closed her eyes, inhaling deep.

He moved his lips down the side of her neck. "I'm starting to feel better."

"I'm so—"

A brief knock on the door preceded the sound of Isabel's voice. "Hey, is Darcy—" She ground to a halt when she saw Darcy and Bryan practically sitting in each other's laps on the sofa. "Oh, boy. I'll just come back later."

"No." Darcy leapt up. "We were—" She couldn't

quite get a lie to her tongue fast enough. And would the razor-sharp Isabel really believe any lame thing she could think of anyway?

"Did you need Darcy for something?" Bryan asked calmly. He hadn't moved.

"We were supposed to meet later for a cooking lesson. I just wanted to make sure we were still on." Isabel's gaze flicked between them. "But if you've got other plans…"

"We don't," he said.

"Whatever Isabel and I make, we'll make enough for you, too," Darcy said quickly, since she could see the growing temper on Bryan's face. Being in charge of a powerful company, he wasn't used to explaining his actions to very many people. And he'd complained to her often about what he saw as his family's interference in his life.

"We were going to watch some of the qualifying," Darcy added into the silence. "I could head over to your place after that."

"Okay, then. I'll see you over there. About an hour?"

Darcy nodded, and Isabel turned and left.

She looked back at Bryan. "Don't you think we should explain to your family about what's going on? About…us?"

"No. They're nosy enough as it is."

"But—"

"It's none of their business."

Darcy said nothing, and since she had no idea what

us entailed anyway, she wasn't sure what she'd say to anybody, either. Including Bryan himself.

Still, the harshness of his response hurt and surprised her.

Looking annoyed, he stood. "Do you want to go to qualifying or not?"

She noticed he'd barely eaten his snack, and his eyes had lost the smoky quality she saw so often when he looked at her these days. The blue had turned cold. "Not if you don't want to."

He returned to his spot on the sofa and turned up the volume on the TV with the remote. "Then I'd rather stay here."

His face was dark, his expression closed. Brooding Bryan was back. Had Isabel's interruption brought this on, or was it the disaster with Lars?

Or was it her? Had the friendly flirting and kissing grown too frustrating?

The happy anticipation that had infused her earlier drained from her body as if she'd sprung a thousand leaks. "I'm going to catch up with Isabel and see if she can get started with her lesson right away."

He turned his head, surprise evident in his eyes. "You don't want to stay here with me?"

"No." She shook her head and backed toward the door, knowing she was trying to escape her own thoughts, as well as him. "No, I don't think I do."

She rushed out with a lump in her throat, which she forced herself to swallow. She caught up to Isabel just as she was opening the door to her and Cade's motor home. "I've got a few minutes now? You want to get started early?"

Isabel held open the door. "Sure."

"You might miss Cade's qualifying," Darcy said as she walked inside.

Isabel shrugged, though her gaze was sharp and probing. "Those flirty fans annoy me anyway."

Isabel probably knew the Garrisons better than just about anybody. Maybe she could give Darcy some insight into her confusing emotions, without getting too personal. It seemed important to remember Darcy was an employee. Not family.

And Bryan had said what went on between them was none of his family's business.

"So what are we making?" she asked Isabel.

"Scones."

Darcy's eyes widened. "Seriously?"

Isabel rolled her eyes. "Cade goes on and on about his mother's buttermilk biscuits, which I've tried, but never can get to work for me. It's entirely possible I'm pounding the dough too hard." She seemed to dismiss the idea with a wave of her hand. "So, I'm raising the stakes. Blueberry scones for breakfast."

"No problem. Scones originated with the Scots, but we Irish haven't fared so badly with our interpretations."

Isabel showed Darcy the recipe, and she saw Isabel

had gathered all the necessary ingredients and laid them out on the counter.

Darcy set the mixing bowl in front of her student. "The most important thing to remember is that *cooking* is about tasting and adjusting flavors to suit you, but *baking* is science. No adding, no messing with the formula, or you'll get a big gloppy mess."

Isabel nodded. "Did that already."

Together, they mixed the dough, kneaded and rolled it out, cutting it into small triangles before sliding it in the oven for baking.

"You want to tell me about that little scene I walked in on?" Isabel asked as they drank coffee at the kitchen table and waited for their creations to cook.

Darcy had known the moment she walked in the door that she'd never get away without the subject of her and Bryan coming up. She'd come inside anyway. But now she didn't know how to begin. "I'm not sure I should," she said finally. "Bryan doesn't want to talk to anybody about it."

"Uh-huh." Isabel sipped her coffee. "And what do you want?"

She *had* to talk to somebody about it. She was nearly bursting with excitement, confusion and anxiety. "We've started kissing," she said abruptly.

"And?" Isabel asked when Darcy didn't elaborate.

"That's pretty much it. Well, other than having dinner together and the training sessions."

"So you're dating."

"I don't know if I'd call it dating…exactly."

"So you're making out, but not going out?"

"I guess so."

"That's all right with you?"

Darcy sighed. "It's pretty wonderful actually."

Isabel stared at her in silence for a full ten seconds. "My brother-in-law, Bryan Mitchell Garrison—tall guy, scowls a lot, orders people around—*he* put that dreamy look on your face?"

"He did." Darcy sobered, thinking of the way he'd retreated earlier, the way she panicked when she thought too much about what they were doing. "But he can be so frustrating."

"Now, *that's* the guy we all know and love."

Darcy nodded. "We have a lot of issues."

"Together or separately?"

"Both, I guess. But we haven't known each other long enough to have too many problems with whatever our relationship is at the moment. The past is a bigger thing—my husband's death, his ex-wife."

"You've both been through a lot."

"I think we're both pretty damaged by it all."

"Doesn't mean you can't heal. He smiles more," she added. "Since he met you, I mean."

"He'd never admit it, but the diet and exercise have helped."

"He looks better. And while the smiling is a little weird, we're all really grateful you were able to get through to him. Nobody else seemed to reach him."

"I can be tough when I need to be."

"He respects that." Isabel leaned back into the booth. "In fact, I bet you've rocked his gloomy little world."

Darcy felt her face heat. "There are times I think we could really make something of this."

The timer for the oven sounded, and Isabel rose to take out the scones. The inviting scent of baking bread and sweet blueberries filled the motor home. "If all else fails, bake these scones. Wow, that smells amazing."

"I'll take him some."

As Isabel scooped a few onto a large piece of aluminum foil, she commented, "There are times you still miss your husband, I'm sure."

Oh, yes, Isabel was sharp.

"I do." But the warmth of the coffee, and the friendship she'd formed with Isabel made the admission almost comfortable. "I feel guilty a lot. Being with Bryan seems like a betrayal."

"You don't think your husband would want you to move on with your life?"

"Sure he would. But I just…can't. I can't let go of what I had before, with Tom. Maybe I won't ever," she added in a whisper. "Can I really drag Bryan into all that drama?"

"He doesn't look like a reluctant man when he's with you. And he has drama—or at least trauma—of his own."

Darcy nodded. "His failed marriage. There's a lot for him to deal with still." She didn't mention the revenge pact, since she'd promised Bryan she wouldn't talk about their routine with anybody. But his desire to prove he'd moved on seemed to give his ex a continued significance in his life. "What if he can't forget her?"

"I don't think he will. Just like you won't forget your husband. That doesn't mean he wants to be with her. And it doesn't mean you can't be together." Isabel's gaze cut to hers as she handed Darcy a hot, buttered scone. "Why don't you lean on each other and see what happens?"

Could things be that simple?

"And, for pity's sake," Isabel continued, "he should certainly be able to come up with an actual date."

AT THE KNOCK on the door, Bryan called out, "It's open."

Darcy walked inside, holding a foil-wrapped package, and the breath he'd been holding for nearly two hours finally escaped. She barely glanced at him, however.

He flipped off the TV. Cade had qualified third; the other GRI teams sixth and fifteenth.

He couldn't care less.

Carefully, he set the remote on the side table. "I wasn't sure you were coming back."

"Me, either."

Still not looking directly at him, she set the package on the counter, then opened the fridge and began pulling out salad ingredients.

"I thought you were making dinner at Isabel's."

"She wanted to make scones. I brought you some to have for breakfast."

"No cheese omelets?"

She didn't smile as he'd hoped. She reached into the fridge again and pulled out the bottle of white wine she'd used to make a marinade the night before. After pouring two glasses, she handed him one. "I think we could both use a break from the protein shake regimen tonight."

She turned away and started chopping. He held his glass, staring at her back. Why did he have to be such a jerk? Wasn't it time he admitted when he was?

He set his glass aside and stood. Sliding his arms around her waist, he pulled her back against him and pressed his lips to the top of her head. "I'm sorry about earlier. Constantly surrounded by well-meaning family and this whole mess with Lars has got me crazy."

"Plus a healthy dose of sexual frustration?"

His hands tightened at her hips.

She turned her head, glancing back at him. Those golden eyes that somehow saw everything, good and bad, regarded him silently for a long moment.

Getting real.

"Just when things get interesting between us," she said finally, "I pull back."

"Or Isabel barges in."

"It's not enough for you, is it?"

He brushed her hair off her face. "I won't deny I want more, but, hey, I'm a guy." The corners of his mouth turned up. "I'm willing to wait until you're ready."

"What is this? What are we doing together?"

"I have no idea, but I don't want it to stop."

Unsure of her frame of mind, he eased forward slowly, brushed his lips across her cheek, then, when she didn't slap his face, turn her head or move, he kissed her. He didn't linger, though he wanted to. She was right when she'd said they were both wary of relationships, just as she'd sensed how much he wanted her in his bed.

But if he wanted her to stick around, which he definitely did, he'd have to be smart about what he did and said. He'd have to make an actual effort to keep her in his life. To talk to her and share his thoughts and feelings.

Nearly everybody else around him was either paid to be there or related to him and had little choice. He was nice to very few of them. That had to change. He had to find a way to make peace with his past, let go of his resentment and appreciate the ridiculously good life he had.

He took the knife from her hand, then pulled her close, pressing her check against his chest. "Forgive me?"

She laughed. "I like how you disarmed me before you asked that question."

"Sometimes I'm smart. Other times, I'm not."

"I think that's true of everybody." She leaned back. "You're forgiven. Let me get this salad made, we'll do our yoga, then eat."

"Yes, ma'am."

Reluctantly, he let her go, then started down the hall toward his bedroom.

"I got you a present," she called. "Why don't you put it on?"

Sitting on the bed, he found a plain brown bag. Inside, was a white T-shirt. Real Men Do Yoga was printed in bold black letters across the chest.

She *had* to be kidding.

He stared at the shirt for several long moments, then, with a sigh, pulled off the one he was wearing and put on the new one. "The things a man does for a little kissing."

After slipping into a pair of sweatpants, he walked back out to Darcy. "I'm never wearing this shirt outside this motor home."

She grinned. "But, oh, my, Mr. Garrison," she said in a fake, sweet, high voice, "look what big muscles you have." She blinked rapidly. "Can I have your autograph?"

He crossed his arms over his chest. Nice was one thing; sappy was a whole other deal. "If you tell anybody I wore this shirt, I'll…" He couldn't think of anything terrible enough to do to her.

She slid her fingertip across his forearm. "You won't show me your big, strong muscles?"

"Darcy, I'm serious. I'd never live down this shirt in the garage."

"Are you going to threaten never to kiss me again?"

He paused. "Let's not go crazy."

"Relax, Mr. Macho. I won't tell."

After setting the salads in the fridge, she got out the yoga mats, and they moved through their poses. She added a few new ones. Difficult ones, which told him he might be forgiven for his earlier behavior, but she wasn't forgetting quite yet.

They ate dinner—grilled chicken from lunch sliced over fresh lettuce, cucumbers and tomatoes. Being Darcy, she also threw in some sliced, roasted almonds, dried cranberries and alfalfa sprouts. With the generous addition of Italian dressing it was actually pretty great. And the treat of having wine was even better.

"About earlier…" he began, wanting to settle things once and for all. "With Isabel, I mean. She obviously wanted to know what was going on between us."

Looking amused, Darcy sipped her wine. "Obviously."

"I didn't say anything to her, because my family asks way too many questions. They think they know what's best for me. Never mind I'm a grown man and can think for myself. Anyway, I didn't want to you to feel awkward, but—"

"Oh, I doubt they'll ask too many questions, since I explained everything to Isabel already."

He paused with his fork halfway to his mouth. "You—" He set down his fork. "Explained what— exactly?"

"That we were kissing."

"Kissing?" His face heated. "That's way too much information. Now Isabel will tell Cade, then she'll tell Rachel, who'll tell Parker. And if any of them tell Sam, or my mother, I'll—"

"Well, I didn't see any point in not explaining what was obvious when she walked in."

Her voice had taken on an aggravated edge, and he certainly didn't want this conversation heading down that road again. "In the future, would you mind keeping things simple? You could have just told her we were dating. She doesn't need to know details."

"Since when are we dating?"

Now he remembered why he'd decided he was through with women. They were the most confusing, frustrating creatures God ever created. "Since last week."

"No, we've been kissing since last week. I don't remember any dates."

He wondered if there was any more wine. No, that probably wasn't a good idea. His head was already spinning. "What do you call this?" he asked, gesturing toward the meal in front of them.

"My job."

"But…" He tried to find a logical argument for why that wasn't true and came up empty.

"A date, Mr. Garrison, consists of you calling up the woman of your choice, asking her to dinner, a movie, some social event, then picking her up and bringing her to that destination. After the meal/entertainment, you take her home, and—if you're lucky—receive a kiss good-night. Women need romance."

Caught somewhere between annoyance and embarrassment, he said, "Take your cell phone and go stand outside."

She raised her eyebrows.

"Would you *please* take your cell phone and go stand outside—for just a minute?"

"Can I finish my dinner first?"

Now, she was being a smart aleck. "Would you mind doing this first, please?"

She laid her napkin on the table, scooped her cell phone off the kitchen counter, then strode outside.

Bryan trotted back to the bedroom, found his own phone and called her. "Hi, Darcy," he said cheerfully when she answered. "It's Bryan Garrison. Would you like to come to my motor home for dinner tonight?"

"I'd love to."

"Great. I'll pick you up in about thirty seconds."

She giggled.

He ran back to the living area, opened the door, and when she would have walked inside, he shook his head. Instead, he scooped her into his arms and took her inside himself. After setting her gently on the floor, he swept his hand toward the table. "Dinner's ready. Please enjoy."

"Thank you." She slid into the booth on one side, and he sat on the other.

"Oh, look there's wine," he said, lifting his glass. "To us."

"To us," she echoed, then tapped her rim with his.

As the ring of crystal sang, he sipped, then told her, "Now, you can tell them we're dating."

She seemed pleased with his efforts. "I guess I can."

"And no more telling anybody related to me—by marriage or blood—what actually goes on during our dates. Agreed?"

"But what if I need to vent to somebody?"

"Why would you need to vent? I'm not going to—" Okay, realistically, was there any *possible* way he wasn't going to make her mad at some point in the future? "I'm sure you've got friends."

"None who know you."

"I'll introduce myself. Can we get on with this?"

Darcy shook her head. "I don't think I've ever had a romantic date that involved the words *can we get on with this.*"

Bryan scowled. "How about if we get right to the kissing part? I'm good at that."

Either she sensed his complete and utter frustration, or she'd decided he'd suffered enough. She swept out of her seat, then crossed to his side, moving in next to him. With her hand on his thigh, she leaned over and kissed him so thoroughly he saw stars.

"Better?" she asked when she leaned back.

"Much." His heart threatened to jump from his chest, but he fought to keep his tone light. "I think I'll like dating you, Darcy Butler."

"I think you will, too." She stroked his cheek. "But we'll need lots of practice."

So they practiced by talking about the race weekend while they finished dinner. Bryan cleaned up, then they decided to watch a DVD. She'd really liked the mystery/action one they'd seen together earlier in the week at his house, so he picked something along the same lines.

They sat in his recliner, side-by-side, their legs entwined, and lost themselves in the adventure and historical setting of the movie.

As the credits rolled, he looked at her. "How am I doing so far with the dating?"

Her hand glided up his chest, then curled around the back of his neck. "Pretty amazing."

So, as seemed to be the norm for them when they were together and not focused on something besides each other, the kissing commenced.

While Bryan had given the dating instructions a great deal of consideration, the kiss at the door—and ending the date there—was going to be a problem. Letting her go seemed impossible.

But he forced himself to pull back.

Sexual frustration was indeed destined to be his state for the immediate future, but not only was she not ready, this was their first official date.

His mother had raised a gentleman. Or tried to, at least. He had a shower—complete with hot and cold water—and he wasn't some randy teenager.

Still, he didn't want her to go.

It's late, he reminded himself practically. He worried about her driving back to her hotel alone. Was there a way to kiss her at the door and not have her leave?

He cupped her cheek in his hand. "Stay with me."

Her eyes widened.

"I'll sleep on the couch," he added quickly.

"But—"

He laid his finger over her lips. "I know it's not part of your planning for our first official date, but I worry about you driving alone this late at night. Plus, I know you'll be here before dawn to help cook breakfast for the guys. Staying here saves you time."

Her gaze searched his. "So you're being practical *and* considerate?"

"Sure."

She laid her palm over his forehead. "Are you sick?"

He grabbed her wrist and tucked her hand around his neck. "I'm hot, all right." He tightened his grip on her waist. "Stay. I'll even kiss you at the door."

"Okay." She tucked her head between his neck and shoulder. "I'll stay. But can we sit here for a few minutes first?"

"Whatever you want."

And for the first time in a long time, he realized he was more concerned about someone else's comfort than his own. Not the race team management, where he always thought about how much harder he could work to make GRI successful, but about a woman. One who intrigued, challenge and amazed him.

For her, for the feelings she inspired, he was willing to sacrifice a great deal.

CHAPTER TEN

"HEY," BRYAN SAID briefly, before covering her mouth with his.

While Darcy had become intimately familiar with his lips over the last five weeks, even she was a little startled by the abrupt—though exciting—opening to their date.

As had become the norm lately, she didn't ask him why, or doubt her decision to throw herself headlong into a relationship when they both still had so many personal issues to deal with, when she still panicked at the sound of sirens and ran straight to her secret stash of chocolate when her guilt threatened to overwhelm her. Instead, she leaned into him, laying her palm directly over his heart, reveling in its rapid, erratic beat.

One of his strong, capable hands cupped her cheek. She'd seen those hands turn a wrench, sign crucial documents and brace his body doing a push-up. They always fascinated her. Just as everything about him did.

And some part of her realized that only a man as

smart, confident, complicated—and, let's face it—wounded could have broken through the self-imposed protective wall she'd erected. The one she'd built out of impenetrable steel.

Maybe it was only right that a man once known as "Steel" should be the one to change everything.

When he leaned back, she had to brace herself against him to keep from losing her balance. The man did know how to knock her back on her heels.

"Wow," she managed to say. "Hard day?"

His hot, bright gaze held hers. "Not anymore."

"Did you want to put on a show for my neighbors?"

He glanced around, as if only then realizing they were still in the open doorway of her apartment. "Not really, no."

After striding inside, he closed the door and maneuvered her back against it, kissing her again.

She finally laid her hand on his chest and stepped back. "Hey, hotshot, we'll be late meeting everybody."

"So?"

And there it was—that barely banked desire mingled with frustration that had become the norm as of late. Though Darcy knew the solution was a confirmation of their chemistry and feelings, a further commitment to their relationship—sex, in other words—she feared giving in to the impulse of her body's needs. Her mind was too busy supplying various scenarios where she fell into his bed and panicked, forever damaging all they had together.

Yet how much longer could she expect his patience to hold?

To diffuse the tension, she smoothed her hand down her fluttery, pale peach top and jeans. "I guess you like my new outfit."

He glanced down at her, clearly noticing what she wore for the first time. "Nice."

She raised her eyebrows.

"Beautiful," Bryan corrected quickly. "I brought you a rose." He patted down his blue shirt and jeans. "Which I apparently left in the limo."

"Limo?"

"I thought I'd have a beer or two and would rather not drive. Plus, it's a party, right?"

The Garrison siblings were all meeting up at a Lake Norman bar and restaurant. Parker, who generally served as the family social chairman, had encouraged everybody to get together and celebrate Cade's success. He'd won two races so far this season and was tops in the championship points.

Since the races for the next two weeks were at the track in nearby Concord, they were all getting together for a rare Thursday night in town.

A teasing light replacing the frustration in his eyes, Bryan slid his arm around her waist. "I can also focus on you instead of driving. Good idea, yes?"

Her heart stuttered. This dating business was pretty amazing.

After a slightly rough start, Bryan quickly got the

hang of the romance thing. He brought flowers when he came to pick her up. He brought gifts of T-shirts, hats, cups, even kitchen utensils—all decorated with the car number and logo of one of the GRI drivers. This was especially helpful, since she could now show her team spirit at the track—though, more often than not, she wound up wearing stuff from multiple drivers, so as to not offend anybody.

He sent her sweet text messages in the middle of the day just to say he was thinking of her. He helped her cook, and he pushed through his workouts without a scowl, complaint or argument.

His confidence had zoomed through the roof. In the twelve weeks they'd been working together, he'd dropped twenty pounds, lost multiple inches from his waist, gained lean muscle mass and dropped his percentage of body fat by ten percent. The women at the track had certainly noticed and spent as much time clamoring for his autograph and attention as they did Cade's.

That part, actually, wasn't so pleasant for Darcy.

One night, when she was at Isabel and Cade's, teaching them to make chocolate-covered strawberries, Bryan dropped by unexpectedly, saying he wanted to help. They all had a great time, talking around the kitchen island, doing things regular couples did.

Not that all their time together had been without problems. Family, work issues, the hectic racing schedule had all caused conflicts. Worse, her ability to hide her guilt and anxiety seemed to be cracking. She'd find Bryan staring at her oddly at times, and sometimes he'd ask her outright if she was okay, as if he sensed she was holding back not just physically, but emotionally, as well.

So an air of uncertainty, guardedness and tension lingered between them. Neither of them seemed to believe that the peaceful, happy days would last.

"Are we dressed for a limo?" she asked.

He tugged her outside. "I doubt the fashion police will pull us over." After locking her door with her keys, he led her down the stairs to the parking lot where a long, gleaming black car and uniformed driver waited with the back door open.

Obviously, her middle-class upbringing would never get used to taking limos for casual outings or firing up the company jet instead of slugging through the commercial airport like everybody else.

Still, the Garrisons were as grounded and easy to be around as anybody she'd ever known. Even Parker, whose luxury hotel chain was world-renowned and who could probably buy GRI several times over, had a special quality of being able to relate to people from valets and mechanics to CEOs and track owners.

That was part of the appeal of NASCAR racing, too. People from every walk of life, profession, income bracket, age group, all came together for entertainment and thrills, all followed their drivers with the passion of a mother protecting her child.

"Hey, you with me?" Bryan asked, squeezing her hand.

She realized the luxury car was moving and strived to set aside her troubled thoughts. "I'm here." Looking over at him, she wondered if he'd been watching her with the look on his face she'd seen a little too often lately. "How are things with Lars?"

"Quiet." His eyebrows drew together. "It makes me think he's up to something."

Lars, even after his I-should-be-driving-the-car-full-time stunt backfired, had continued to be a problem. "Surely he's learned his lesson about going to the media," she said.

"About negative things, sure. Now, he just brags."

Lars was winning. He'd won the last race—at Darlington, no less—and though Cade had finished second, jumping him to the top spot in the championship points, winning that particular race had raised Lars's status tenfold among everybody in the garage.

While the staff at GRI was thrilled with the success, they were leery of their young, rebel driver's attitude. They worried his ego was spinning out of control.

"You'll manage him," she said, patting his leg.

"Oh, you have great confidence in my coddling skills, do you?"

"Not exactly. But he's scared of you, so that'll work just as well."

Bryan shook his head. "That kid isn't scared of anybody, or anything—that's half the problem."

"Well, he's scared of you."

A calculating look slid into his eyes. "That's certainly interesting."

Personally, Darcy would hate to be the object of that heated speculation, but Lars had been such a distracting pain in the butt for GRI, she figured he had it coming.

They arrived at the restaurant minutes later. The limo and Bryan got several speculative looks from other arriving diners. As they passed a group of two couples walking through the door, Darcy heard one of the guys whisper Bryan's name.

She didn't think often about Bryan's fame. By now, she was used to the reporters at the track, but having regular people recognize the man she was seeing was still a strange and rare occurrence. Feeling awkward about the stares, she held tightly to Bryan's hand as he led them into the restaurant and to the reserved table in the far corner of the room.

With its rough-hewn plank walls, clean-lined decor, long, wide bar and beautiful view of the lake beyond the back deck, Midtown was an easygoing neighborhood place patronized by lots of racing people and the Garrison clan's sporadic hangout. With them being out of town four days out of seven, it was hard to be a regular anywhere.

Thankfully, at the table, she found familiar faces. Parker and Rachel were already seated, with the waitresses and manager fluttering around them, probably wondering if Parker was buying the joint. Come to think of it, maybe he had.

They both rose as she and Bryan approached.

Parker kissed Darcy's cheek. His alluring green eyes gleamed. "There's an extremely likely chance that we'll be forced to thrash the male population of Mooresville tonight, Bryan. Are you prepared to defend our wildly attractive women with your life?"

Darcy giggled. Rachel rolled her eyes. Bryan simply shook his head.

Parker said things like that. In an era of knights and chivalry, defending the castle with a blade and a metal shield, he would have fit right in.

"I doubt we'll have to resort to fisticuffs," Bryan said seriously, then grinned, no doubt proud of his own historical reference.

As Rachel complimented Darcy's hairstyle, Cade and Isabel arrived.

There were friendly greetings all around, then Isabel planted her hands on her hips. "Where's the beer?"

"On its way," Parker assured her, pulling out her chair as Cade signed a few autographs for fans several feet away in the main room. "I guess the meeting with Splash didn't go so well."

The company who made Splash laundry detergent was the primary sponsor of the Kevin Reiner/Lars Heiman car for GRI. Needless to say, the Lars dramatics over the last several weeks had not made them happy. Still, with his recent win, the car was up front, on TV and being talked about constantly in the media. They couldn't be totally unhappy.

Isabel groaned and gratefully accepted the bottled beer offered by the waitress, who left an ice-filled bucket containing more bottles in the center of the table. She also brought Parker a glass of deep red wine and Rachel and Darcy glasses of white.

Isabel sipped her beer, then smiled as Cade slid into the seat next to her, softening the look of annoyance on her face. "The Splash people are so used to Kevin—his down-to-earth personality, his professionalism, his connection and loyalty to his fans. I *do* think Lars will eventually get all that, but his media mistakes are piling up."

"How'd he get along with the PR consultant?" Rachel asked.

"They hit it off well," Isabel said. "This PR guy is really young and hip," she explained, obviously for anyone who wasn't up on his credentials, which Darcy wasn't. "He consults with music labels all the time. Like getting pop stars out of their latest 'wardrobe malfunction' scandal or whatever."

"And Lars enjoyed the attention," Parker said.

Isabel rolled her eyes. "He *loved* it. He was practically glowing by the end of the meeting."

"The squeaky wheel gets the grease," Rachel commented.

Isabel nodded. "That seems to be his strategy."

Parker raised his wineglass in a toast. "How else are you going to outshine a legend like Kevin?"

Whether Parker was acknowledging Lars's intelligence or insolence, Darcy wasn't sure.

"What about that smarmy agent of his?" Cade asked. "Where'd he come from?"

Isabel's eyes narrowed. "I have no idea, but he needs to go. Fast."

"He's renegotiating his contract early," Parker said. His gaze moved to Bryan, who'd—typically—said nothing during the discussion so far. "You need to watch him."

Bryan simply nodded.

Isabel took another sip of her beer. Her expression was fiercely annoyed. Darcy could see her "Scary Isabel" nickname had been well-earned. "Well, if he—Lars, I mean—gives me that conceited smirk one more time, I won't be responsible for my actions."

Cade linked his hand with his wife's. "Damn, though. He can drive a race car."

There were reluctant murmurs of agreement about that evaluation. Though some said he didn't have enough seasoning and car control.

Throughout the debate on Lars and his talent, or lack thereof, Bryan still remained silent. From previous talks with the family, Darcy knew that at some point the others would look to their leader for his evaluation and expertise.

He was a strong, respected and admired man. Just

a few of the reasons Darcy was so attracted to him. So why couldn't her mind overcome the memories of her heart? Why couldn't she give in to the intense feelings she had for Bryan?

"But can we afford to lose him?" Cade asked, thankfully drawing her from her personal worries.

Bryan's moment, apparently, had come.

"I don't care how talented he is," Bryan said, his eyes bright with annoyance. "He keeps screwing up, he's gone."

Testimony, assessment, judge, jury, verdict. Case closed.

Oh, wait. There was no jury. Just the judge.

That hard line was a place Darcy knew she and Bryan would never agree on. She always considered people worth saving or helping. Where he wanted to step back from those he didn't agree with, she wanted to embrace their differences.

Or at least find a way to prove her point in a gentler way.

But no couple was alike in every way. If everybody was the same, life would no doubt be very dull.

"I agree the situation isn't ideal, Bryan." Rachel, seemingly the only one brave enough to challenge her brother, leaned forward. "But sponsorships are expensive, and he's winning. How can we—"

"Isabel just said our sponsor isn't happy," Bryan said evenly. "I don't care how many races he wins. If he can't represent GRI the way everyone else on our teams is expected to, I'll fire him."

The conversation swiftly moved away from Lars.

"Did you hear Dad ordered flowers for Leanne?" Cade asked the group.

Rachel shrugged. "What's so weird about that?"

"He ordered them from the florist Mom's dating."

Rachel choked on her wine. Her gaze darted around the table. "Why do you think he did that?"

Cade shrugged. "Don't know. But I know he didn't call up the shop and place an order. He went down there, asked for the owner and had the guy lead him around the place while he asked advice about picking out an arrangement for the woman he was seeing."

"Who told you this?" Isabel asked.

"Dad did," Cade said, looking amused. "Said he'd always led the family by example, and he wanted us kids to realize that divorce could be amicable, that he and Mom were happier apart. He wanted everybody to get along."

"Sounds like he was trying to convince himself more than you," Darcy said.

When every gaze at the table fell on her, she wished she could call back her words. She barely knew Mitch Garrison.

"Why do you think that?" Isabel asked.

"Well, he…" She glanced at Bryan, wondering with uncharacteristic timidity if the women he dated normally butted into family business. Since he simply looked as attentive as the others, she continued. "Taking time out of his day to pick out flowers for a woman he's dating doesn't seem completely out of character, but—"

"Oh, yes, it does," Rachel said. "He wouldn't know a petunia from a carnation."

"As opposed to a piston from a carburetor," Parker said.

"You can hardly mistake a piston for a carburetor," Isabel pointed out.

"Let her finish."

At Bryan's quiet, but firm words, her starving libido metaphorically thumped her on the back of her head. *He's hot* and *thoughtful. What more do you want?*

She cleared her throat. "It seems obvious he chose that specific florist for a reason. Obviously, to check out this guy. I mean, really, he didn't go there just for flowers." She paused, considering. "Though I'm sure Leanne appreciated the effort anyway. So then he makes a big deal of telling you all about how great his relationship is. If everything was so great, wouldn't that be obvious? Why does he need all the public declarations about it? And to his own son, who probably thinks it's weird to discuss his dad's love life in the first place."

She nervously ran her finger along the stem of her wineglass, even though she was certain her assessment was correct. "He's jealous."

"Dad's jealous," Rachel said slowly, probably

wanting to clarify Darcy's long explanation—she tended to ramble when she was uneasy. "He's not happy Mom's dating the florist."

"And things are apparently not all carnations and roses in his relationship with Leanne," Parker added. "I do believe you've analyzed the situation quite nicely, Darcy."

Darcy sipped her wine and tried not to gulp in relief. Her own love life was a strange mix of desire, companionship, tenuous restraint and yoga poses. Who was she to talk?

"Are you sure your only expertise is *physical* therapy?" Cade asked, angling his head.

Darcy shrugged. "Therapy is therapy in a lot of ways. I tend to encourage push-ups rather than long discussions about feelings. Sometimes, it amounts to the same thing, though."

"And she's good at finding motivation," Bryan said, his gaze meeting hers. "She knows just the right button to press."

Since that button, for him, had been revenge against his ex-wife, Darcy wasn't thrilled with the reminder. Their past relationships were too prevalent in their lives. And danged if she knew how to make them go away.

Rachel lifted her glass. "That sounds like pretty great news to me." When nobody else immediately joined her, she stared at all of them in disbelief. "We all want Mom and Dad to get back together. They *be-*

long together. Y'all are honestly telling me you're not happy?"

Cade glanced down at the table, then back at his sister. "Yeah, but we don't want Dad to be miserable."

"Who said he was miserable?" Isabel asked, lifting her beer bottle to join Rachel's wineglass. "You guys all hate that your parents broke up. Maybe this is the first step to them reconciling."

The men all frowned.

"Jealousy is a miserable thing for a man to go through," Cade said.

"Since when have you—" Isabel stopped. Both she and Rachel lowered their toast. Isabel's gaze moved between Parker and Bryan. "Okay, fine. Sorry I brought it up."

Darcy, of course, knew about Bryan's resentment of Chance Baker. But she also knew why the subject was sensitive to Parker. As perfect a couple as he and Rachel were now, she'd spent most of last season dating a neurosurgeon from Atlanta.

Since Darcy had gotten to know Parker well, she thought—but didn't point out—that Rachel dating the wrong guy had motivated Parker to finally accept and declare his feelings for her. So, really, the jealousy thing had helped them get together. Maybe it would be the same for the senior Garrisons.

But since the idea of Bryan and Nicole's reconciliation put a boulder in her stomach, she managed to keep her mouth shut about that possibility.

"Okay, now *that's* interesting," Isabel said suddenly.

Darcy, along with everybody else at the table, turned.

It was Chance Baker, walking into the bar. Alone.

Without Nicole, his manager, his father, his agent or his crew chief hanging on to his arm, Darcy hardly recognized him.

But several women in the bar did.

They strutted toward him in short-skirted, avaricious groups of two or three, eventually surrounding him. He soaked up the attention, and as he slid his arm around a girl on each side, the manager rushed over to accommodate them with a table.

Away from the one where Darcy sat in the far corner with the Garrisons.

The guy was clearly no dummy. She made a mental note to ask Parker later if he really had bought the place.

"Maybe Dad's love life isn't the only place there's trouble in paradise," Rachel said, then raised her glass again in another attempt at a toast.

While his siblings clinked their glasses together, Bryan leaned back in his chair, drumming his fingers on the table.

A relationship between two people as vain, selfish and superficial as Chance and Nicole couldn't last. He was surprised they'd managed to hold things together all this time.

But could this possible personal issue make a difference on the track? He needed to update Sam, let him know the Baker team might be vulnerable. Cade was first, but Chance was third in the standings. Any advantage was welcome.

"You're not toasting trouble for Chance?" Darcy asked him as she leaned toward him.

"Sure. I'd like to see him finish forty-third in the next race."

"That's not the kind of trouble I meant."

The revenge quest.

Would he like for Nicole to see him in a popular female fan moment, like the one Chance just took advantage of?

Maybe. Things had certainly started out that way between him and Darcy. His motivation for getting into shape had been about showing his ex what she'd given up. So many weeks later, though, he wasn't sure how much he cared what anyone thought, except him—and Darcy.

Still, a refrain beat in his head. *She left me for* him. That weak-headed, self-centered, egotistical jerk.

What's wrong with me? Why wasn't I good enough?

The fact that Chance could still race and Bryan couldn't was the most obvious, logical reason, but Bryan couldn't help the lingering whispers, making him wonder if there'd been more. Had he really been such a lousy husband? Had he ever meant anything to her at all?

Shrugging, he drank from his beer bottle. "Whatever."

"You're calmer than I would be. If my ex had broken up with the woman he'd left me for, I'd be opening champagne."

"No, you wouldn't. You're too nice."

"Unlike you, No Second Chances Garrison."

"Why would I give her—"

"I mean, with Lars."

"I'm giving him a second chance. Right now. I'm not willing to give him third and fourth chances. And what makes you think Chance and Nicole are broken up?"

She stared at him. "If they aren't now, they will be when she finds out about him coming here."

"I'd be willing to bet she's prepared to give good ol' Chance a certain amount of leniency when it comes to flirting with fans."

"And if it went beyond flirting?"

He shrugged. Who knew what kind of relationship they really had? From his own experience with his ex, he couldn't imagine it was based on honesty and sincere commitment.

"Did you ever cheat on her?"

"No."

"How long were you married?"

"Two years." Would he have seen through her charade if they'd stayed together longer? He liked to think so. But then two years was time enough to get to know somebody. "Why all the questions?"

"She was a big part of your life once. She changed you."

He started to deny it, just on principle, but he'd been *getting real* with himself for a while now, so he'd sort of gotten the hang of it. "I guess so. But I don't like to talk about her."

"Too painful, I guess."

"Not really. It's more like I feel stupid. And angry. Why didn't I see her for what she is?"

"What is she?"

"A user."

Darcy nodded in apparent approval. "Beauty can be blinding."

"You're beautiful, and I see you clearly enough. How long have we known each other? Three months?"

"I don't look anything like her. I'm certainly not blinding."

Need for Darcy rushed over him in a wave. He wanted her in so many ways, and yet there were barriers between them he wasn't sure they could overcome. Would her love for her husband always be between them? Or were the qualities that he'd lacked with his ex the same ones that kept Darcy from consummating their relationship?

He stroked his thumb across her chin. "You are to me."

"What are you two whispering about over there?" Rachel asked.

"Trouble for Chance and Nicole," Darcy said quickly, as if not wanting anyone else to know exactly what they were discussing.

Which was fine by Bryan, but he wished he hadn't made her so sensitive about the issue of telling his family about their relationship. He was getting pretty good at the romance stuff. What did he have to be self-conscious about?

"It's weird," Cade said, furrowing his brow. "They seemed made for each other."

Rachel glanced back at Chance's table. "There's not a whole lot of depth there for a long-term commitment, though. They probably just argued, and Chance came where he knew he could publically soothe his thin and fragile ego."

"Whatever," Isabel said. "Who cares? It annoys me to give either one of them the consideration of a two-minute discussion."

Rachel faced forward again. "I guess you're right."

Isabel gestured with her beer. "I'd rather focus on the possibility of this personal wrinkle in the Bakers' perfect world translating to the track."

Bryan did so love his sister-in-law's ruthless mind.

"Hear, hear," Parker said as he topped off wineglasses and handed out fresh beer bottles. "Let's talk about the upcoming races in Concord. And getting Cade back in Victory Lane."

CHAPTER ELEVEN

"YOU WANTED TO SEE ME?"

Sitting on the couch in the back of the hauler, Bryan stared hard at his troublesome driver. "I do." He swept his hand toward the other end of the sofa. "Have a seat."

As soon as Lars had flopped into place, Bryan rose, slid his hands into the front pockets of his perfectly pressed black pants, then rocked back on his heels and said nothing.

Darcy had said the kid was scared of him but only now did Bryan truly believe.

Lars's eyes widened and his face went pale.

Bryan had dressed with purpose that morning. Black and white. Ironed and collared shirt. Dress shoes. He'd shaved. The only time he looked this way was when he held a formal press conference.

And that's exactly the image Bryan wanted dancing through his young driver's mind.

Lars's normal cockiness returned quickly. "So, what's up?"

"Nothing's up, but my patience is low." He paced

the length of the sofa, then back. "I understand you went by the shop yesterday."

Lars shrugged jerkily. "Just wanted to talk to the guys."

Bryan paused and glanced over at him. "Oh, right."

"Hey, we could be running better, you know. I wanted to tell the guys what I thought about—"

"What *you* thought?"

Lars's eyes blazed with anger. "Yes."

Bryan's blood chilled another ten degrees, and he raised his eyebrows.

"Yes…sir," Lars corrected with obvious reluctance.

Though Bryan felt strange demanding what he considered a title for his father's generation, he needed to remind this kid just who was in charge. Had he really been this insolent and willful at nineteen?

Probably.

"What's your job title?" Bryan asked him.

Lars paused for a long moment, then sighed. "Driver."

"Do you like your job?"

"Yeah, sure." He met Bryan's gaze for a second. Whatever he saw there had him looking away quickly. "Uh…yes, sir."

"Do you want my job? Or maybe one of the engineers'?"

"No, sir."

"How about the chassis specialist you had such

an in-depth conversation with yesterday? You want his job?"

"No, sir."

"I'm glad, because you're not remotely qualified." He paced back and forth twice. "So, in review, if you want to keep your job as driver, you'll do that and nothing else. The guys you so helpfully gave advice to have more degrees than you have fingers and toes. They have more combined years of experience in racing than laps you've taken on the track in your entire career." He paused, his anger abating, though his frustration remained. "This is your dream job, dammit. Act like you belong here."

Lars's shoulders slumped. "Yes, sir."

"If you have a problem or a suggestion, you take it to your crew chief. But you should know your credibility with the team is lousy. I'd keep my thoughts—other than direct questions about the car's handling—to myself for now. Instead, I advise you to *listen*."

"I can do that."

"Fine. Head out to practice."

Lars, for all his immaturity, apparently had a hint of steel. As he rose, he held out his hand and shook Bryan's. "I appreciate your candor, sir."

Bryan nodded, then, as Lars wrapped his hand around the doorknob, he added, "You step out of line one more time, you're out. You got me?"

"Y-yes, sir."

Good grief, he'd made the kid tremble.

Maybe it was necessary, but he wasn't entirely sure he was comfortable with his actions. Plus, he'd given the kid a third chance.

It was all Darcy's fault.

The moment he walked into the motor home a few minutes later and found her sitting at the table, reading cookbooks, he pulled her into his arms and twirled her around.

"Why are you so happy about firing that kid?" she asked, sounding annoyed.

He set her on her feet and kissed the tip of her nose. "Who says I fired him?"

"You did. A few weeks ago, when he was already pushing the limits of your patience with his second chance."

"Well, I didn't."

"Why not?"

He felt weird telling her that he didn't want her to be disappointed in him. He'd never expressed his feelings well and now was no exception. "I didn't feel like it. I only came by for a kiss. Do I get one or not?"

She waggled her finger at him. "You certainly don't."

"Then I'm going out to the practice session."

He let go of her and started toward the door, but she snagged his hand. "What happened?"

"Okay, fine. I scared him."

She smiled triumphantly. "Aha! So I was right."

"Yes, you were right, Miss Brilliant Darcy. I intimidated him—"

"You do that well."

"It's a gift. And scared kid that he was, he folded like a bad poker hand."

"But you didn't fire him."

"No. I'm still not completely sure why I didn't. Except…"

She slid her hands up the row of buttons on his shirt. "Except…"

"He's a good driver. He *could* be great." He paused. "And I knew you'd want me to be kind."

Her eyes glowed. She hugged him tight against her, and he absorbed her comfort like a sponge, even as the feel of her womanly curves added an edge of torture.

How much longer could they go on like this?

"You're a good man, Bryan Garrison."

He closed his eyes at her praise, grateful for her support, but disappointed in himself for knowing it wasn't enough. But he'd never idled in Neutral in his entire life.

After a moment, when he was sure he could smile, he leaned back. "Then I deserve a kiss."

She laughed, then kissed him with an enthusiasm that rocked him back on his heels. "Go to practice."

"Mmm." He slid his lips across her cheek. "I could be a few minutes late."

Even as he said the words, a knock on the door interrupted.

Reluctantly, he stepped away from Darcy. Forced

to do this with increasing regularity, his tone to the intruder was more annoyed than usual. "Yeah? What?"

The door opened, and Sam stuck his head around the corner. "Did you fire him?"

"No."

At Sam's thunderous look, which was sure to be followed by a tirade of advice about how Lars was bringing down all the GRI teams, Bryan held up his hand. "We've come to an understanding."

"Uh-huh," was Sam's telling and doubtful response.

"I'll be right there." When Sam retreated outside, Bryan pressed his lips to Darcy's one last time. Didn't she feel the straining hunger? Or did she not want him as much as he wanted her?

His patience felt strained to the limit, and yet every day he went along with his promise to wait until she was ready. He smiled and pretended he was fine with the way things were going. And he was at a loss to figure out what she needed that he hadn't given her.

Leaning back, he noted the glaze of desire evident in her amber eyes. *When?* he wanted to ask, though he bit back the impulse. "After qualifying, it's just you and me, right?"

"Aye. I'm making bangers and mash."

Bangers and what? "You're making—" He stopped and shook his head. The direction of his thoughts was obviously way too carnal these days.

"It's an English dish—sausages and mashed

potatoes with gravy. I've adapted them for a healthier interpretation."

His stomach growled. "I *like* mashed potatoes and gravy."

Her eyes danced with amusement. "I'm sure you do. You'd better enjoy them, too. It's your big indulgence for the month."

"For the *month?*"

She punched him lightly in the stomach. "You didn't get that six-pack on potatoes and gravy."

He kissed her forehead. "True." As he headed to the door, he looked back at her.

Man, she was beautiful.

He started to tell her so, but wasn't sure how to find the right words. "Bake the kid some cookies if you have time," he said instead. "I was pretty hard on him."

"You really like that girl, don't ya?"

Walking toward pit road as the drivers were taking their parade laps, the race at Dover about to begin, Bryan stared at Sam. "She's not a girl, and, yes, I do."

Sam grinned. Well, he showed his teeth, which was a smile for the taciturn crew chief. "Touchy about her, too, aren't ya?"

"Does this conversation somehow relate to winning this race?"

Sam hunched his shoulders. "She's feedin' you too much of that rabbit food. No other reason a man should be so grouchy talkin' about his woman."

Oh, there was another reason, all right. One Bryan was even less reluctant to discuss in a professional setting.

Sex.

Specifically, the lack thereof, as Parker might put it.

After the sausages and potatoes dinner the night before, she'd hustled out so quickly he'd been tempted to check for skid marks on his floor.

He was aware they both had emotional baggage and taking their relationship to that level would make their easy companionship much more serious. She wasn't some casual one-night stand. Sleeping together would imply commitment, but, hell, they had that already.

He had no urge to see anyone else, and she apparently didn't, either. So they were in an exclusive relationship.

Without the fun stuff.

"You really think Lars is gonna keep his mouth shut?" Sam asked, dragging Bryan from his personal thoughts.

"He'd better."

"He could be a great driver."

"So everybody says. We'll see."

Parade laps finished, the drivers and teams were called to pit road for the prayer, singing of the national anthem and military flyover. They were staples of each and every NASCAR-sanctioned event. The solemn moments always made Bryan think of his father and grandfather and their early racing days.

Wooden bleachers had transformed into modern entertainment facilities. A guy with a microphone and binoculars had turned into a state-of-the-art broadcast booth. The local beauty queen singing to fans in a covered tent had become infield concerts by international superstars.

And still the cars went around, counterclockwise, each driver desperate to see the checkered flag first.

With or without all the hoopla, that simple event would always draw race car drivers and fans, because it meant something to all of them. Memories of fun times with family, crazy times with buddies, celebrations of friendship, realizations of dreams.

All of them bonded by the sheer, raw appreciation of a skill nearly everyone had on some level. Driving a car wasn't rocket science. And yet it was.

It was poetry *and* science. Heart and technology.

He knew of no other event that encompassed those opposites so thoroughly.

As the sound of jet engines faded, he headed toward Cade's car. "This one's yours," he said briefly as the safety director handed his brother his helmet.

Cade grinned, and Bryan turned away from the circle of crew members, plus Sam and Isabel, who'd sent their driver off to his race.

After stopping by Shawn's and Lars's pit boxes, Bryan climbed the war wagon of equipment— containing everything from wrenches to flat-screen computer monitors—behind the small stretch of pavement where Cade would bring his car in for servicing.

By habit, he glanced around for Darcy, but didn't see her.

Sometimes she hung around the pit box. Other times, she watched the race from the motor home. Though she enjoyed being close to the action, she always seemed self-conscious about being anywhere in public.

As the team president's sort-of-undeclared girlfriend, he could hardly blame her.

Something had to change.

Didn't it?

Yet he enjoyed his life more than he ever had. Meeting Darcy, going through the training and physical therapy had healed and strengthened more than his body, it was helping him let go of his past as a driver. He finally accepted that things would never be the way they had been before. And, in some ways, that was good.

As a driver, even the eldest in the family, he'd never anticipated running the company. He'd always assumed if anybody took over from his parents, it would be Rachel. But while she enjoyed being Cade's business manager, and she was certainly a vital part of the business side of GRI, she'd since told him she didn't want to be in charge. She liked leading, not directing.

To him, that meant she liked being bossy and voicing her opinion, but didn't particularly want the responsibility of making all the decisions.

Personally, he liked being in control.

Part of his driver's mentality, no doubt. He'd managed to translate that fierceness on the track to a fierceness in business meetings. He thrived on it.

Gentlemen, start your engines!

As the call echoed through the grandstands of the one-mile concrete oval, Bryan shook himself into his role at the moment—keeping his teams focused and on-target. All three had qualified in the top ten. They'd all practiced well. They were due for a win.

With the added stress of Lars and his antics, they could all use a boost.

The cars rolled off pit road under the bright sun to the cheers of thousands of fans. The crews behind the wall hovered, in a tense, anticipatory pattern, waiting for the moment when their every move and breath would help or hurt their teams. Cameras and reporters recorded every moment for the TV audience.

As the green flag flew, Cade, who'd qualified third, immediately jumped to the outside of the second-place car. He was even with the other car's door by the time they rolled along the backstretch of lap one.

The crowd roared.

Bryan leaned back in his chair, though he wanted to jump from it.

By lap four, his brother was in the lead. He gave it up a few times—during one green-flag pit stop and a couple of cautions where a few people changed two tires—but each time he gathered his speed and sailed past his competitors with a smoothness that spoke of his skill at the wheel and the entire team's dedication to building a kick-butt race car.

Bryan wandered down pit road during the race, checking on the other GRI teams, encouraging their over-the-wall guys and consulting with the crew chiefs.

There was one point when Cade and Chance battled for third place. They drew up alongside each other, door-to-door several times. The crowd rose, as one, to its feet. The TV and radio commentators followed every move. The past tension between the families was discussed. The tangles over the last few years between these particular drivers were analyzed.

Even though his heart was hammering, Bryan listened, outwardly dispassionate for the cameras and spectators, as Cade's spotter described the action through his headphones.

"Outside, outside. He's on the door." Long pause. "Outside. Rear."

As Chance fell to Cade's back quarter panel, his car wiggled. Obviously spooked, he tucked in behind Cade, and, over the next dozen laps, fell back several spots. On lap 221 he blew a tire, sending him to the back of the field after he'd pitted to fix the problem.

Later, when Cade's car streaked down the front-stretch, heading toward the finish line first, nobody was surprised, though the friends, supporters and team members in the No. 56 pit didn't let go of their collective breaths until the checkered flag waved. Then, they exploded.

Laughter, high fives and leaps among men who normally wore an expression of intent focus was an interesting, amazing sight. Sam even embraced Bryan—briefly.

As a bonus, all the GRI teams finished well. Jogging with the rest of the No. 56 crew to Victory Lane, Bryan glanced at the scoring pylon, which showed Shawn finishing eighth and Lars ninth. He hoped Parker was already planning the victory party.

In Victory Lane, Cade scooted from the car, stood on the window frame and pumped his fists in the air among a spray of Go! and confetti. Isabel kissed her husband as he dropped to the ground, and the live media interviews commenced.

After a minute or two, he called Parker over, then Bryan. Backing away as his dad walked up, Bryan looked around for Darcy. She should be there. She was part of the team, too.

Almost as soon as the thought occurred to him, he saw her, standing off to the side, next to Parker and Rachel. He watched his brother-in-law lean over and gently kiss her cheek.

That guy is smooth.

Bryan used to think he could hold his own charming women, but Parker was in a whole other league. Darcy was clearly impressed. Should Bryan strive to be more like Parker? Was that the key to taking their relationship to the next level?

She needs romance.

Smiling, he appreciated the interference of his conscience—for once. Okay, fine.

He'd managed the romantic and impulsive first-date invitation, hadn't he? He'd remembered to bring flowers, to ask her which movies she preferred and to respect her opinions. He'd even been kind and generous to his troublesome young driver, for Darcy.

All he needed was to think of some romantic way to seduce her.

DARCY WRIGGLED THE CORK from the champagne bottle with a satisfactory pop and a group cheer from her fellow passengers.

With the GRI company jet hovering comfortably at cruising altitude as they flew from Delaware back to North Carolina, she filled glasses and joined in the toasts. Bryan had told her that wins should always be celebrated, since you never knew when you'd get another one.

"How did you have time to order all this?" he asked her, standing at her side, obviously impressed by the elaborate seafood buffet, complete with breads, salads, slaws and the best North Atlantic crab, shrimp and lobster available.

Darcy grinned. "I ordered it Friday."

"Friday? But how did you know…?"

"The Irish believe in God and country, leprechauns and fairies, kings and destiny. And, naturally, a really good party." She sipped her champagne and immediately felt her head spin. She'd been too nervous to eat all afternoon and needed to hit the buffet soon. "Parker and I have been conspiring with the pilot for weeks to hide the champagne in case of a win. That, combined with access to such amazing seafood, seemed like destiny. We were prepared to celebrate finishing sixth, twentieth or even forty-third."

Bryan squeezed her hand. "I prefer first."

"I imagine you do. Parker brought home coolers full of seafood to host a party for everybody at GRI this week." She glanced at Bryan, noting the flushed, happy expression on his face. "With presidential approval, of course."

"You have it. Tomorrow's good. I assume Parker has all the details under control."

"Naturally."

"And probably roped you into cooking everything, too."

"He asked. I accepted. Frankly, with all those top-shelf ingredients, it's a pretty easy job."

"Even if it wasn't, you'd do it for Parker, though, right?"

Looking up at him, she searched his gaze. "That's an odd question."

"He's very charming and persuasive."

"Sure."

"Women like guys like him."

"Much to Rachel's annoyance, I'm sure they do. Why does that matter to—" Her eyes widened as a wild thought occurred to her. "You're not…jealous?"

His eyes took on a familiar—though not so common lately—jaded expression. "No."

"You don't think I like Parker, do you? Romantically, I mean."

"No."

But there was something about Parker that bugged him. She would have loved to find out what, but Isabel shouted for a toast, and the opportunity to talk to Bryan alone didn't occur until she was unlocking the door to her apartment. By then, she'd forgotten all about everything else since Bryan's mouth covered hers as he steered her through the doorway.

"Great party," he murmured against her lips.

"Thanks, I—"

But he distracted her again with another kiss, and her heart began the familiar accelerated beat that came with touching Bryan. Like a gas pedal beneath the foot of an impatient driver, it revved, straining against the limits she'd imposed.

"You need any help tomorrow…" he began, then paused to kiss her again. "You only have to ask."

"Okay. I'd like—"

His arms tightened around her as he lifted her off her feet, and she was unable to finish again.

"Are we going to talk or not?"

"Not." His lips trailed a path down her throat. "I have other things on my mind besides parties."

She fought for breath. "We could talk about racing."

"Not thinking about that, either."

"Impossible."

"Around you it's difficult to keep my mind on work."

Before she knew it, he'd maneuvered her to the sofa. And while they'd made out plenty of times on his motor home couch, she sensed a new urgency, a barely controlled power that had her pulse pounding in anticipation and panic.

At her request, they'd been careful to keep the physical part of their relationship easy and fun. Bryan had buried the intensity that was a vital part of his personality for months.

But that need was bubbling to the surface, like a volcano's heat, forming cracks in the foundation of something that had seemed solid ground only moments before.

She laid her hands firmly on his chest. "Bryan, I—"

When he pulled back slightly, either because of her words or their urgent tone, she scooted away from him and stood. "I'm sorry. I—" Embarrassed, her heart pummeling her with excitement and her soul aching with guilt, she turned her back on him. "I…c-can't."

"Okay."

Despite his undoubted efforts at staying calm, she heard the strained disappointment in his voice.

He was a smart, successful, incredibly attractive man. He could probably have any woman he wanted.

She closed her eyes and prayed he'd understand. Hugging her arms tightly around her waist, she cleared her throat and forced herself to face him. "I'm sorry. It's not you, it's—"

He held up his hand. "I get it." He leaned forward, bracing his arms on his knees.

She crossed to him and knelt. "I haven't…been with anybody since my husband died."

He gave her a half smile. "I figured."

"Will you give me more time?"

Gently, he slid his palm down her face, cupping her jaw. "Of course."

Desire still glittered in his dark, smoky eyes, but tenderness lurked there, too. Still, how much longer could they go on this way? What if her panic attacks never went away? What if she couldn't ever be intimate again?

"I should go," he said, clasping her hand and bringing her up to stand beside him.

"Yeah," she said lamely. "It's late."

She walked him to the door both reluctantly and eagerly. The moment she was alone, she knew she was going to fall apart. The signs were familiar by now.

Her body was burning with a feverlike heat. Her pulse raced. Her eyes burned. Her shoulders ached, as if a hundred-pound weight had suddenly settled on them.

What gave her the right to be so happy when Tom was gone? How could she take pleasure in another man when her husband could never touch her again? How could she have a warm bed when he had a cold grave?

It was wrong. Just plain wrong.

Blinking back the tears that threatened, she managed to face Bryan at the open door. "I'm s—"

"Kind, beautiful Darcy," he said quietly, then pulled her close to kiss her temple. "You've done nothing wrong."

She closed her eyes, absorbing his comfort, even though guilt clung to her like fog.

He leaned back after a moment, kissed her quickly, then left.

She gripped the doorknob, forced herself to watch him walk down the hall toward the staircase. When the sob in her chest could no longer be contained, she shut the door, pressed her back into the wood, then sank to the floor and let the tears fall.

They tracked hotly down her face, dripping off her chin. She didn't even bother to wipe the wetness away. With heaving breaths, she drew her knees to her chest and let the emptiness and hopelessness and injustice that she should continue to feel this way consume her.

Memories assaulted her.

The first time she'd met Tom—at an elementary school community appreciation day. She'd talked about the importance of nutrition; he'd spoken of fire safety. She remembered the way his smile was always quick and bright, the caring and tenderness he had for kids, the softness of his kiss, the scent of his cologne.

All of that was gone, living only in her memories.

Was she now trying to replace him? Would Bryan slide smoothly into Tom's place in her life? Or did her cold and broken heart even have room for anybody else?

Tom was supposed to have been by her side forever. Now that he wasn't, couldn't be, what was she supposed to do? How was she supposed to act? To feel?

Her sobs echoed around the apartment, though no one was there to hear her sorrow.

She wanted something—some*one*—steady in her life. Didn't there have to be a point where the guilt eased, and she could truly move on? When she could think of Tom smiling down at her from heaven instead of imagining him brokenhearted that she was betraying the intimacies of their marriage vows?

And was there any possible way Bryan could deal with all this uncertainty and emotional chaos? He had his own past to overcome. She didn't see how she could expect him to handle her issues, too.

He's strong. So strong.

She slumped over on her side, her face pressed to the cool tiles in the foyer. The tears still rolled across her cheeks, but her breathing was coming in short, calmer hiccups of grief.

Maybe someday she wouldn't have to pretend she

was handling everything so well when she really wasn't. Maybe a time would come when the idea of sharing herself body and soul with another man wouldn't send her into a crumbling panic.

Maybe Bryan was that man.

Drawing a deep breath, she pressed her palm against the cool tiles. She prayed and hoped. She suffered and ached.

And though she knew there was a secret stash of double-fudge ice cream hidden in a nonfat yogurt container in the freezer, she didn't even want that comfort.

Tom had nothing anymore. Maybe she shouldn't, either.

CHAPTER TWELVE

NEARLY A MONTH after Cade's win at Dover, Mitch Garrison walked out of the drivers' and owners' motor home lot in Loudon, New Hampshire, and saw Darcy heading in.

Since he rarely had an opportunity to talk alone with the woman who'd been such a positive influence on his oldest son's life over the last several months, he flagged her down.

"Hey, Mr. Gar—" she said, then stopped abruptly. "I mean—Mitch."

"It's not too hard to remember, is it?"

"It feels weird." Her delicate-looking face turned pink. "My grandmother would be horrified by my manners."

He smiled teasingly. "Your grandmother would tell you to listen to your elders."

"Pardon me, but you don't seem like much of an elder."

"Racing keeps you young at heart. And if I'm not old, I don't need the Mr. G stuff, do I?"

She angled her head. "That's very clever."

He winked. "How do you think I got all those trophies?"

"Fast and smart, are you? I can see where the guys and Rachel get their skills."

"Actually, their mother had a bit more to do with their smarts than I did." Because talking about Barb made him sad and regretful, he changed the subject. "Are you busy right now?"

"No. I'm all done with the lunch rush and everybody else is talking about either track bar adjustments or marketing campaigns. My head was spinning, so I thought I'd head to Bryan's motor home for a while. Do you need something?"

"Just a track charity event. Would you mind coming with me? Leanne's at a dermatology convention this weekend. It'll give me a chance to share humiliating stories about Bryan, so you can use them against him when he's being a pain in the butt."

Smiling, she linked her arm with his. "With that kind of offer, how can I do anything else?"

"So, you really have my junk-food-loving son eating healthy?" he asked as they walked through the infield toward the hospitality village. "Actual green stuff?"

"Yep." She leaned close and whispered, "He even likes most of it."

"Doesn't seem possible."

"I had to bully him into trying some things, but when he saw the results, he was a lot more cooperative."

"And his knee is better?"

"He saw the orthopedist last week, who said his range of motion is better, and he's much stronger. He'll never be one-hundred-percent again, but the doctor says Bryan has far exceeded his expectations."

"Thanks to you."

She shrugged. "He did the work." She glanced at Mitch, her eyes twinkling. "I just held the whip and chains."

Mitch could see where this woman, with her elfin features and bright spirit, could get a man to do anything she wanted him to. She seemed an odd match for Bryan—who'd always gone for the more sophisticated and reserved type—but they fit in an unexpectedly lovely way, too.

And she didn't remind him at all of his ex-daughter-in-law. The fact that they were both blondes was the only thing they had in common. Nicole's beauty had blinded them all to her nasty side. And while Darcy was certainly beautiful, her looks seemed to glow from within.

Barb had those kind of looks. Whenever she walked in a room, her smile touched every corner. The kids had inherited that quality from her. Cade especially. Star quality. The kind of person that drew everyone else to them.

When had her smile stopped working its magic on him? When had he stopped noticing how beautiful she was? How lucky he was to have her by his side?

Of course if the obsessed way he looked through photo albums was any indication, Barb's smile had never lost its true power over him.

Darcy cleared her throat. "You know I don't really have whips and chains, right?"

Mitch laughed. "Too bad. We could have sent Lars over whenever he gets too full of himself."

"You could bring it up at the next strategy meeting."

"I think Bryan's decided Lars is out of opportunities for helpful meetings."

"Yes, he has. It's a good thing Lars has taken his advice." She was silent for a moment, then she asked, "You sure there's not more on your mind than Bryan?"

They walked a bit farther, seeing groups of fans who were headed to and from the campgrounds, either to the hospitality tents where they themselves were going, or into the grandstands for qualifying, which was due to start in a few hours.

Mitch steered Darcy away from the crowds. This was a private conversation.

"You're a very intuitive woman," he said finally.

"Are you worried about Rachel or Cade?"

"No. My kids are happy and healthy. Including Bryan. You've been a real blessing to our family."

Her gaze darted to his briefly. "Thank you. All of you are special to me, too. Are you—"

"I'm afraid I've made a mistake."

She didn't seem at all fazed by his blurted confession. "With who? About what?"

"My wife. My *ex*-wife," he corrected and still felt the pain of saying it. "Barb."

"You're not happy she's dating that florist."

Visualizing that smarmy guy's hand sliding along the lower part of Barb's back, he clenched his jaw. "No."

"I don't blame you. She's a lovely woman, and he seems really interested in her." When his surprise obviously showed on his face, she continued, "I get a lot of chances to stand back and observe people. Plus, I'm really good at reading faces. It helps when I need to know if I can physically push a client further or need to pull back."

"Or when you need to tell him he's full of bull."

Her gaze darted to his. "Then, too."

When she didn't elaborate, he said, "I appreciate honesty."

"Are you sure about that?"

"This is like a conversation between a driver and a crew chief—I have to know where the car's going off track if I'm going to finish the race anywhere near the front."

She nodded, then stopped, turning to face him. "Do you still love her?"

He couldn't think of a single thing to say. He wasn't a man who discussed his feelings easily, and yet Darcy seemed the perfect confessor. She was close to the family and knew all the players, but she could also be objective.

"If you do love her," Darcy went on, "I think you need to tell her. If you don't…"

"What?"

"Stuff your jealousy. *You* left *her.* If you can't be happy with her, she deserves to have someone who can."

"You're very direct."

"I know." She sighed. "It's good in some ways, lousy in others. I'm sorry if I offended you, I—"

He held up his hand. "Don't apologize. You're right. I can see why Bryan values you so much. And I don't know what I feel exactly. But I know I don't like that damn florist."

"Well, in my honest opinion…" She glanced at him, obviously looking for his approval, so he nodded. "You can't go to Barbara and tell her that. For one, she'll slam the door in your face. For another—"

"I've lost the right to say anything."

"Yeah, I think you have."

They encountered more groups of fans heading toward the hospitality area. Inevitably, Mitch was recognized.

Though he always enjoyed the fans, and appreciated everyone who remembered him, as more people gathered, he regretted not bringing one of the PR reps or crew members to help him move through the crowds.

Concerned about Darcy, he looked around and was surprised to find her next to him still. She was so small, surrounded by fans shoving autograph books, hats and T-shirts over her head for him to sign.

"Okay, folks," she said in a loud voice. "Mr. Garrison needs to go now."

Then she grabbed his arm and started walking. The progress was slow at first, but either the sound of her authoritative voice or the sheer determination on her face had people moving out of her way.

"Mr. Garrison has a commitment in the hospitality area," she kept repeating as they worked their way through the pack. "Please check the GRI Web site for his appearance schedule. Thank you for your support."

Some of the fans moved with them, still babbling excitedly about the first race they saw, or explaining they, their dad or their aunt Mildred were *huge* fans. Mitch kept signing autographs, and Darcy kept them moving.

When they reached the security gate to the hospitality village, several security people rushed forward to help with crowd control. Mitch signed some last-minute autographs, then followed a track volunteer to the tent where his appearance was scheduled.

"Everyone's so jacked up about you coming, Mr. Garrison," the volunteer said as he led Mitch and Darcy into the back of the tent, to a blocked-off area behind the stage.

Mitch nodded. "I was glad to do it. Nobody's more vital to our communities than our firefighters."

"Firefighters?"

At Darcy's shocked tone, Mitch turned toward her. "Sure. That's who I'm meeting with today. The track organized an appreciation—"

He stopped as her face turned white. She swayed on her feet.

Mitch grabbed her arm. "Are you okay?"

"I—"

Her eyes were wide, the pupils unnaturally dilated as she stared out at the rows of chairs and the men and women starting to file into the tent.

"Darcy?"

The sound of her name was barely out of his mouth when she crumpled at his feet.

He braced his hand underneath her neck at the last second, preventing her from hitting her head on the ground. The quick reflexes he'd had all his life apparently hadn't deserted him completely.

As Mitch knelt beside her, grateful the stage blocked the audience's view of them, the volunteer gaped. "Oh, boy. I don't— What should I— What's wrong with—"

"I don't know." And before the guy could ask any more questions Mitch didn't have the answers to, he said quickly, "You have a tent full of firefighters, most of them probably paramedics, too. Go find one."

The volunteer's eyes darted from Mitch to Darcy, then to the gathering of event attendees only a few feet away. "M-my brother-in-law's out there somewhere," the volunteer said, his voice shaking.

"Find him."

As the volunteer rushed off, a spark of panic surged through Mitch. What had happened to her? Why had she fainted?

Before he could do anything more than grasp Darcy's hand in his, a woman knelt next to them. "Is there anything I can do?"

Though his mind was racing and his heart pounding, he noted she wore a chef's jacket. Part of the catering staff, no doubt.

"Ice?" he suggested. "A cool washcloth maybe? I think she just fainted."

Though why she'd passed out so suddenly, he had no idea. Darcy was the healthiest person he knew.

"On my way," the caterer said, leaping to her feet and striding away.

Mitch stared down into Darcy's pale face and willed her to open her eyes. "Darcy?" He patted her cheeks gently. "Darcy, it's—"

"What happened?"

As a young man with light brown hair dropped beside Darcy, Mitch leaned back. "She fainted."

The man, presumably the volunteer's brother-in-law and a firefighter-medic, pulled back Darcy's eyelids, then slid his fingers around her wrist, while looking at his watch. "Did she hit her head when she fell?"

"No, I caught her."

"Is she on drugs? Any kind of medication?"

"Not that I know of." He considered the question

more thoroughly. "She doesn't take illegal drugs. She's a nutritionist and rehabilitation trainer."

"When did she last eat?"

"I don't know. She usually has lunch with the team, though. That couldn't have been more than half an hour ago."

I need to call Bryan.

The thought zipped through Mitch's mind as the medic continued to take Darcy's vital signs and assess her condition.

"I'll be right back," he said, lurching to his feet and drawing his cell phone out of his pocket.

His fingers froze on the keys. Bryan was most likely working in the garage. He wouldn't answer his cell phone. Ditto for Sam or any of the other team members.

Rachel. Or Parker. Better yet, both.

He dialed Rachel first. She picked up before the first ring was over. "Hey, Dad, how's—"

"How quickly can you get to Bryan?"

"Last time I saw him, he and Sam were in Cade's garage stall. Why? What's wrong?"

"Get him and bring him to the hospitality village. Darcy fainted."

There was a shocked gasp, then she said, "We'll be right there. I'm heading toward Bryan now. What happened?"

"I don't know. I asked her to come with me to an event honoring firefighters and the next thing I know, she's—"

"Dad," Rachel interrupted quietly.

"What? Maybe she didn't eat lunch. She's always cooking, but I assume she eats, too. Did you see her? What—"

"*Dad.* Her husband was a firefighter, and he was killed in the line of duty two years ago."

"Oh. Oh, man." Mitch's heart contracted. Regret crashed over him. "I knew she was a widow. That's all. I didn't know…."

"It's okay. Hang on."

He heard muffled conversation, drowned out once by a revving engine, then Rachel was back. "Bryan and I are coming. Is anybody giving her medical attention?"

"I'm in a tent full of firefighters, honey. I got that much handled."

"Good. And don't worry. I'm sure she'll be fine."

Mitch signed off, then closed the phone, looking back at the medic and Darcy, lying so pale and still on the concrete floor.

What have I done?

BRYAN CALLED on every cell of self-control he possessed and stifled the urge to burst into the hospitality village and shout at, curse or pummel the first person he saw.

He clenched and unclenched his hands as he and Rachel rushed along the back side of the tents, dodging catering staff with trays, carts and trash bags.

No one questioned their presence and everybody—obviously noting Bryan's coldly determined stride—got out of their way.

When they reached the tent, a nervous-looking volunteer approached them. "Right this way, Mr. Garrison."

"A woman in a golf cart is going to pull up here any second," he said briskly, trying to focus on the things he could control and not on what he couldn't. Like Darcy unconscious on the floor. "Make sure she has a clear space to park until we come out."

"Y-yes, sir."

Then, as the volunteer laid his hand on the tent flap, Bryan heard her voice.

"I told you, I'm *fine.* I have things to do, so—"

"Ma'am, you're sitting right here until your pulse rate is lower," answered an unfamiliar male voice.

The medic Dad had found, no doubt.

"My pulse rate would go down if you people would stop prodding me and let me get up," Darcy said, her voice rising in both volume and annoyance.

Bryan always heard doctors were the worst patients, but he'd bet PTs could give them some stiff competition. But angry and frustrated was much better than pale and passed out as far as he was concerned.

When the volunteer looked at him questioningly, Bryan held up his hand. He needed a second to let his heart settle back into its normal place in his chest. For the last ten minutes, it had clawed its way to his throat.

"Bryan will be here any minute," his dad said in a soothing tone from inside the tent.

"What's he going to do?" Darcy asked scathingly. "You two are already holding both my hands."

"I think I finally see the side of her that whipped you into shape," Rachel said quietly from behind Bryan.

"She's tough."

"But probably embarrassed. I know I would be. Let's get her out of here."

"Dad still has his appearance to get through. You stay here with him. He's shaken more than she is, I'm sure."

A golf cart pulled up beside them. Huntington Hotels' PR rep Emily Proctor was behind the wheel. "Is everything all right, sir?"

"I think so," Bryan said, relieved—and not for the first time—by the efficiency of Parker's staff. "I'll be back in a second." He pushed back the tent flap.

Darcy sat on the floor with a blanket wrapped around her shoulders. His dad hovered on one side and the medic on the other.

"I think she needs a little air," Bryan said.

Her gaze darted to his, then she bowed her head. "I can't believe they called you."

Crossing to her, he knelt beside her as his dad moved out of the way. He caught her chin in his hand and turned her face from side to side. He noted the golden sparks in her eyes—ones that only seemed to appear when she was ticked off or aroused. "You look pretty steady to me."

"Pulse just spiked," the medic pointed out, still holding her wrist.

Darcy flushed, and Bryan assumed he was the cause of her sudden rise in heart rate. The idea made him smile.

"I'll make sure it comes down," he said to the medic. "One of the docs will see her this afternoon."

The medic frowned. "She needs to drink her juice."

Darcy shook her head. "Too much sugar."

"Low blood sugar is probably the reason you passed out in the first place," the medic argued.

Darcy glared at him. "No, it's *not*. I told you, I had a perfectly balanced meal less than an hour ago. Now, *go away*."

Bryan grasped her hand and pulled her to her feet before she clobbered the guy. "I'll take charge of her," he said to the medic. "Thank you for your help."

Shrugging, the medic rose. "You sure she's not a doctor?"

As Bryan led her out of the tent, he accepted the tossed-out advice from his sister and his father with a nod. Darcy's pain certainly wasn't physical, though he'd taken steps to make sure his instincts were true.

He'd complimented her often on the graceful way she'd handled the troubles in her past, but, looking back, he realized maybe she'd appeared to handle things *too* well. He wore the chip of resentment from his past—his divorce, the accident—on his shoulder for all to see. Darcy had tried to bury hers along with her husband.

Neither of their grand plans had worked so well.

When she saw the golf cart, she halted. "I can walk."

"I'm sure you can." Sensing she'd been pushed to the point of total retreat, he plucked her off her feet and set her in the front seat. "Right now, though, you'll like riding."

"Let's go, Emily," he said once he'd settled on the bench in the back.

Emily took off.

The ride to the motor home lot was silent among the occupants of the cart. A couple of people called to Bryan, but he simply waved. He had a situation on his hands that was much more serious than the perfect balance of a race car.

The fact that he ranked Darcy above racing was more telling than any long-winded self-evaluation he could think of.

And pretty damn scary.

"Did you make the phone call?" he asked Emily as she pulled the cart to a halt beside his motor home.

"Yes, sir. ETA less than ten minutes."

"Thanks. And we appreciate the ride."

Darcy gave Emily a sincere thank-you, then rushed inside the motor home without even glancing in his direction.

O-kay.

He'd been ornery toward her plenty of times. He supposed it was time to return the favor.

"I don't want to talk about it," she said the moment he opened the door.

"I wasn't going to ask you about it." He settled on the sofa. "You can give the doc all the details when he gets here."

Standing in front of him, she planted her hands on her hips. "No doctors."

"Too late. He's already on his way."

"I guess that's who Emily called."

"It is. Have a seat."

"No."

"You might as well relax 'til he gets here."

"No."

He wanted to drag her down to the sofa. He wanted to hold her and assure her everything was going to be all right. He wanted to hold her and calm himself. But coddling had only made her mad.

Thankfully, the doctor arrived.

Darcy sat through his brief exam without complaint. She answered his questions, and, within a few minutes, he pronounced her healthy.

"You probably just got overheated," he said, offering her a lollipop, which she took with a scowl.

Bryan thanked him for his time, and after he closed the door behind the doctor, he turned to see Darcy tapping her foot in annoyance.

"I've never fainted in my life," she said.

"It's not a big deal," he said, careful to keep his tone casual as he returned to his place on the sofa. "I passed out after racing dirt cars when I was a kid a couple of times."

"That's *passed out,* not fainting. Overexertion, heat exhaustion, blah, blah." She raised her arms, then let them drop in a gesture of complete frustration. "I *fainted.* Like some weak-minded, weak-kneed female."

"But you are female."

She waggled her finger at him. "Don't debate word choice with me, Bryan Garrison. You know what I mean."

"But—" He stopped. Let her rant. If somebody tried to tell him he'd fainted, he'd probably slug them. "Fine. I know what you mean."

"It was just the unexpectedness of seeing all those firefighters in one place. It reminded me of family gatherings at the firehouse, everybody joking and razzing each other." A smile teased the corner of her lips. "Then I realized the last time I saw that many firefighters in one place was Tom's funeral."

Oh, boy.

"They were all dressed up, carrying his casket with such delicacy and duty."

A lump in his own throat, Bryan watched as tears welled up in Darcy's eyes, and he fought the urge to wring his hands. Was there a man in all of history who knew how to deal with a woman's tears?

Parker.

He glanced at his phone, sitting on the kitchen counter.

No. He couldn't bring Parker into this. Darcy was already angry and embarrassed enough. Besides, if they were dating, then these were the kinds of issues significant others were supposed to talk about. It wasn't all intimate meals, kissing and not-having-sex.

"Do you want to talk about Tom?" he asked tentatively.

He really didn't, but if it would make her feel better to get out all her deep-seated, lingering emotions of love and sorrow about her dead hero of a former husband, he was willing to—

Dear heaven, why had she tossed out all the alcohol?

A conversation like this should involve liquor and dim lights and possibly sad songs.

And somebody with way more sensitivity than him.

"No, I don't want to talk about him," she said, narrowing her eyes. "Didn't I say I didn't want to talk about it?"

Good. Even if he had liquor, it was barely two o'clock in the afternoon. And stone sober, he wasn't about to point out that she was the one doing all the talking anyway.

"They put a cold cloth on my forehead—that, apparently, was what brought me around, by the way. They brought me juice and held my hand. I am not weak."

"I know you're not."

"In fact, I bet I can do more push-ups than you."

"You probably—"

To his disappointment, she dropped to the floor. "Come on. Not chicken, are you?"

"No. Darcy, please get up." The pain she'd been trying so hard to hide, that he'd seen only a glimmer of in all the months they'd known each other, was finally showing on her face. Her eyes glittered with tears, ones she was fighting with a desperate kind of anger that made his own heart ache in response. "Don't do this."

"Do what?" she asked, starting her push-ups.

"Pretend you're okay."

"Of course I'm okay. Didn't you hear the doctor?" Three more push-ups. "Overheated. *Pfft.*"

He crossed to her, kneeling beside her. "Darcy, stop." Five more push-ups. "No."

"Stop and look at me."

"Don't you have a qualifying session to go to?"

"Not right now. Darcy, it's okay to feel sad. It doesn't make you weak. You can—"

A sob broke from her throat. But she kept doing push-ups.

He laid his hand on her shoulder, and she jerked back into Child's Pose, sitting on her heels, her chest resting on her thighs.

When her body started shaking, he grabbed her by her waist and pulled her into his lap. "It's okay," he murmured as she cried against his chest, her arms clenched tightly around his neck. "I'm right here. You're not alone."

She cried harder.

He didn't leave her. He didn't go to qualifying. After a while, through hiccupping sobs, she asked for chocolate and confessed she had a secret stash in her bag. Later on, he convinced her to eat some soup, but she wanted more chocolate and told him about the hiding place under the passenger's seat of the motor home.

He was so worried about the bleak look in her eyes, he didn't comment about the sugar content.

Instead, he carried her into his room, tucked her into bed and lay beside her while she drew shaky breaths and her tears soaked the front of his shirt. He'd never felt more helpless and yet more needed in his life.

The violent weeping abated as it grew late and shadows filled the room. He rubbed her back, and the tightness he'd held in his stomach all afternoon eased slightly when she pressed her lips lightly to the base of his throat.

"I don't deserve to be happy when he can't even be here at all," she said, her voice choked from crying and slurred from exhaustion.

He kissed her temple. "Yes, you do."

CHAPTER THIRTEEN

DARCY LAY IN BED, listening to the rumble of stock car engines circling the track. Extending her hand to the space beside her, she noted the sheets were cool.

Where had Bryan slept? The last thing she remembered was falling asleep in his arms.

Yes, you do.

He thought she deserved to be happy. He wanted her to be happy.

And while she felt raw, puffy-faced and exposed, she also felt strangely better. Cleansed. Comforted.

Sharing an emotional breakdown with a man she cared about, but had only been dating a short time, should have at least felt awkward. But some deep instinct inside told her he was the only one she could trust with her pain.

Maybe it was all the months of physical therapy and close contact during exercise, meals and "getting real" conversations. Maybe it was simply because of the man he was.

After her solitary crying spell a few weeks ago, she'd hoped she'd finally cried out all her despair. For two long years, she'd lived in fear of those horrible episodes never stopping. And now, after months of keeping a tight rein on her emotions, she'd broken down twice in a month.

Her eyes burned. Would she ever be whole again? *Stop.*

She forced herself to sit up. Closing her eyes, she rubbed her temples. And, taking her own advice for once, she called on her yoga training. She crawled to the floor and worked through a few simple poses, forcing her mind to empty, her breathing to steady and her heart to beat in a slow, measured rhythm.

During those quiet moments, a truth finally moved through her.

She wouldn't ever be the same, but she could be a whole person again.

Tom, who was so generous and kind, wouldn't expect her to stand still. He'd want her to be happy. Just as she wanted the same for him. Heaven wasn't full of pain, that she knew, so she could at least rest easy on that belief.

Last night she'd turned a corner. Taken a step forward. The past seemed further away, instead of clawing at her heels. And knowing Bryan was so close, so supportive, made looking down the road ahead much easier.

With one, last, cleansing breath, she opened her eyes.

The first thing she saw was a glass of water sitting

on the bedside table. As she reached for it, she also saw several chocolate bar wrappers.

She nearly dropped the glass.

The chocolate. She bowed her head, not believing she'd let that secret escape. What had Bryan thought about Miss No Sugar Thank You hoarding candy?

Gulping water to soothe her raw throat, she frantically searched for some justification—other than her emotional weakness—for needing to hide chocolate every-freakin'-where.

She also realized she was wearing her polo shirt from yesterday.

She waved her hand, hoping her conscience would shut up. Bryan was a true friend and gentleman—even if traits like those weren't entirely cool in this century. The fact that he'd cared for her was comforting, yet she was embarrassed to have been so far gone she hadn't even thought to drag on her own sweatshirt and sweatpants.

Stop.

Her conscience had apparently ignored her command to be quiet.

Still, it—or was it she?—was right. Embarrassment wasn't something she could feel with Bryan anymore. They'd been through emotional ranges during the last several weeks that a lot of couples never had to explore in a lifetime.

He'd held her while she grieved for her former husband. And while he probably felt as odd about that experience as she did, it just seemed to add another layer of bonding between them.

She stood and noticed her bag sitting on the dresser, her jeans folded neatly on top. She dragged them on quickly, and though she'd have loved to take a shower and dig out fresh clothes, she decided she ought to get the awkward, morning-after-breakdown moment over with.

Walking down the hall, she could see into the kitchen/living area. Bryan was nowhere in sight, but Rachel was picking up discarded chocolate wrappers.

"Some party last night, huh?" she asked, obviously hearing Darcy's approach.

Knowing her face had to be beet-red, Darcy muttered, "I have a problem with chocolate."

"Don't we all?" Rachel shrugged and tossed the wrappers in the trash. "And, hey, better a sugar rush than a hangover, right?"

"I guess so."

"I made coffee. You want some?"

"Sure. Thanks."

"Bryan went out to the practice session," she said as she crossed to the pot on the counter. "He thought you might like some company other than his this morning. You want sugar?"

"No, thanks." Darcy opened the fridge and drew out the cream. "Just a little of this. You?"

Rachel peered at the carton's label. "Organic, low

fat, no sugar added, huh?" She extended her own mug. "Sounds yummy."

Darcy smiled as she poured the cream. "It's better for you."

"I should hope so." Rachel leaned back against the counter and blew across the top of her steaming cup. "You want to talk about it?"

Remembering Bryan had quietly asked her the same thing yesterday, and she'd returned only anger to him, Darcy sighed as she settled at the dining table. "I'm not sure what to say."

"There's no shame in grieving."

"There's shame in fainting."

"Yeah." Rachel slid into the bench seat across from her. "I guess there can be. The Garrisons are a pretty sturdy lot. You think we'll look down on you now?"

Darcy nodded, then sipped her coffee. The hot liquid soothed her throat, but not her pride. "You or Isabel would never faint."

"You've obviously never seen us after Cade wrecks. We're not too steady on our feet, believe me."

"But I work for GRI. I shouldn't be bringing my personal problems—"

"Whoa." Rachel held up her hand. "Employees are like family around here, and you're much more than that, regardless." Blue eyes, brighter than Bryan's, focused on Darcy's face. "I haven't seen Bryan this happy since the last time he crawled out of a race car in Victory Lane. You're the reason."

"He's worked hard, t—"

"*You're* the reason," Rachel insisted. "Personally, I think you're amazing. Strong, smart, compassionate, determined. Anybody that can handle Steel Garrison for months on end has serious spine."

"I don't feel very strong."

"I understand that, and I'm not saying I wouldn't feel self-conscious about passing out in public, but you won't get anything from my family except support and respect. I promise."

"Thanks." She squeezed Rachel's hand and felt a little more of her tension and worry drain. "If I had to be rescued, I'm glad you guys were the ones."

"Hey, when the matriarch says move, we all mobilize immediately." She angled her head. "I can't believe I called myself that. I spend too much time listening to my husband."

"But you are the leader."

Rachel scowled. "Matriarchs are old women."

"Not necessarily, and I'm Irish. I know about these things."

"Are you embarrassed to see Bryan now?"

"I don't know." Darcy glanced out the window. Part of her felt closer to him than ever; part of her thought she was laying too much significance on a simple crying jag. Part of her was terrified she was going to lose him if she didn't get herself together. "Maybe a little. I'm more worried about what brought on all this grief."

"You lost your husband—suddenly, tragically—anybody would—"

"No." She shook her head to clear it. "I mean, yes, I did. But I've spent two years working through losing Tom, and I've been doing okay. The panic attacks and crying were losing steam. The reason I'm such a mess is because I feel so guilty."

"Guilty? But why—" Rachel stopped and nodded. "Bryan."

Surprised she understood, Darcy's gaze darted to Rachel's.

"You guys have been growing pretty close over the last few months. You have strong feelings for him. You…want him."

Darcy pressed her lips together briefly. "Yes."

"So you two haven't…" Rachel raised her eyebrows.

"No. It's weird, right?"

"I don't think so. These days sex is definitely casual for most people, but it doesn't have to be for you. It never was for me—though it took me a while to convince Parker of that."

"It did?"

"Oh, yeah." She smiled, obviously with remembrance. "For him it was all about illicit invitations and keeping everything simple and temporary. Charming, but empty."

"And you didn't want that?"

"I didn't even like him then. But we became friends, and I began to see more in him." Her tone softened; her face glowed. "Eventually, I realized he was everything."

"You two are great together."

"Yeah, we are." She caught Darcy's gaze. "Maybe you and Bryan are, too."

"Maybe." She certainly cared about him more than any man since her husband. "But there's my past and his divorce, and we've been thrown together in this weirdly intimate situation with the training and rehab. I'm not sure we'll last the season. Or even the month."

"But maybe you will."

"I don't see how if I'm afraid to sleep with him."

"He'll be patient." When Darcy dropped her jaw, Rachel laughed. "I know. Not normal for my brother. But he will if he cares enough, and I think he does."

But Darcy knew his patience was holding on by a thread. As for caring, she had no idea how he felt. They'd carefully skipped around those kinds of conversations. They were content. Or had been. Her emotional breakdown had kind of thrown things off stride.

And she was deeply concerned that his divorce—being *rejected*—was something he might never get over.

Did she want a man who was still hung up on his ex-wife? Did he want a woman who still fainted and cried over her deceased husband?

In short, they were a mess.

"Try not to get too stressed over it," Rachel said as she rose. She rinsed her mug and set it in the dishwasher, then turned back to face Darcy. "It's only love."

As Rachel well knew, there were truckloads of implications in that four-letter word. The past, the present, the future. *Everything*.

She forced a smile. "Yeah, only."

"I'm here if you need me. Isabel, too."

"So everybody knows about yesterday? Me fainting?"

"Only the family," Rachel assured her. "Dad blabbed."

"There are races to focus on," Darcy said, a different kind of guilt assaulting her. "The teams running for a championship, dealing with Lars. Nobody needs to worry about me."

"But we do." Rachel smiled gently. "Besides, if you think you're guilt-ridden, you should see Dad. He's a complete mess. He's anxious to apologize, and he's been bugging me since yesterday about what to get you."

"He doesn't have to get me anything. It wasn't his fault."

"I was going to recommend truffles."

Darcy considered that prospect for less than two seconds. "Tell him I'm going to need at least twenty-four, and I like the coconut and raspberry-flavored ones best."

Rachel laughed. "Like I said—smart." She opened the door. "Don't forget we're here for you."

Darcy cupped her hands around her coffee mug. "Thanks. But I hope you won't be dragging me off the floor again anytime soon."

"We're here for more than that."

After Rachel closed the door behind herself, Darcy did something she never did. *Nothing.* She sipped her coffee and listened to the cars loop the speedway and the track announcer talk about the upcoming NASCAR Nationwide Series race, as well as the positions of the drivers practicing at the moment.

She should probably go for a run but decided she was due for a day off. At the moment, all she wanted was Bryan. Maybe she'd feel awkward, maybe she should be embarrassed, but she also knew she'd feel steadier once she saw him.

By the time the door swung open a while later, she'd made chicken salad for lunch, then turned on the TV and settled on the couch to watch the race coverage.

"Hey," Bryan said, walking through the doorway and toward the fridge. After pulling out a bottle of water and drinking from it, he moved toward her. "You feel okay?"

She extended her hand, and he grasped it, sitting beside her on the sofa. "I'm good. Better now that you're here."

He smiled slightly. "You sure about that?"

Leaning forward, she kissed him, and the raw, jagged edges of grief, regret and confusion receded. It was as if he'd breathed life into her again. She laid her hand on his chest and was comforted by the strong, steady beat.

Whatever they had to manage from their pasts, to overcome for future happiness, she knew she wanted to try. She'd helped heal Bryan's body, maybe she could find a way to repair their hearts.

"Thank you for yesterday," she said when she pulled back.

He smoothed her hair off her face. "You're welcome." Then he flung his arm around her waist and hugged her tight.

Surprised by the stark emotions rolling off him, she didn't know what to do except wrap her arms around his neck and hold on.

"You scared me," he said, his voice rough.

"I'm sorry."

"Try not to do that again."

"I'll do my best."

"I didn't realize you still missed him so much."

"I don't." She leaned back to look at him. "Though, I guess I've been repressing a lot lately. Probably not a good idea. But it was more than that. It was the guilt of me moving on. Meeting you, getting close to you."

He said nothing for a long moment. "The fact that I want to sleep with you made you faint?"

"No, the fact that *I* want to."

"Ah." His eyes brightened suddenly. "You do want to?"

She trailed her finger down his chest. "Sure. Now that you're all svelte and sexy."

He frowned. "Just because of that, huh?"

She pressed her lips to his. "There are a few other reasons."

"Can I have a list?"

"I'll make one ASAP, but is it okay if we move past my emotional crisis now?"

"Yeah." He smiled. "What's for lunch?"

"CHICKEN SALAD, HUH?" Bryan asked as he stared down at his plate.

Taking her seat across from him, Darcy shoved his shoulder. "Eat it. It's healthy."

He poked at the lettuce. "It's chick food."

"It is not."

"What're you feeding the teams?"

"I'm not feeding them anything," she said primly, forking up a bite of her own scoop of chicken salad.

He stared at her. "But you know what they're having."

"It's good chicken salad, you know." She pointed with her fork. "I even put in the roasted walnuts you like so much on regular salads."

"You know what they're having."

She sighed. "They're having chicken."

"What kind of chicken?"

"Grilled."

"With…?"

"Slaw and potato salad."

"Is there barbeque sauce on the chicken?"

She bit her lip.

"I know you. I know your meal pairings. When you have slaw and potato salad, there's barbecue sauce involved."

"Fine then. Yes."

"And ribs? I bet they're having ribs, too."

"Possibly." She stabbed more chicken salad. "Cade's jack man is six-four, weighs at least two-sixty, works out two hours every day and loses three pounds a weekend during the races. They can't feed him chicken salad."

"But I can have it."

She leaned forward, sliding her hand up his arm, sending the familiar tingles of desire straight to his gut. "*You,* my amazing boyfriend boss, are an evolved man."

He wasn't sure whether he was being flattered or patronized. He glanced from her hand to the chicken salad, then back to her eyes. "I want this on my list."

"List?"

"The one that records the reasons why you want to sleep with me."

Her eyes lit with sparks. "Done."

"And I want an expiration date on the sex."

She stared at him. "Excuse me?"

"You know, *I will sleep with Bryan by this date and time.*"

"You don't want to let things just happen, you know, naturally?"

"No."

She was silent for a long moment, during which he held his breath. He'd been kidding about the expiration date. Well, sort of. "What date and time did you have in mind?" she asked finally.

He glanced at his watch. "Now's good."

"I—" She set down her fork, then her gaze searched his face. "You're messing with me."

"Yeah," he admitted with a grin.

He'd been so worried about her the night before, about her emotional state, how her breakdown would affect their relationship. Would he never measure up to her former husband? No matter what he did? No matter how much time passed?

And yet he had no right to expect more from her. After all, he was using his own ugly past as motivation to change his future.

"But if there's no sex, then I want a cheeseburger."

"Now?"

"For dinner." Maybe if he kept a teasing attitude, his body would have the strength to follow suit and forget about the injustice of the exchange he was offering. "And every two weeks from now on." When she said nothing, he added, "You get chocolate. I want a cheeseburger."

"Okay, that's just not fair."

He shrugged. "At least I haven't brought up the way you've been hoarding the stuff around here like a squirrel. And not sharing, either."

"'Cause you're too nice to do that," she said sarcastically.

"Exactly."

She scowled as she picked up her water glass. "If you want the cheeseburgers, you'll have to cut calories or increase exercise somewhere."

"Do I? I'm in maintenance mode, right? I don't need to lose more weight. Just keep a balance."

She paused with her glass hovering at her lips. "You listen to me way too closely."

Laughing, he linked their hands. "You're the only woman on the planet who's ever uttered those words."

"Possibly."

"I'll make the burgers tonight."

"But I'm supposed to—"

He shook his head. "If you're about to tell me that's your job or I can't figure out how to grill meat by myself, I'm going to have to turn in my man card. I'm eating the dang chicken salad. Let me do dinner."

"Do I get to lounge on the sofa watching sports on TV?"

"I'd rather you hover by my side and tell me how great a cook I am."

"As long as you return the favor."

After lunch, he suggested they go out to watch

some of the on-track activities. She agreed, though tentatively. "Are you sure nobody knows about yesterday?" she asked as they stepped outside.

"Of course people know. Not that I told anybody. Or Dad or Rachel. But a medic worked on you, plus there was the hospitality volunteer and—"

"But Rachel said nobody knew," she protested, her voice high and alarmed.

"When you're associated with my family you're going to get talked about. It's part of the deal." Glancing at her pale face, he pressed his hand into the small of her back and urged her toward the garages. He really needed to talk to Shawn about his practice session that morning, which hadn't gone well, but he didn't want to leave Darcy alone in the motor home with her sorrow and stash of chocolate bars. "Rachel probably didn't want you to worry."

"I think I'll go back to the motor home," she said, turning. "I could start dinner."

He steered her back the other direction and kept a tight hold on her hand to be sure she didn't run off. "It's barely one o'clock, I know you like watching the races and I'm in charge of dinner. Forget about yesterday. It's not like people are going to be whispering about you behind their hands."

She didn't look so sure, but she walked along beside him. As they started to round the corner of the garage stalls, she shook her hand free of his. "This isn't a date," she said, her eyes looking to his for understanding. "We need to be professional."

Though he nodded, he was surprised by his reluctance to let her go. He wasn't a big PDA guy, and with any woman he'd dated in the past, *he* would have been the one to ask for distance. Maybe it was simply the lingering protectiveness he felt toward her because of yesterday.

As they walked into the main hub of the garage area, he saw lots of familiar faces. He spoke to a couple of people as he made his way to Shawn's stall. The NASCAR Nationwide Series drivers were taking their parade laps around the track, preparing for the start of their race, their immediate vicinity was free of media and fans.

Bryan found Shawn talking to his crew chief, Kyle, at the back of his race car. "How are things?" he asked after they'd greeted Darcy.

"I can't drive it through the center of the corner," Shawn said, his voice tight with anxiety.

Shawn, who'd grown up in Southern California, had always reminded Bryan of a surfer—shaggy blond hair, casual, live-and-let-live philosophy. Unfortunately, he didn't look so laid-back at the moment.

He wanted desperately to make the Chase for the NASCAR Sprint Cup. With Kevin as defending champion and Cade's own intense drive to win the championship, having only missed it by a few points the previous year, Shawn longed to prove he belonged in the GRI stable of elite drivers.

Bryan remembered his own ferocious need to demonstrate he was worthy of belonging to his family of champions, so he understood as probably few could.

"What've you done?" he asked Kyle.

"We tried Cade's setup," he said.

Shawn sighed. "We think that's why the last practice was so lousy."

Cade and Shawn had a completely different style of driving, and each setup was tailored to a particular driver. If the guy behind the wheel didn't have the feel he wanted, the car was going to the back pretty quickly, no matter how brilliant the engineers, mechanics and other support personnel. Shawn's team must have been fairly desperate to try that particular tactic.

"Don't panic," Bryan said. "We'll figure something out."

Had his absence yesterday caused their worry to intensify? His dad hadn't been around, either. Darcy's collapse had distracted them all.

Times like this reminded him how difficult it was to balance his personal and professional life. He'd focused on his career, no doubt ignoring his wife too often, and wound up divorced. His parents had made things work for a long, long time, but they, too, hadn't lasted.

But his brother and sister were managing. Hell, thriving.

Was it all a matter of the right timing, or the right person?

He shook off the personal thoughts. "Let me look at your notes," he said to Kyle, reaching for his clipboard.

"I'll let you guys handle—" Darcy glanced at Kyle's scribbled chart of tire pressure, wind tunnel results, dyno testing and resulting track speed "—all that. I'm going over to Shawn's hauler. I need to find out if they got all the supplies for tomorrow's lunch."

"I'll find you in a few minutes," Bryan said.

As their gazes met briefly, she nodded. Professionally. Boss-to-employee-like. After all they'd been through in the last day, the detachment was odd.

He didn't like it one bit.

"Hey," Shawn called as she started to walk away, "the chicken was great. Thanks."

Kyle grinned, then elbowed his driver. "Sure it was. But the ribs were even better."

Darcy's gaze darted to Bryan's. Her face flushed. He'd known they'd had ribs.

When she was gone, Bryan gave his full attention to Shawn and Kyle. There was a final practice late that afternoon, so they had only one, short opportunity to try out the new strategy they came up with before race day.

Retreating to the back of the garage and the computer, they talked through their plans, consulting with mechanics and engineers and calling Sam, Cade's crew chief, at one point to get his thoughts.

To start a race with an ill-handling race car, basically putting the driver and team into a hole they had to dig out of before the first lap was even complete, rarely led to a successful finish.

Still, Bryan occasionally found himself glancing into the area between the garages and haulers, looking for Darcy.

At one point, he saw her talking to Chance Baker, of all people. He ignored every instinct he possessed that told him to run to her, separate her from the man who seemed determined—or destined—to interfere with Bryan's life at every turn.

By the time he'd finished his meeting with Shawn and Kyle, she was standing behind the car, waiting for him.

"What did you talk to Chance about?" Bryan asked, heading out at a brisk pace.

"Nothing much. He wanted to know why I'd taken the job with you instead of him."

"And you said?"

"That my friendship with Parker inspired me to go with GRI instead."

He glanced at her. "*Is* that why you took the job?"

"Yes." She paused. "I didn't know you then—"

"And I wasn't very nice to you. Parker had to be the only incentive."

They reached the end of the garage stalls. A group of Cade's crew were heading the opposite way. They smiled, and Darcy waved, but Bryan didn't stop or acknowledge them.

"What's wrong with you?" Darcy asked.

He didn't answer, but his heart rate picked up speed, as did his stride.

"Are you mad I talked to Chance?"

"No, of course not." But he was. Irrationally, the idea of Chance talking to Darcy, of him being anywhere on the planet near her, was maddening. And why? It's not as if he was jealous of that little jerk.

"He asked me a question, and I answered it," Darcy said, her tone pushing toward annoyance. "Nothing personal. What was I supposed to say?"

"*Get lost* is the first thing that comes to mind."

Once they passed by the guard at the drivers' and owners' motor home lot, she grabbed his arm and turned him to face her. "So you're mad I talked to him."

"I said I wasn't."

"You're mad about something."

"I'm—" What was he exactly? He pushed his hand through his hair, resisting the urge to tug. Frustration and aggravation permeated his every pore. It was the upcoming race. It *had* to be. He was taking on Shawn and Kyle's frustration with the car. One glance at Chance Baker talking to his woman couldn't—

Oh, man.

His woman?

"I think Nicole left him," Darcy said, breaking into his disturbing thoughts.

And it just gets better. Or was it worse?

When he didn't comment, but started walking again, she asked, "If that's true, how do you feel?"

"Am I supposed to congratulate her, or commiserate with him?"

"Don't be flip. My…episode happened because I was suppressing my feelings. They built up and—"

"And your knees were suddenly weak?" He flung open the door to his motor home. "Come on, Darcy. That was entirely different."

She stared at him in disbelief. "No, it's not. Are you really going to stand there and tell me it doesn't matter to you whether or not your ex is still hooked up with Chance?" She held up her finger before he could speak. "Try to remember I'm the person who set you on your revenge quest."

He stared at the floor. He couldn't deny the truth to those all-seeing golden eyes. "Okay, fine. Maybe it matters. But at the moment Nicole doesn't concern me near as much as you." He met her gaze. "I don't want you talking to Chance. I don't even want you near him." Lifting his hands, then letting them fall, he confessed the humiliating truth. "There you go. I'm a possessive, jealous idiot."

CHAPTER FOURTEEN

DARCY'S MOUTH WENT DRY. "Jealous? You're jealous of Chance."

"Yes." Bryan hissed out the word. "He has what I'm supposed to have—a successful driving career, endless opportunities for fame, fortune, glory, trophies and championships. He also has my wife."

Braced against the counter, Darcy tried to order her thoughts. She supposed she should be flattered Bryan was possessive of her. It was the *my wife* part that she couldn't get past. He still thought of Nicole as belonging to him.

A lump rose in her throat that she fought to talk around. "Would you—"

"He took my wife," he said harshly before she could get out her question. "He's not taking my girlfriend."

Her gaze jumped to his. "You don't seriously think I'm interested in dating Chance Baker, do you?"

"If he tried to hire you, would you accept?"

"No."

Her simple, immediate response seemed to startle

him. "What if he offered you triple the money?" he asked.

Darcy closed her eyes. Her heart contracted in her chest. "No." She forced herself to look at him. "You think I'm here for money?" she whispered. "You think this is just a job to me?"

"I don't know."

Dear heaven, she had no idea his ability to trust was so damaged by that selfish witch he'd been married to. "I know I've got problems. I know I'm not the easiest person to deal with sometimes. I'm demanding and prideful." She clenched her fist by her side. "But I am not *her.*"

He turned away, then sank on the sofa, bracing his elbows on his knees. "Told you I'm an idiot. I'm not trying to compare you to her. I didn't mean to—"

"Would you take her back if she asked you?"

He looked up. "No. No way."

She didn't completely believe him. Not that he was lying. He was telling the truth as he considered it now. But if Nicole came to him with tears and apologies, criticism of Chance and the way he'd treated her—whether that was true or not—Bryan would be tempted.

If for nothing else than to say he'd won.

"I'm sorry." He snagged her hand and pulled her down beside him, then drew her into his arms. "I really messed this up."

She inhaled his familiar, wood- and spice-infused

scent, and her heart ached. She was trying to move on with her life only to fall for a man who might never truly be hers? How stupid was that?

Yet she couldn't seem to stop herself from taking the risk anyway.

"You could argue with me a little about the idiot part," he said after a moment.

She pressed her cheek against his neck. "No, I really don't think I can."

Leaning back, he cupped her face in his hand. "Then will you forgive me and let me make you dinner?"

"I can do that."

He kissed her softly. "I don't want to talk about them anymore today."

"Who?"

"Nicole and Tom."

She angled her head. *Tom?* "What about Chance?"

"I *definitely* don't want to talk about him. I barely acknowledge he breathes most of the time, but today I had to restrain myself from punching him out. I thought I'd gotten past that urge."

"The past sneaks up and bites you when you least expect it."

"I guess it does."

She'd used the *I don't want to talk about it* tactic with him, then proceeded to blab endlessly anyway. She doubted the same would work with him. And she knew they needed to talk about Nicole, just as she'd confessed her guilt about Tom. If she and Bryan were going to make anything meaningful out of their relationship, they had to settle their pasts first.

After yesterday, she felt as if she was finally moving forward, and while he'd done so physically, she didn't think he'd fully come to terms with how much his ex's betrayal had scarred his heart. Or how much he craved Nicole's acknowledgment that he was a better man than Chance.

But it had been an emotional couple of days, and they needed to set aside some of the unanswered questions and just enjoy each other.

"Okay," she said. "Let's start the grill and table everything else—her, him, the past, fainting, all of it."

"I can make a really great cheeseburger, you know."

She shrugged. "If you say so. I'm not much of a judge. I haven't had a cheeseburger in years."

His jaw dropped. "Years? How do you survive?"

"You're never really going to completely leave your red-meat-and-potato-loving ways behind, are you?"

"I doubt it." He rose, pulling her up beside him. "You'll just have to hang around to make sure I stay on the sort-of straight and narrow."

The future.

Even the thought of anything beyond the next twenty-four hours used to make her sad. She'd planned a future once, and it had crashed to pieces. Even so, she couldn't imagine not coming to the track with Bryan each week, working out with him, sharing meals with him, having him around to touch and hold.

And while he meant the comment casually, to her, realizing she could begin to finally think in that direction, was an incredibly bright spot in an otherwise tumultuous weekend.

"As long as you supply me with chocolate, I'm all yours," she said lightly.

After a quick grin, he kissed her.

While he started the grill, she poked through the fridge for some veggies and fresh fruit to go with the burgers. If the man was determined to eat high-fat, high-calorie, at least she could provide some nutrition.

During the prep work, Cade and Isabel showed up—since their motor home was next door, they'd smelled the grill. Then Parker, Rachel and Mitch arrived. Before long, all the drivers, wives and kids on the row had wandered over, offering Bryan help at the grill, meat, side dishes and drinks to add. In no time, a full-fledged block party was underway.

With the last half of the NASCAR Nationwide Series race still rolling around them, there was a lot of good-natured jeering about who would win, who was doing well and what that meant for the race tomorrow.

Darcy was in her element.

She fed people who were hungry, even making miniburgers for the kids whose eyes widened in fear and awe at the size of the half-pound ones the adults ate. She ran between the kitchen and the tables that had been pulled together outside, offering appetizers, drinks and minimal comments about her and Bryan.

He'd been right. Everybody knew about yesterday.

But there were no snide remarks or leering curiosity. Everyone seemed to have an uplifting story to share about the life of their loved one or friend, shared memories of tributes and families who'd found strength among the racing community whenever they needed support.

It was so similar to the firefighters' mentality she'd been part of for so long, she had to blink to realize she was in the company of women who'd cheered, supported and practically helped drive the car for their husbands to celebrate multiple racing championships. On a regional and national level. Nearly all their lives.

There were couples who'd just started out in the world of NASCAR racing; there were couples who'd been together thirty years.

"It's hard to believe that when we come back here in a couple of months, it'll be the first race for the championship," Kevin Reiner's wife, Kim, commented as the kids tossed around a football, and the guys argued the differences between gas and charcoal grills.

"Is it weird to think Kevin won't be in the running to defend his title?" Rachel asked.

"A little," Kim said. "But the kids and I like having him home more. He and I have been on the road together for nearly twenty years. It was time."

"Does he actually sit on the sofa and watch the races on Sunday?" Darcy asked. Even after four and a half years of retirement, Bryan never seemed to sit still during a TV broadcast.

"Oh, yeah." Kim smiled. "The neighbors come over and we have cookouts like this. Of course Kevin spends half his time shouting at the TV. Either the commentators say something he doesn't agree with, or a driver he likes or doesn't like is doing something smart or dumb, depending."

To Darcy, Kevin was always charming and teasing, but she knew he had to have an intense side, as all drivers seemed to.

"Hey, Darcy," Kevin called out, as if he knew they'd been talking about him. "You're a master chef. Isn't a charcoal grill better?"

Apparently they were intense about grills, as well as racing.

She glanced at Bryan, who'd just cooked his burger masterpieces on charcoal. She generally preferred gas because it was easier to use and cooked more evenly. All that lighter fluid and fire must be a guy thing.

"Grilling is all in the seasoning and marinade," she called back. "The grill just provides the heat."

They all stared at her for a couple of seconds, then turned to each other and resumed the debate.

"I think you just put fuel on that particular fire," Rachel said to Darcy.

"Naturally." Isabel rolled her eyes. "She didn't agree with one side or the other."

"You can't be neutral in this sport," Kim added.

"What sport?" Darcy asked. "We're talking about cooking. It's not rocket science." Thinking about the guys on the GRI teams, though, the way they hovered and offered advice when she helped cook lunch, she reconsidered. "They do take food very seriously."

"Didn't Big Dan make you audition before he'd let you touch his grill?" Rachel asked.

"He did." But that seemed so long ago. Now, she and Big Dan were a formidable, well-balanced cooking team. She'd become part of GRI. Practically part of the family, according to Rachel.

But she'd only signed on for the season, and Bryan had made his fitness goals. He knew the rehab exercises so well, he really didn't need her help. Would there come a time when she wouldn't be part of the team? Would she and Bryan continue to date past the terms of her job? Or would it all be over at the end of the season?

Rachel laid her hand on Darcy's arm. "Are you okay? You look a little pale."

"I'm fine." She shoved aside her troubled thoughts. This afternoon was supposed to be about relaxing. "Great, actually. I'm going to get another bottle of water," she said as she rose. "Anybody else?"

When everybody shook their heads, she moved toward the motor home door, then slipped inside. As she grabbed a bottle from the fridge, she thought about the last couple of days and all that she and Bryan had shared and been through.

He'd been amazingly supportive and caring. And while he probably wouldn't describe himself as patient, he had been—about her crises over the past and her inability to be intimate.

But if they were going to move forward, if she wanted to truly be part of the team, she was going to have to think beyond next week and consider her future. What she wanted, where she wanted to go, who she wanted to be with.

"Hey," Bryan said as he opened the door. "You okay?"

She sipped her water and took in the long-legged, broad-shouldered length of him in his fitted navy T-shirt and jeans. "Yep."

And feeling better by the second.

"What're you doing in here by yourself?"

"Thinking about you," she said, smiling as she walked toward him. She slid the tips of her fingers up his chest. "This was supposed to be our relaxing evening alone."

His eyes lighting like blue flames, he wrapped his arm around her waist. "The smell of the grill drew too much attention."

"Your burgers were great."

"Yeah? You didn't miss the tofu and alfalfa sprouts?"

"Not today." She glared at him with mock sternness. "But it's back on the program tomorrow. We run at seven."

"A.M.?"

"Definitely." She looped her arms around his neck. "Unless…"

He drew her tight against him. "Unless…?"

"Any chance we can have a relaxing *evening* alone?"

"Hmm." He brushed his lips across her cheek. "I think we can manage that. But what in the world would we do all by ourselves?"

"We'll think of something." She grinned teasingly. "A movie maybe?"

"As long as we share the popcorn bowl with you sitting in my lap."

"Then we'll have to watch something we've seen before. You always distract me."

As his eyes turned smoky, he brushed her hair off her face. "Or we could skip the movie and move straight to the fun part."

She leaned forward, pressing her lips against his. Putting a little effort into the kiss, she found her pulse pounding, her blood heating. His hands, braced at her hips, tightened.

"Maybe we could run a little later," she said softly when she pulled back, knowing she'd taken another step into her future.

ALMOST BEFORE BRYAN BLINKED, the company plane had touched down in Indianapolis, Indiana, the last weekend in July. One of the most prestigious trophies of the season was on the line in three days.

Everything was heightened for this race. Though

it seemed the level of competition could jack no higher, it always did. Worldwide media, teams and fans invaded the town and the track with the fervor of a religious movement. Sponsors and business partners held special events. Drivers smiled for the cameras, while their insides jumped like a pond of frogs.

On Cade's particular team, Sam was worried about the engine. Bryan was worried about fuel mileage. Cade was simply worried.

While he had three wins for the season so far, and two other drivers had two each—including Chance Baker—Cade had had some bad finishes lately and had fallen to fourth in the championship standings. He was so edgy, no one wanted to be around him— apparently including his wife, since she sat beside Darcy in the pair of seats in front of Bryan.

As he rose to depart the plane, he stepped back so they could slide in front of him.

He touched Darcy's shoulder, and she turned her head to smile at him. His heart jumped, as always.

She let Isabel out in front of her, then reached back to squeeze his hand.

Moments like these were ones that made him realize how vital she'd become to his life. He wasn't sure he'd ever shared a bond with anyone like the one he had with Darcy.

And yet everything was also unsettled.

Over the last few weeks, they'd established a pattern. She went to and from the hotels near the track with Parker and Rachel. Parker always made sure Darcy had a room reservation, and Bryan felt better knowing she wasn't making those trips—on unfamiliar roads and often at night—alone.

The schedule also gave his dates with Darcy a deadline. When Parker and Rachel were ready to leave the track, Darcy went with them. And while he'd taken more cold showers over the summer than he'd had in his life, he'd nearly convinced himself that his ability to maintain a platonic relationship with a woman he wanted more than he needed to take his next breath was a test of his yoga skills.

He focused as often as possible on work, which he at least understood. Except when she smiled at him. Or touched him. Or breathed in his vicinity.

Hell, he was in a world of trouble.

But on Friday afternoon following practice, he smiled as he walked through the garage area.

The expression was a rare occurrence pretty much anytime, but when his teams were running lousy, a good mood was usually nonexistent. But today he was going home to Darcy.

He hadn't thought about home in a long time. He had a house; he had a motor home. They'd both been professionally decorated, and he'd added little. His ex-wife had influenced his surroundings way more than he had, and he hadn't bothered to change much since she'd left.

He had a home he'd grown up in, but that wasn't the same since his parents' breakup.

His stagnant position stemmed back to his accident.

His very identity had changed in a moment of screeching tires and crashing metal on the highway. He was a race car driver, then suddenly he wasn't. He'd lost his career, his wife, his fire, his ambition, his physique, his confidence…everything.

Darcy had brought it all back. And though things would never be exactly the way they were before, he'd regained much of what had been missing in his life.

He could handle anything that came his way. He could face a practice session where his teams were running eighteenth, twenty-second and twenty-fifth for one of the biggest races of the year.

Wincing, he turned down the row of motor homes where his was parked. Well, the *idea* could still be painful, even if he was confident about being able to deal with the situation.

He opened his door and lifted his credential lanyard over his head, tossing it on the kitchen counter to his left. "Hey, what's—"

"Hi, Bryan."

He blinked, but his ex-wife was still sitting on his sofa.

Leggy, glossy and blond, she smiled at him as she stood. "How are you?"

He was… He seemed to have lost his voice. As well as the anger he usually associated with her. "Fine," he finally managed to say.

She moved toward him, her long, tanned legs closing the distance in two strides. "You certainly look good." Brushing her fingertips down the front of his T-shirt, her gaze connected with his. "Really good."

Glaring at her, he stepped back. "I'm busy. Do you need something?"

She moved toward him. "Just you."

What?

He barely stopped short of asking the question out loud. What the devil was going on with her? The desire in her eyes, the longing in her voice, was something he'd dreamed about for a long time. Suddenly she was delivering his wish?

When he'd needed her the most, she'd run. Bolted to his family's greatest rival and crippled his recovery from the accident. She'd only wanted a driver, not him. For better or for worse be damned.

And yet, the guy he thought he'd buried in the last few months, the angry, selfish man who'd started out on a fitness quest purely for revenge, looked at her and wondered. What did she want from him? Why was she here? Did she now regret leaving him? If so, how much?

"Do you really?" he asked, his tone cynical. "What happened to Chance?"

Her eyes brimming with tears, she looked away. "He's gone. I'm not sure he ever cared about me at all."

"No kidding."

She dragged her gaze back to his. "He's not like you."

Finally, something he could agree with. "No, he's not. Look, Nicole, if you came here to—"

She pressed herself against him, backing him against the wall. Her perfume, an exotic, musky blend of flowers, washed over him, teasing his memory with times when he'd desired her with a fever.

"What do you say, Bryan?" she whispered, her lips nearly touching his. "Wanna take a walk down memory lane?"

CHAPTER FIFTEEN

DARCY PAUSED with her hand on the door latch of Bryan's motor home.

"I love him," she whispered, hoping when she said the words aloud for the first time they'd sound wrong.

They didn't.

Crap.

Darkness had settled over the track, but the heat hadn't abated. She'd give up chocolate for a month for a cool breeze.

On second thought, that was a rash promise. She might need a truckload of it before the night was over.

Deciding she'd been a chicken long enough, she flipped the latch and opened the door. Cool air washed over her as she peered into the darkness. Confused, she started to call Bryan's name when she saw him, pacing near the front of the motor home. He had a bottle in his hand.

He stopped and turned toward her. "Where've you been?"

She closed the door behind her. "Hi, to you, too."

"I was getting worried," he said, though he didn't

move toward her. No welcoming kiss, no hug or teasing smile.

"Is that why you're alone in the dark, drinking?" she asked, heading toward the fridge for a bottle of water. She needed something to ease the dry panic in her throat. Gulping, she noticed two empty beer bottles sitting on the kitchen counter.

"I felt like having a beer," he said defensively, aggressively.

"Looks like more than *a* beer to me."

"So you're my mother now?"

Ignoring her pulse's bump of irritation and worry, she flipped on the track lighting over the sofa. "What's wrong?"

He looked away from her and resumed pacing. "Nothing."

"Are you concerned about the practice session?"

"No."

"Is everything okay with your family?"

"Yes."

"Are you in pain?"

Pausing briefly in his restless movement, he shook his head. "No."

"Then it must be about Nicole."

He ground to a halt, then drank from the bottle. "I… How did you—"

"I saw her leave."

"But she left hours ago."

"I know. I walked around a while before I came

back. I couldn't—" She cleared her throat as images of what might have gone on between Bryan and his ex danced cruelly through her mind.

Oh, but isn't that moment the reason you realized you loved him?

Sure. Yippee.

Since that was also the moment she realized how much he could hurt her, how much of him obviously still belonged to Nicole, she couldn't find the hope to be positive.

"I needed to get my thoughts together before I came back," she managed to say.

"Yeah, I can understand that." Suddenly looking depressed instead of angry, he sank onto the sofa and pushed his hand through his hair. "I'm sorry."

Her hand clenched around her water bottle. "What are you sorry about?"

"For jumping down your throat when you walked in. I'm not mad at you. I'm mad at myself."

"Why?"

"For letting her tempt me."

Darcy's legs trembled. She remembered having the same reaction to a group of firefighters barely a month ago.

But she wasn't going to faint. Not now. No way.

She'd faced her own past; she could face Bryan's, as well. And even though she realized he held her heart in his hands, she wanted to trust him with it. She wanted to fight for them.

Would he really betray her with the woman who'd broken his heart? Who'd hit his confidence like the suddenness of a bomb exploding? Who was a constant reminder of all he'd lost?

Not now. No way.

She set her water aside and crossed to him. He stood as she approached and yanked her into his arms. "Dammit, Darcy. I'm supposed to be over all this."

Pressing her face against his neck, she drew in the scent of his cologne's warm cedar fragrance, welcoming her into his embrace like a comforting blanket. "Yeah. Let me know when that happens. I'd like to join you."

"Nothing happened," he said, squeezing her tight.

She leaned back and studied him. "Nothing, huh?"

His gaze darted away, and when he looked back at her, his eyes were clear and focused. "She…she made an offer."

"And you wanted to accept."

"Yeah."

Her stomach dropped, and she wiggled her way out of his arms. "I need to go."

"Please don't." He grabbed her by her wrist. "I wanted to accept for a *second.* I wanted her to regret leaving me. And she does. Or so she says."

A shiver of fear went through Darcy's body. "Does she? So you dived into the beer to celebrate?"

"No." He tugged her down to sit beside him on the sofa. "No." He set his beer bottle on the side table. "I was confused because I didn't know how to tell you. How to explain. I'm furious at myself for being tempted. For forgetting, even for a second, that she's the enemy."

"Because she left you for another man or because that other man is a member of the Baker family?"

"Both."

She closed her eyes briefly and fought to accept the idea that personal and racing issues blended. The rivalry with the Bakers had started long before she arrived, and she wasn't likely to affect any change.

But her concerns were personal at the moment, and she couldn't care less about GRI, trophies or championships. Her heart was on the line. Her heart, which had jumped with such fear when she'd seen Nicole slip out of Bryan's motor home that she'd darted out of sight and run away from him and her feelings.

Maybe I should have kept running.

But, no, even as that thought raced through her mind, she pushed it away. She was done trying to escape from pleasure and pain. She was constantly proving to people how strong she was physically— challenging every available male to a push-up contest came to mind in particular—and it was time to prove her strength in other ways.

It was time to let her love for her husband rest in peace. It was time to leave the past behind and take a risk. Her love for Bryan, which felt so fresh, new and scary was already being tested.

But she could handle that, too.

She swallowed the tears clawing their way up her throat. "So, on some level, you still…want her. But what does she mean to you? What do you feel for her?"

He slid his thumb across the back of her hand. "I wish I could say nothing. I'd *hoped* she meant nothing." His gaze flicked to hers. "But after tonight, I have so many regrets."

She wanted to shudder, but refused to give in. "Okay."

"I should have been a better husband—more attentive, more sensitive. But, in a way, I'm also glad I wasn't." His eyes burned brightly blue. "Because I never would have met you."

Her breath caught; her heart thumped like crazy.

"I don't want her." He cupped her cheek. "I want you."

Studying his handsome, so familiar and cherished face, a smile tugged at her lips. She leaned toward him. "Same goes."

Their mouths met, and as she wrapped her arms around his neck, the relief that he'd seen through whatever scheme his ex had cooked up made her light-headed.

And while his confession was a balm for her heart, she didn't believe for a moment that everything was all roses, champagne and proposals. Certainly neither of them were ready for that.

But they were ready for the next step.

Gripping his hand in hers, she pulled back and rose. "I've spent the night in your bed twice. I was alone both times. I'd like to try it with you there this time."

He searched her gaze. "Are you sure?"

"I'm sure."

Tucking her against his side, he led her down the hall.

AS LIGHT PEEKED THROUGH the blinds in the bedroom, Bryan slid his hand across Darcy's bare stomach and pulled her back against him. "Morning," he mumbled next to her ear.

"Already?" She pressed her face into the pillow. "Make it stop."

"No early-morning jog?" he teased. "There's a lake."

"No jogging. I'm exhausted. You kept me up half the night."

He kissed her shoulder. "Want me to help wake you up?"

She turned her head. Sparks of desire were evident in her golden eyes. "You could do that."

He proceeded to show her just how happy he was to accommodate her needs.

AFTER DRAGGING HIMSELF out of bed and sliding on a pair of jeans, Bryan headed into the kitchen to start the coffee. If Darcy was going to be the lazy one, somebody had to get breakfast and their day started.

With the coffee brewing, he pulled the egg carton

out of the fridge and reflected on how precious these stolen moments with Darcy were. His crazy life. How long could he have lasted before he burned out? How long before his family's company became a burden instead of a joy?

Darcy had certainly changed him.

But was he good for her?

He dragged her all over the country and rarely spent any time with her, other than during meals and exercise. He was moody and stressed about Cade's quest for a championship. They'd been testing so often during the early part of the week, he hadn't taken her out much when he was home.

And while he was thrilled she'd spent the night in his bed, he worried that he'd somehow pushed her into a decision she wasn't ready for. Would she have guilt and regrets? Would she think of her husband? Compare Bryan to him?

He'd been honest with her about Nicole, but had he been wise in confessing his brief temptation? Had Darcy slept with him to prove she was the one he desired?

The possibilities made his stomach clench.

"Can't even think positively for ten minutes, can you, mate?" he muttered to himself as he pulled out the omelet pan.

When he walked into the bedroom a bit later with coffee and a cheese omelet, she was still lying in bed, her eyes closed. "Do I smell food?"

Obviously not asleep, though. He sat on the edge of the bed, and she dragged herself up, pushing her tangled hair out of her eyes. "At your service."

She reached for the plate and mug, taking a sip before setting the coffee on the bedside table. "Do I get sexy early wake-up calls and breakfast in bed every morning from now on? Clearly, I should have jumped you long before last night."

Though it was wonderful to see her relaxed and happy, he couldn't let his doubts linger. "Do you feel okay about last night?"

Her eyes danced. "I'm much better than okay." She fed him a bite of eggs. "Gee, Bryan, you could flatter yourself a little."

"I'm glad I can, but I was thinking more about how you feel emotionally."

"We've had sex and now you want me to talk about my *feelings?* Good grief, you'd better get out there with your testosterone buddies ASAP, or they'll revoke your man card."

"They probably would." He met her gaze and made sure his stare was serious. Was she avoiding talking about how she felt on purpose? "We waited a long time to take this step, and I want to be sure you're okay with your decision."

Setting aside her plate, she linked her hand with his. "I'm fine. Truly. No regrets."

"So you didn't sleep with me because of what I told you about my ex?"

She angled her head. "Huh?"

Her simple confusion was a great relief, but he needed to be sure. "I told you I wanted you, but did you need me to prove it?"

Golden stars sparked in her eyes. "I only needed you to touch me. If there was any proving going on, it was on my part. I wanted to show you how much you mean to my life. I wanted to finally put the past behind me."

He searched her gaze. "And have you?"

"I have."

Kissing her softly, he closed his eyes to enjoy the relief and promise of her words. "I'm glad," he said when he leaned back. "My jealousy over your deceased and heroic firefighter husband was getting to be kind of pathetic."

"His memory will always be important to me, but you have absolutely no reason to be jealous."

"I'm the first since him, though, right?"

"You are."

"And you didn't think about…" he trailed off, feeling stupid for bringing up the subject, but as long as they were letting go of the past, they might as well really do it.

"No." Smiling, she laid her hand on his bare chest. "There's plenty of you to concentrate on."

"I have to keep up with you and those push-ups, don't I?"

She picked up her plate and offered him another

bite of omelet. "I'm not challenging you anymore. You've beaten me the last three times."

"Remember when I could barely do five?"

"Sure." She sipped her coffee, then handed the mug to him. "It was only a few months ago."

"It seems longer. It's weird imagining my life without you."

"Of course it is. Who'd feed and nag you?"

Again, he got the odd sensation that she was deliberately making their conversation casual. He, however, was concerned. He wanted to make sure she was satisfied and happy. He needed reassurances that they were secure as a couple.

Hell, maybe he *did* need his man card revoked.

"Who'd nag me?" he asked, going with her teasing tone. "Oh, just my mother, my sister, the crew chiefs, engineers and fabricators. Carmen, our office manager, being the mother of three, is also an expert. Even my dad—"

"You need to release some of that tension." She took the coffee mug, setting it and the empty plate aside. "Should we go jogging around the lake or…" She glanced back at the rumpled bed.

An insatiable Darcy was beyond enticing. And burning calories could be accomplished in ways besides running.

WHEN RACE MORNING DAWNED, Bryan woke with his stomach clenched.

Despite the fact that Darcy lay next to him, her breathing deep and even, her beautiful face relaxed with sleep, he couldn't stay in bed.

Life couldn't be all shared cheese omelets, cool sheets and heated sighs.

At least not *his* life.

He slid out of bed, then leaned over and brushed the back of his hand across Darcy's downy cheek. He inhaled the scent of her tropical-fruit-and-vanilla perfume, which he'd actually discovered the night before was a lotion she used twice daily—one he'd generously volunteered to rub on her to make sure she covered all the important spots.

After a quick shower, he dressed in jeans and a GRI candy-apple red polo shirt. No matter what happened that afternoon, no one could deny where his loyalties were placed. He recalled vividly the morning he'd gotten up six years ago without a trophy from Indy, but by the time he'd gone to bed—in the champagne-soaked wee hours of the morning—he had that precious goal checkmarked.

Finally.

At the moment, and especially now that he was retired, he was incredibly proud to have his name as part of the long and storied history of the grand track. All the greats had kissed those famous bricks, and he wanted the same for Cade.

The excitement, anticipation and nerves his brother

would feel that day were familiar to Bryan. They'd once been his life, too, after all.

He knew Cade had eaten his traditional night-before-race meal of lasagna and garlic bread sticks. He'd wake up and go through his morning routine in an exacting order. He'd wear his lucky socks and hunt down Parker to make sure he was carrying the lucky penny. He'd do nothing out of the ordinary or anything to tempt Fate.

Was it all just a bit silly?

Sure, but Bryan would never tell a driver that. He'd done the same thing. Just as those before him had, and those who'd come after him would.

Has it really been six years since I won here?

It meant he'd been retired for nearly five full seasons. His entire career in NASCAR Nationwide and NASCAR Sprint Cup Series had only spanned that time period. In an odd way, he still thought of himself as a driver, not an owner.

Darcy woke up as he was tying his tennis shoes. "I thought I was the early riser in this relationship."

Crossing to the bed, he sat beside her. He tucked her tousled hair behind her ear on one side, then leaned down to kiss her. "Sympathy stress for Cade."

"Hmmph. For Cade, huh? How about you?" She sat up and stretched her arms over her head. "No Indy win for GRI since you took over as head honcho."

"You've been talking to Rachel."

"Actually, it was your dad who shared that tidbit."

He sighed. "I'm so glad I don't have to worry about some slick-talking dude like Parker coming along and stealing my girlfriend. I can count on my own father for that."

"He brings me chocolate, and I listen to his dating woes. It's a beautiful relationship." She curled her arms around his neck. "And don't worry about Cade. He'll be fine."

"Is that right?" Since she'd insisted on sleeping in a baseball-style shirt with Cade's number and colors, he knew he wasn't the only one trying to send positive vibes his brother's way. "I'd be happy if Shawn or Kevin won, too, you know."

She kissed him briefly. "No, you'd be content." She climbed out of bed.

"You don't have to get up for me."

"Hey, I'm a supportive girlfriend. I'm here for you in your needy and desperate times."

"I'm not needy or desperate." He watched her hips sway as she headed toward the bathroom. "I have you in my bed at night, in the morning, and actually the afternoon could be fun, too."

"Exactly. I'm used to losing sleep."

He leaned against the door frame of the bathroom while she started the shower. "So you're reluctantly dragging yourself awake as a show of devotion to me and my anxiety?"

"Well…"

"You're cooking breakfast for the teams, aren't you?"

Whirling, she planted her hands on her hips. "Who've *you* been talking to?"

"Big Dan. I was going to wake you up before I left if you weren't already."

She pouted briefly. "I'm still concerned about your anxiety."

He kissed her forehead. "Don't be. We're going to win, you know. I can feel it."

"Don't say the *W* word to Cade—or anybody on the team."

"Right. The jinx." He reluctantly turned away. They had their last off weekend coming up at the end of next month, and he mentally made a note to ask Parker for a good island spot to take Darcy. He'd love to pamper her and spend huge chunks of time with her while she wore nothing but a bikini.

"Can you give me fifteen minutes?" she asked. "We'll go together."

"Sure." He shrugged. "I need my breakfast, too."

As she tossed a washcloth at him, he closed the door and headed to the kitchen. He started the coffeepot, then peeked out the window.

He saw no one moving along the rows of motor homes, but he knew there were plenty of people stirring inside. The garage would open within minutes. The team members—from engineers to front tire changers—would arrive, driving in from their hotels, anticipating hot coffee and the rush of adrenaline. Express planes would bring in the families and crews who hadn't come for the whole weekend. The media center lights would flicker on, and the stories would begin to unfold.

After the lousy practices, Cade and the other drivers had qualified well. His brother was starting fourth, which was critical, since the race was rarely won by anyone not starting in the top fifteen.

Would he be the story of the day?

True to her word, Darcy appeared in the kitchen a few minutes later. She wore jeans and her No. 56 red-and-white shirt, the Huntington Hotels logo emblazoned proudly across her chest. Her eyes were bright, her lips glossy pink.

He handed her a disposable cup full of hot coffee.

She took a sip, then hugged him. "You're my champion."

"At least until my dad steals you away from me."

"Jealous?"

He opened the door and led her out into the muggy morning air. "Intensely."

"Don't worry." She linked their hands. "We'd wait a respectable amount of time before we ran off to Vegas and eloped."

"Funny. You're really funny." He drank his coffee as they walked through the compound toward the garages and pushed away the ridiculous image of Darcy hugging his father in any way other than friendship. He wouldn't put such a vile manipulation past his ex, but Darcy? No way. "You said Dad had dating woes. I thought he'd let his resentment of the florist go. He and Leanne seem inseparable lately."

"They're…okay."

"So, what's going on?"

Darcy glanced at him. "Do you really want to go into this on race morning?"

"I guess not. Is there a quick summary?"

"He's looking for a way to reconcile with your mother."

Bryan ground to a halt. "Not on race morning."

"I assumed not. So we table the discussion." She tugged his arm, getting him moving again. "But your mom's coming today, so in between all those critical fuel mileage calculations, you might want to glance around and notice how your dad acts around her."

"Between fuel mileage calculations, I'll be pacing, talking to my drivers, talking to my crews and crew chiefs." He sighed and fought the battle between being an owner and a son. Surprisingly, the son won. "How do you know?"

"I don't *know*. It's a gut instinct."

Darcy's gut was usually right. On some level, he and his siblings had never given up hoping for reconciliation between their parents. To Rachel, it was practically a quest. For years, Bryan blamed himself for the breakup, as his accident seemed to be what brought everything to a head. But Rachel had sat him and Cade down last summer and explained that while his accident had been a catalyst, it had simply been a reminder of his dad's mortality.

His dad was afraid he was missing out on life. He'd moved out to reclaim his youth. And even last year, his sister suspected their father regretted his decision to turn his back on decades of marriage. He just didn't know how to go back.

Better than anybody, Bryan understood regret. He understood how it felt to be abandoned the way his mother had; he understood his father's desire to live life as if you were invulnerable. But how could they realistically repair their marriage? How would either of them ever be able to trust the other again?

Would *he* ever trust again? He was crazy about Darcy. Their bond as both friends and a couple was strong. He couldn't say he'd ever been friends with Nicole.

Could that make the difference? Could he and Darcy last long-term? Wasn't the idea that he was even considering her and the words *long-term* together a sign that he, like his father, was letting go of his past? That he could move beyond old pain and resentments?

"Here's where I need to peel off," she said as they reached the garage. She glanced up at him and squeezed his hand. "Wish Cade my best."

"I will. And save me some breakfast."

Her grin flashed. "I'll do my best. Your guys are a hungry bunch."

"But I'm the boss."

"Uh-huh. How about *you* tell them that at mealtime?"

With more reluctance than he wanted to admit, he let her go. He actually stood still, watching her walk away, her hips swaying before he shook himself from the melancholy thought that he'd miss her. He liked having her by his side.

Melancholy? *There's no melancholy in racing.*

Dismissing his weird thoughts, he headed to Cade's garage stall. As expected, Sam was there, gulping coffee along with his team. The car chief and one of the crew members were checking each and every part and piece of the car to be sure everything was accounted for and in its proper place before it was due to go through the tech inspection process mandated by NASCAR. Bryan joined Sam in his silent stare at the car, as if they could push it to the front of the field by a sheer force of will.

"How are we?" Bryan asked the crew chief.

"Good as we can be. Cade's edgy."

"I noticed."

"Seen him this morning?"

"Not yet. Expect him any minute, though."

"You check the war wagon inventory?"

"Twice."

"You talk to the other teams about their fuel mileage?"

"'Bout the same as Cade's."

They stared at the car again.

"How are we?" Cade asked when he walked up a few moments later.

"Good as we can be," Sam said again.

"Is that good enough?"

Sam shrugged. "Maybe."

Cade paced.

"At least everybody qualified well," Bryan said.

"So did a lot of other fast cars," Sam pointed out.

"What fast cars?" Cade asked. "Faster than mine?"

Bryan wasn't in the mood for Cade's manic energy. If his brother didn't slow down a little he wouldn't have enough energy to drive four hundred miles.

Before Bryan could point out that fact, Emily, the PR rep for Huntington Hotels, stopped in front of him and Sam with plates of steaming hot egg-and-cheese breakfast sandwiches.

"Darcy made you a protein shake," she said to Cade. "Do you want it now?"

"No, thanks." He waved his hand. "Too nervous."

Bryan and Sam thanked Emily and shook their heads at their driver. He'd have to eat something before the race. "We can always call Isabel. She'll force him to eat."

"Good idea." Sam glanced at Bryan's plate. "I got bacon on mine."

"I see that. And when you can't button your pants because all that fat has settled on your belly, I know who to call to work it off."

"I guess you do." Sam took a bite of his sandwich, chewed thoughtfully, then announced, "If you don't marry her, I will."

"Apparently, you'll have to fight my dad for her."

"Fight?" Cade asked urgently. "Who's fighting with Dad? Not Mom again?"

Bryan pointed to the other side of the car. "Go pace over there."

CHAPTER SIXTEEN

"IT'S YOUR DAY," Bryan said as he leaned against the window frame of his brother's race car. "You're going to win."

Cade's eyes widened. "Are you crazy? You'll jinx me."

Bryan smiled and shook his head. Darcy was absolutely never wrong, as she'd predicted Cade's exact reaction that morning. "I didn't tell you that earlier, because I was afraid you'd starting hopping around the garage instead of just pacing a hole in the floor. But you could use the jolt of confidence now, I think."

Cade stared through his windshield. "It's just another race. I don't know why I'm so worked up."

"Because it's not just another race."

"Counts the same amount of points as all the others."

But Indy was special. And Cade's team could use a boost. The heated days of summer had slowed their momentum, which they'd need heading into the Chase for the NASCAR Sprint Cup. Turning his head, Bryan glanced down the seemingly endless front straightaway toward Turn Four. How many drivers had taken that final turn and imagined the finish line being farther away than Mars?

Countless.

"This race is about history." He met his brother's nervous gaze. "We could be the only family in NASCAR with three Indy wins."

"But no pressure," Cade snapped back sarcastically.

"You live for pressure." Bryan tapped his shoulder. "Go get 'em."

Gentlemen, start your engines.

At the immediate roar of sound, Bryan stepped back, allowing Isabel to move in and squeeze her husband's hand one last time. One of the crew members fastened the safety net over the window, then the cars began rolling behind the pace car.

Turning toward the pit area, he noted Isabel's worried expression, mirroring Cade's, so he patted her shoulder, too.

As he put on his headset, he saw Darcy waving at him. He waved back and wished for another good luck kiss—though they'd indulged in several less than an hour ago. Instead, he climbed his way into the command center hovering over the pit box and sat next to Sam, knowing Darcy was headed back to the motor home to watch the race. If Cade was in contention to win, she'd promised to come back at the end to support the team.

The team was well-fed, energetic and ready to go, so her job was over. Which really wasn't her job at all, just something she volunteered to do every week. He frowned. Shouldn't he offer to compensate her for that time? The whole issue of money between them was strange, given how their relationship had changed over the course of the season.

But as the green flag waved, his personal issues had no voice, since the packed grandstands roared as fiercely as the engines. They were all a part of history, too, and Bryan hoped they'd be telling their grandkids how they saw Cade Garrison's first Indy win, live and in person.

During the race, he visited both Kevin's and Shawn's pits, as well, making sure their crew chiefs were on top of everything and didn't need help from him. At one point, as Chance Baker came off Turn Two, his car wiggled, the back end nearly sliding out from under him.

Cade happened to be right next to him.

"Go low, go low," Cade's spotter announced over the radio.

Cade swerved and avoided contact with the other car.

Bryan clenched his jaw.

But as the race wound down, he put aside worries about Chance and his banzai driving and focused on Cade's track position. Since it was notoriously difficult to pass at Indy, if they didn't make a bold call on pit road on the last stop, he didn't see how Cade would win.

He ran the idea by Sam, who'd already been think-

ing along that line, then he went by the other GRI
teams' pits to find out their strategy. In the end, he and
Sam decided Cade was the only one who'd take two
tires. Shawn's position for getting in the Chase was
too precarious to take a risk and Lars's team had tried
two tires earlier, only to have him lose several positions once he got back on the track.

Just as they were all contemplating green-flag
stops, the caution flew for debris fifteen laps from the
end of the race.

"Two tires," Sam said into the headset.

"Two?" Cade answered back, clearly concerned.

"You need track position," Sam returned firmly.

Bryan held his breath as Cade pulled his car into
the box below him. Any mistake during the stop
would negate the risky call.

"Go, go!" the gasman yelled as he jumped back.

Cade's car roared off second.

The green flag waved, and Cade had passed the
leader within a lap. The crowd was on its feet as he
blazed across the Start/Finish line in first place, eight
laps to go.

Bryan and Sam exchanged a glance, but said nothing. Left to hope that he'd made the right recommen-
dation, Bryan leaned back in his chair, alternately
watching the monitor and the track and listening to
the spotter call information to his brother.

On the last lap, going into Turn Three, the driver
in second surged toward Cade's bumper, making a

run for the lead, he pulled alongside the tire, but by the time they'd rounded Turn Four, Cade had put distance between them.

"Hold your line," Bryan said over the radio. "You're almost there."

Everything seemed to move in slow motion except his heart, which was pounding in his chest like a war drum. But when the checkered flag came down, waving over Cade's car, the world exploded in flashing lights, roars of sound and speed.

Hearing Cade's whoop of excitement through the headset, Bryan grinned and gave Sam a quick hug.

After scrambling off the pit box, he found his dad, Rachel, Parker, Isabel and Darcy all huddled together in a group hug of celebration. The crew members were high-fiving each other. Cameras and microphones seemed to be everywhere.

"This is a big win not only for your driver, but your family," a TV reporter asked Bryan. "How do you feel?"

"I'm proud of everybody at GRI. They all worked hard and deserve this win. I know Cade is thrilled."

"Your family has made history. Your father, you and now your brother all have Indy trophies."

"Yeah." He smiled. "We've done well."

He'd never been very effusive with reporters, and when his dad walked by, the TV crew wrapped up and rushed over to him.

Bryan, meanwhile, found himself face-to-face with Darcy. He pulled her to him in a tight hug and lifted her off her feet. He couldn't explain how incredible it felt to have her there as part of the win, part of the family. Though Cade and GRI had already won three times that season, a lot had changed between him and Darcy over the summer.

Within seconds, they were unfortunately separated. The family and team members were urged by the officials toward the celebrations in Victory Lane. More interviews and pictures ensued. But Cade's megawatt smile as he climbed out of the race car was worth all the attention Bryan usually shunned.

Bryan kissed the bricks. Then he kissed Darcy.

With cameras flashing everywhere that probably wasn't wise. Darcy would be a source of speculation and gossip. Not that everybody who went to the track each week didn't already know they were seeing each other. And it wasn't as though he wanted to hide, but their relationship was private.

Still, he insisted she be part of the pictures.

"Come on," he said, tugging her hand as she tried to move away.

"The *team* is supposed to be in the pictures."

"And you're part of the team."

It was more than that, of course, but he didn't know how to explain, or even fully understand it himself. He only knew he wanted her as part of the picture he'd hang in his office and enjoy for years to come. And having her stand beside him felt pretty damn good.

THE LAST RACE BEFORE the Chase for the NASCAR Sprint Cup was about to begin.

As Mitch walked the familiar path through the garage area toward Cade's hauler, he reflected on what had passed and what was to come.

Cade, Chance and another driver exchanged the top three positions nearly every week. Shawn was holding tight around the seventh to ninth spot, and even though Kevin and Lars weren't able to contend for a championship, that team had finished in the top fifteen for the last five races.

As the heat intensified on the GRI Chase contenders—or possibly because Bryan kept a tight rein on him—Lars had kept his mouth shut unless he was supporting his teammates. Cade had won two more races since Indy, and Shawn had gotten his first win of the season. Lars was one of the first people in Victory Lane to congratulate them.

Over his nearly forty-year career in racing, some things never changed—drivers fought for wins, owners and crew chiefs obsessed over details and teams that stuck together won championships.

On a personal level, Mitch had asked the entire family, including his ex-wife, to meet him for some professional pictures he wanted taken. Though everybody had a separate job to do in order to make sure the race went off as planned, he'd insisted, as all their pictures lately seemed to be missing one person or another. Looking through the scrapbooks that Barbara had meticulously kept over the years, he knew he couldn't let one as important as this get by them without the memories documented.

And as a way to get Barbara to himself for a night, he thought it was pretty smart.

Two weeks ago, he'd broken up with Leanne, and she didn't seem surprised. She'd obviously known for a while that he wasn't committed to their relationship, and he was through trying to fool himself as to the cause.

He wanted his wife back.

He'd screwed up and thrown away the best thing in his life. Hard as it was for him to admit a mistake, he was forced to. While his kids were off finding happiness and success, he'd been acting like an idiot, searching for something he'd already had.

The love of a lifetime.

So, he'd just fix it. He'd find a way to get her back. He'd make her see that her forgiveness and love were all he thought about. Simple, right?

Thinking of Barbara's cool stare when he'd seen her at the Atlanta race the weekend before, he wasn't at all sure. He had a lot of making up to do, a lot of proving that this decision wasn't flippant, but something he'd been struggling with, really, ever since he'd left in the first place. He'd made a terrible, terrible mistake, and he'd do whatever he had to in order to make it right again.

With determination and dedication, he'd gotten

everything in life he'd ever wanted. Career. Family. Friends. He could do this, too. He had to—

"Oh, my gosh, you're Mitch Garrison!" a shocked voice said as a pair of lovely young women stepped in front of him.

Smiling, he signed their autographs and thanked them for remembering the old-school guys who were still hanging around the track.

Being an adored NASCAR legend isn't too shabby of a life, either, he thought as he walked away, sliding through the back door of Cade's hauler.

Several of the team members were standing around, probably hoping the grills Big Dan had lit outside would soon burn with dinner. Darcy would no doubt be itching to get out there and help him.

Mitch had insisted Darcy be present for the pictures, which she'd worried about and Bryan had simply nodded about. His eldest child was notoriously closemouthed, so Mitch wasn't sure how serious his and Darcy's relationship was. But he personally thought his son was crazy if he didn't grab that amazing girl with both hands and run to the altar.

Even if Bryan somehow lost his mind and didn't, though, this picture was a reflection of their family as it stood now, and Darcy was a part of that. In the future, he hoped all his kids would be happily married, and he hoped grandkids would follow. He hoped there were championships and race wins and business and personal successes.

He closed his eyes briefly as he approached the door to the back-room office. *I hope Barbara will talk to me.*

When he opened the door, Rachel was busy rearranging the sofa and directing people around the room. "I'm *not* sitting beside him," Barbara was saying. "We can sit at opposite—"

"Dad!" Cade called, rushing toward him. "We were just talking about where everybody should go."

Glancing at Barb, Mitch knew exactly where she'd like him to go.

Reconciliation wasn't going to happen overnight— much as he'd like it to. He was fine with them standing apart in this picture, since he had every confidence they'd stand together again in the future.

It was kind of like racing at Talladega. You knew the finish line was your goal, so it was up to you to bargain, maneuver, charge or coax—anything to get the prize. Naturally, while avoiding accidents along the way.

Calm—he'd run a lot of those races at Talladega, after all—he walked over to Rachel and kissed her cheek, then gave the same greeting to Isabel and Darcy. Finally, he moved toward Barb. She stood in front of the sofa with a tense, suspicious look on her face, as if wondering what he'd do next.

He'd done that to her. He'd turned his generous, loving wife into a cynic.

He grasped her hands and brushed his lips across her cheek before she could evade him. "Thank you for coming," he said simply, then let her go.

When he turned around, everybody was busy looking somewhere else.

With the photographer's help, Rachel directed the shoot. He wound up as far away as possible from Barb in every shot. He deserved the cold shoulder, but he was still proud that he'd been a strong enough man over the years to assure his family's loyalty, to endure the uncomfortable pauses and know that he would make things right again.

To deserve her again.

As the kids rushed off to do their jobs, he stepped in front of Barb before she could walk out of the room. "Have dinner with me tonight."

"Have…what?" she whispered in disbelief.

"Dinner. I have reservations. Will you come?"

"No, I—"

"You don't already have plans. I checked with Rachel."

Her gaze cut to his. The anger and distance he saw there made him realize how incredibly far he had to go. "Why?"

"Why, what?"

"Why are you asking me out to dinner?"

"I'd like to talk to you."

She crossed her arms over her chest. "So talk."

"I…" He'd hoped to have this moment over a candlelit table. "I made a mistake." He cleared his dry throat. "With us. With you. I—" He forced himself to meet her gaze. "I'm sorry. I'm sorry I've been such an idiot. I had everything I wanted, and I went crazy. I don't really know how to explain." Self-conscious, he slid his hands in the pockets of his pants. "Bryan's highway accident threw me, messed me up. The way his life changed in an instant, and we all knew nothing would ever be the same…."

"But I was there for him. For you, too. And you kept running away from all of us."

"I've been trying to recapture my youth. I thought I needed to do that alone."

For a moment, her eyes glistened with tears. "We're never going to be young again, Mitch."

"Yeah. I know. I know that now. But—"

"And it's too late to apologize."

"Maybe so, but I'd like to try."

"Don't bother." She opened the door, moved out, then shut it in his face.

He stood alone, silent with shock, realizing the true extent of his loss for the first time and doubting he could ever go back.

As the laps wound down in the Richmond race, Darcy left Bryan's motor home and headed toward pit road. Since Cade was so high in the points standings, he'd been guaranteed a spot in the Chase before the race even began, but Shawn's team had to finish well to get in. With him running tenth, she figured chances were good and that there'd be a significant GRI party that night.

She moved quickly out of the drivers' compound,

sending a text message to Parker as she walked, asking him if he wanted to leave right after the race to get the party prep started at Cade's house—the usual gathering spot for friends, family and the team after a big race.

He answered back quickly, saying he and Rachel were leaving as soon as the checkered flag fell and they'd be grateful for her help. She picked up her pace, but because of her distraction, she almost didn't see the blond-haired woman strolling several feet in front of her.

Nicole.

She'd been absent from the track ever since Indy—the night she'd come on to Bryan. The rumor around the garage was that she and Chance were history. In fact, Darcy had seen a striking brunette on Chance's pit box only last week in Atlanta.

So what is she doing here?

Suddenly the idea of going with Parker and Rachel and leaving Bryan at the track wasn't so comfortable.

Watching Nicole head down pit road, possibly toward Chance's pit, Darcy fought to ignore the sinking in her stomach and turned the other way.

Bryan had spent the last six weeks showing her how important she was to him. He'd told her he wanted her, not Nicole. When he thought of his ex-wife, he apparently thought only of regret. Being jealous over a woman he had nothing to do with, and even avoided, was nuts.

Still, she was.

Because Nicole had had something from Bryan that Darcy didn't.

Commitment.

Not so long ago, the idea of contemplating a future with a man other than her late husband would have been laughable. Now, it was all she wanted. Practically all she thought about.

And yet, on some level, she was content to drift, to hold her love for Bryan tight against her, not taking the risk of saying those words, fearful he didn't feel the same way.

There was no denying they were a couple, and everyone they knew thought of them that way. Earlier that day, she'd posed in family photos, which seemed a little crazy and surreal, but no more so than the race-winning pictures in Indy, Pocono and Bristol that she'd been a part of.

Bryan had shrugged off her concerns, telling her she was part of the team. She was a paid member of the team, in fact. But when an event rolled around for just the family to attend, she was part of that, too. Yet she wasn't family.

She was being paranoid. She definitely didn't want to act like some of the young drivers' girlfriends, who obsessed constantly about hard card versus paper credentials and wondered about the true status in their man's life.

She wasn't flighty and pathetic. She was a confident, strong-minded, thirty-two-year-old woman.

Of course, she also had a hard card.

By the time she made her way down the packed pit road, the checkered flag was flying. She glanced at the scoring pylon, towering over the speedway, noting Cade had finished third, Shawn seventh and Lars twelfth. While the winning car headed for Victory Lane, reporters descended on Cade's pit, interviewing Cade, Bryan and Mitch.

The Chase for the NASCAR Sprint Cup had officially begun.

"Did you see that blond traitor is back?" Rachel asked as she, Darcy and Parker stood back to allow the media more room.

Darcy nodded. "Actually, I just saw her heading the other way down pit road. What's she doing—"

"Her and Chance are back together."

"No kidding." Was that good news or bad news? Searching her feelings, she came up with no immediate answer. She only hoped she could find the self-possession to stop worrying about her own life and celebrate with everybody at GRI.

Rachel sighed. "I guess it was too much to hope that he'd date some random bikini model we couldn't care less about."

Parker cleared his throat.

Darcy pressed her lips together to avoid laughing. Parker had dated a few bikini models before he got wise and chased down Rachel.

"I was hoping he'd find a brain surgeon," he said,

his eyes flashing with humor. "There just aren't enough female neurosurgeons in the world."

Rachel glared at him for a moment before shifting her gaze to Darcy. "You want to tell Bryan you're coming with us?"

"Yeah, I should." As she hung back and waited for the reporters to move away, she considered what to say to him.

After the race-winning photos were taken in Victory Lane, the top twelve drivers had to pose for their first official Chase picture. With Bryan having two drivers among them, there would no doubt be some inadvertent encounters with the Baker family. Shouldn't she warn him about Nicole?

"Congratulations," Darcy said when she finally worked her way through the people crowding around him.

His eyes glowing with pride, Bryan pulled her into his arms. "Thanks."

Well aware of the speculation about her and Bryan's relationship—how serious it was, how long it had been going on, how long it would continue— she stepped back quickly. That very personal picture of them kissing at Indy had even shown up on the Internet, which had caused old friends of hers and Tom's to call her up and ask—rudely, she thought— what was going on. She wasn't wild about having any more probing, uncomfortable conversations like those—especially since she didn't know the answers to most of the questions she'd been asked.

The one positive aspect of those questions had been the lack of guilt she felt. She was embarrassed by the picture, but she wasn't racked with shame and uncertainty. She was not betraying the love she'd shared with her husband.

Her love for Bryan simply glowed too bright.

"Are you okay?" he asked, angling his head and sliding his hand up her arm.

"Chance and Nicole are back together," she blurted.

He stiffened briefly, then he shook his head. "Why should I care?"

Did he care? was the big question. "I just didn't want you to be surprised if she shows up later."

"Okay. Thanks." Seeming oblivious to the flashing cameras all around, he linked their hands. "I'm going to be here a while with the press and the team."

"That's fine. I'm going back with Parker and Rachel." When he frowned, she added, "Party prep at Cade's house."

Grabbing her other hand, he drew her close. "So, I'll see you there later?"

"Sure, but, Bryan...I—" She cast a quick glance around. "Do you think this is a good idea?"

"Look at me," he commanded softly.

When she did, the tender, focused expression in his eyes made her heart flip. Chaos reigned round them. Celebrations, disappointments, combinations of sheer exhaustion and relief or utter disappointment could be found within feet of where they were standing.

"Thanks," he said.

Confused, she cocked her head. "For?"

"Just for being here."

Abandonment. His ex had rejected him, his body had betrayed him—both taking away the things he loved. Could he love her as much? Would he allow himself to trust her to stay? To hang around for whatever ups and downs their lives brought?

She swallowed her anxiety over the unanswered questions and pressed her lips to his.

"Big party tonight, people," Rachel said, breaking abruptly into their gentle moment. "You can have her all to yourself later, Big Bry."

Reluctantly, she let herself be led away by Parker and Rachel.

And though she spent the next few hours working side by side with them, arranging the buffet, bar, posters and balloons, all announcing GRI's Chase contenders, part of her was still with Bryan.

A couple of times she thought about his proximity to Nicole, but dismissed her worry each time. Regardless of his ex's hold on his past, of the way she'd had a part in shaping the man he was today, he would never betray Darcy.

Of course that didn't mean he would stay with her, either, but she knew he would be honest if his feelings about her changed.

Whatever those feelings were.

Oh, yeah. You are so completely confident and strong-minded.

Before she could dwell any more on her reluctance to have a meaningful conversation about how she and Bryan felt or where they were going, the crowd arrived.

Fresh from the track or their homes where they'd been watching the race, team members, friends of GRI and family streamed into the rec room in Cade's basement, including, surprisingly, Mitch and Barbara, though in separate groups.

Parker was ready with bottles of chilled champagne and had even arranged for a confetti machine, which popped red, gold and white slips of paper over Cade and Shawn when they walked into the room. To say the least, the mood was ebullient.

Darcy was lighting the burners beneath the buffet trays when Bryan's arms suddenly slid around her from behind.

She jumped. "Are you crazy? I've got a lighter in my hands."

Turning her by her waist, he set the lighter on the table. "Not anymore."

The look in his smoky blue eyes could best be described as…hungry. And she had the feeling that the hot wings, Italian meatballs and mini egg rolls had nothing to do with his appetite.

He kissed her with more enthusiasm than the public setting warranted, and she fell into him, forgetting about everybody around them. Love welled up in her, but her good sense warred with her heart. She wanted a future with him, but she didn't want to be wholly dependent on someone again. She'd had that once and lost it in a flash.

"Geez, boss, get a room."

When Darcy tried to jump back at the sound of the unfamiliar voice, Bryan lifted his head but held her body in place, plastered to him. "I am celebrating. Go away."

Glancing out of the corner of her eye, she saw Cade's car chief walking away. Her face heated. "You're crazy."

He smoothed back her hair. "About you."

Swallowing the urge to push that comment further, to ask with desperate need what, exactly, he felt for her, she scrambled for something impersonal to say. To distance herself from the intimidating feelings that had invaded her heart. "You scared him away."

"Good."

"Bryan, I—" She broke off, biting her tongue. *I love you,* she wanted to say. To shout. But she couldn't force out the confession. She couldn't take that step. "I need to check on the pasta salad."

Before he could protest that lame excuse, she spun away from him and raced up the stairs into the kitchen.

CHAPTER SEVENTEEN

IF SHE'D HOPED to get rid of him, she'd greatly underestimated his determination, since he followed her.

Once, he couldn't do ten push-ups, and there were times he didn't think he had the will or commitment to change that humiliating fact, but he had. And he wasn't about to avoid any other challenge. Especially one involving Darcy.

"Something's wrong," he said, walking up behind her as she stood at the open refrigerator door.

"Not as long as I get more pasta salad downstairs."

When she whirled around with a covered bowl in her hands, he grabbed it and set it on the counter. He led her to the back deck, which, thankfully, was deserted.

There were several people below by the pool and somebody, who'd apparently hit the champagne too hard, was bouncing on the diving board while fully clothed. At the inevitable splash, Bryan looked away and concentrated on the woman beside him. "What's wrong?"

"I just feel weird being in public with you."

"This isn't the public, and you're with me all the time around these people."

"These people work for you." Her gaze shot to his. "*I* work for you."

"So?"

She turned, bracing her arms on the deck railing. "It's weird. I feel…weird."

It wasn't like Darcy to not be direct, to not know exactly, with precise, turn-by-turn directions what she was doing and where she was going.

But then they weren't going anywhere. They were content with where they were. At least he was. Maybe she wasn't. If so, how did he handle that?

He wanted her, but when he thought beyond the moment and toward the future, he could feel his heart resisting. He *wanted* to let go of his fears about trust and relationships, but he couldn't seem to manage to do so.

Up until this moment, he hadn't thought Darcy was ready to, either. Who knew better than them that love and commitment didn't last forever?

Noting there was no lighter in sight, he slid his arms around her from behind, then kissed the top of her head. "You feel pretty great to me."

She laid her hands over his and leaned back into him. "Earlier today, I stood beside you in a *family picture*. It's making me panicky."

Relieved that she didn't expect commitment or promises of happily-ever-after, which he didn't see how anyone could make, much less him, his pulse slowed. "I'd rather you relax. Everybody here is either like family or actual family. There's no line drawn between the two. Big Dan's been in plenty of family pictures."

"Big Dan's a legend."

"You will be, too, if you keep making those grilled ribs and chicken every weekend."

But he knew what she meant. Big Dan had been his dad's gasman for more than fifteen years before he'd tried to retire and take up fishing, then wound up driving Cade's transporter and serving as team chef. He'd been there for the championships, the ups and downs, the victories and defeats. They had history.

But Bryan didn't like to think about history too much. At least not the recent past. He'd accepted the way his life had turned out, but was he truly at peace with it? Would he ever be?

"Did you see Nicole tonight?" Darcy asked as if she'd read his mind.

"Sure."

"Are she and Chance back together?"

"Looked like it, the way she seemed permanently attached to his arm. Do we have to talk about her?" Before Darcy could answer, the mystery of her unsettled, worried demeanor clicked. "You're not concerned about her and…me, are you?"

She glanced back at him. "No. Why would I be?"

"You shouldn't be." He turned her to face him. "It's over between us."

"But you were tempted."

He drew the pad of his thumb down her cheek. "Not anymore."

"And that's it?"

"That's it. And, really, I wasn't ever tempted by her as a person, because she's not worth it. I was tempted by what she represented—my past. The times when I thought I had everything I'd ever wanted."

"But your life changed."

He nodded. "It did. And now I have you." He lowered his head. "Not a bad deal from what I can see."

As he kissed her, he knew that they both had unanswered questions about their pasts and futures, but he'd lived in misery and resentment for so long, he wanted to enjoy the corner he'd turned. He wanted to revel in the victory.

"THANKS, EVERYBODY," Bryan said into the microphone as he looked out at the folding tables full of GRI employees gathered in the auditorium. "Now get back to work."

Everybody laughed, but most of the chairs scraped back as people got to their feet.

The catered barbeque lunch was part celebration/part motivation to keep up the championship-caliber work they were all doing. Cade had won at New Hampshire, Shawn had finished fourth and Kevin fifth. The press had officially dubbed GRI as the team to beat.

Bryan headed back to his office with Cade, Rachel, Isabel and Sam. They were going to discuss Cade's appearance schedule for the remaining races and decide the benefits and consequences of each event. It was important to ride the wave of success and keep sponsors happy, to let those financial partners share the ride to the top, since those rides didn't come along very often.

But Cade had to be rested, alert and ready to race every week. The slightest misstep could cost him the championship.

"Where's Dad?" Cade asked.

Bryan opened his office door and let everybody precede him inside. "Don't know. He said he already had lunch plans today."

Rachel frowned. "That's weird. I asked Mom to come, and she said she was busy, too."

"Maybe they're on dates," Cade suggested.

Rachel took her place at the conference table. "With each other?"

Cade waved his hand. "Nah."

"Could be," Rachel said.

"There was something going on between them at Richmond," Isabel added, sitting in the chair Cade pulled out for her. "Some kind of tension. It made me wonder if they were sleeping together."

Cade stared at his wife. "What?"

Rachel smiled. "Do you really think so? How great would that be?"

"Do we really need to consider Mom and Dad and...*that?*" Cade asked. "It kind of grosses me out."

Isabel rolled her eyes. "Oh, please. Where do you think you came from?"

Cade's face whitened.

Shaking his head, Bryan sat at the head of the table. "I'm sure Sam is fascinated by our family's love life, but can we get back to the small, insignificant matter of the championship now?"

Sam cleared his throat. "For what it's worth, I think your mother is an amazing woman. She and Mitch belong together."

Bryan, along with everybody else in the room, stared at their usually reticent crew chief. It occurred to Bryan, like it must have occurred to his siblings, that their parents' divorce had affected a great many more people than just them. The long-term employees had been there when Mom balanced the books and Dad, who'd just retired from racing, ran the shops. They'd built the business together, from their life savings, a crowded trophy case and sheer force of will.

Many years later, they had championship trophies, multiple teams, hundreds of loyal employees—and a heartbreaking division among the founders.

What was left to do but move on? The company had. Mom and Dad had. Bryan had. Darcy had.

Shaking off the personal track of his thoughts, he addressed the more immediate concern of Cade's schedule. "I guess Parker's willing to be flexible?" he asked, his gaze going to Isabel.

"Sure, but he's given the lion's share of the sponsor dollars to this team. His employees deserve some recognition."

"What if postseason we organize an employee retreat?" Rachel suggested. "Whether Cade gets the trophy or not, it's been a great two years. We could do two different weekends, rotating as many people as possible. Cade could sign autographs and do Q&As."

"Where, exactly, would this retreat take place?" Cade wanted to know.

"The hotel in St. Croix is pretty amazing," Isabel said, then offered Rachel a dazzling, out-of-character smile.

"How are we going to get hundreds of people to and from St. Croix?" Bryan asked, thinking of the scary columns of red ink—signifying negative cash flow—that might entail.

"We could always do New York or Charlotte," Rachel said. "Have the New York appearances when we're there for the banquet."

"There's too much going on that weekend already," Sam said.

"Okay," Isabel said, holding up her hand. "I was kidding about St. Croix. How about we do one weekend in Miami—or maybe a Monday/Tuesday after the last race—and do another in New York, sometime before Christmas? We could entertain all

the executive staff that way and easily fly in anybody else."

Grateful, and not for the first time, for Isabel's
decisiveness, Bryan glanced at Sam. "That work for
you?"

Sam shrugged. "Racing'll be over by then." His
gaze swept the table. "As long as you don't interfere
with the winter work schedule."

Cade groaned. "Can we focus on *this* year? The one
so pressure-packed, I'm about to climb the walls?"

"Tell that to the engineers and fab guys already
building your cars for 2010," Sam said matter-of-factly.

The rest of the shuffling wasn't so easy. Isabel and
Rachel vowed to make deals and promises that would
likely keep Cade so busy next season he'd be lucky
to make it to qualifying each week. When his brother
simply laid his head on the table, Bryan called a halt
to the plans.

"What about bribes?" he asked the group.

Rachel blinked. "Bribes?"

"Gifts," Bryan said. "Autographed cars, hats,
T-shirts, pictures, dog leashes, firstborn children—
anything that doesn't require Cade zigzagging across
the country every other minute."

"Gift bags aren't a bad idea," Isabel said, tapping
her pen in consideration. "We could send a DVD
with a personal message from Cade and record those
in one afternoon. We could apologize for Cade's
crowded schedule, thank them for their dedication
and send along some signed merchandise."

"And food," Rachel said.

"Food?" Bryan echoed.

"Sure." Rachel nodded. "Ooh, Darcy could make those amazing chocolate cupcakes." She glanced at Bryan. "Though maybe we should check with her first."

"I can ask her," he said, wondering why he hadn't been offered any cupcakes.

Isabel and Rachel exchanged a glance. "Consider that done," Isabel said.

"Why's that?" he asked.

Since both of the women seemed reluctant to enlighten him, Cade spoke up. "Wow, dude, are you clueless?"

Bryan leaned back in his chair. "I guess I am."

"She's completely crazy about you," Isabel said.

Rachel patted his shoulder. "She'd make cupcakes for every team in the garage if you asked her."

How they'd worked their way from Cade's schedule to his personal life, Bryan had no idea. He'd do anything in his power for Darcy, and it was nice to hear other people thought the same about her, but now didn't seem to be the right time to talk about it. He definitely wasn't about to pour out his feelings and worries to his entire family.

"What are her plans for next season?" Isabel asked, her direct gaze meeting his.

"I—" He had absolutely no idea. Technically, their employment agreement ran through the last race of the season. He was as strong and recovered from his injuries as he was ever likely to get. Even now, he didn't really need her to work out with him or tell him what he should and shouldn't eat.

"I'm not sure," he finally said.

"I suggest you find out," Isabel said. "We could use her."

"We could?" he asked.

Rachel glared at him. "Bryan Garrison! You're not just fooling around with her, are you? She's an amazing woman, who has done wonders with your snarly self. You should run, not walk, straight to the altar with her, and I can't believe you—"

Sam lurched to his feet, his chair jolting backward. "I have dyno numbers to look at." He practically ran from the room.

Bryan felt heat rise up his neck. "Thanks, Rach."

But his sister, as usual, was undaunted. "You *are* serious about her, aren't you?"

"I only wanted Isabel to give me some concrete reasons why Darcy was good for the team, so I could tell her when I offer her a new contract." Was he going to do that? He certainly hadn't considered next season before this moment. He also noted Rachel's glare hadn't budged. "And I'm as serious about her as I can be about anybody."

"Is this going to turn into a relationship therapy session?" Cade asked, his eyes bright with amusement. "I could be spending this time keeping sponsors happy, after all."

Bryan rose. "Meeting's over."

To say the least, the dispersion was awkward. Cade was way too gleeful to escape without a firm schedule in place, and Rachel was still annoyed.

Isabel stopped at the door. "With or without cute gift bags, bargains and chocolate cupcakes, we're not going to completely eliminate personal appearances over the next few weeks, especially if Cade climbs into the top spot."

"I know."

"Why don't we let Parker help? Maybe he can throw one of those fancy, cross-sponsor parties, Cade can breeze in for an hour, and everybody will be happy."

"That's a good idea. Thanks."

She started to turn away, then glanced back. "With a huge sense of déjà vu, I'll say I'm here if you want to talk."

"Déjà vu about what?"

"Barely a year ago, Rachel and Parker didn't know what the hell to do about being in love either, but I helped clue them in."

Ignoring the way his heart rate sped up, he crossed his arms over his chest. "Who says I'm in love? In fact, I don't really believe in love."

Her eyes reflecting sympathy, she patted his shoulder. "I'm sorry to hear that."

"Why?"

"Repressing your feelings and living in denial never works. Trust me."

I'm fine! he wanted to shout after her as she left his office.

He stomped to his desk. He was terrific, in fact. Everything was great between him and Darcy. They were happy. Why couldn't everybody let them enjoy each other? Not only did they not need commitment and flowery speeches about tingly emotions, they didn't *want* them.

Irritated, he went back to work. He called Parker, who was spending the day at his office in Manhattan, and set up details for a multiple-sponsor event. The smooth style, the outright class that was so much a part of his brother-in-law had intimidated him in the past, but never more so than thinking about his family's… What was it they'd really expressed?

Pity, he decided. They pitied him for not climbing on the happily-ever-after train they'd all boarded.

He'd tried that route, and it had been a flaming disaster. While he could say he'd simply picked the wrong girl, nobody would acknowledge Mom was the wrong girl, and look what had happened to his parents.

Of its own accord, the framed picture of the win at Indy drew his gaze. It would hang there for years, and he'd known that when he'd asked Darcy to pose beside him. Had he unconsciously been making a commitment to the future with her?

No. Ridiculous. It was just an impulse.

He wasn't repressing or in denial about his feelings. What a crock.

His annoyance never abated. He snapped at people all afternoon and finally shut the door to his office, refusing to take calls.

When a brisk knock sounded on his door just after six, long after the office staff had gone home, he stormed across his office and flung open the door. "Look, I told you—"

"Hi," Darcy said.

"Hey." Trying to put aside his irritation, he stepped back and waved her inside.

When he closed the door behind them, she snagged his hand and placed it around her waist, then she looped her arms around his neck. "Long day?"

"Oh, yeah."

She hugged him tight, and he closed his eyes, grateful for her touch. "The Chase. Cade. Strategy meeting. Schedule shuffling. I'm not even going to ask. What do you want for dinner?"

"Are you crazy about me?"

Leaning back, she had a slight smile on her face, though she also looked a little puzzled. "Sure."

"Would you do anything for me?"

"Of course."

She didn't even hesitate. And, for some reason, he felt like a jerk. But he'd do anything for her, wouldn't he?

Even love her? his conscience—which mysteriously spoke in Isabel's voice—asked.

Maybe not. He seemed to be out of stock on love.

"Dinner, Mr. Garrison," Darcy said.

"I don't know—cook, takeout or go out?"

"You seem to be in a pretty impatient, and—can I add?—strange mood." She released him and crossed to the phone. "How about pizza?"

His lousy mood, which had risen the moment he'd seen her, jumped even higher. "Pizza?"

"Thin, whole-wheat crust, all organic toppings, which will mostly be vegetables."

He barely resisted the urge to say *yuck*. "How about a side of spaghetti?"

She sighed, but only a little, and picked up the receiver.

"And I want a chocolate cupcake for dessert."

As DARCY PULLED a batch of cupcakes out of the oven at Bryan's house, she wondered where Kick-Butt Darcy had gone and what alien race had replaced her with Sappy Darcy.

"At this rate, he's going to put the weight back on before the end of the season," she muttered.

But then he'll need you, won't he?

She turned away—from the stove and her conscience. What more did she want? They were a declared, monogamous couple. They practically lived together. He gave her his full attention when they were alone, and she often caught him staring at her when they were surrounded by other people. He spent as much time with her as possible, even amid the chaos of the Chase, and Cade finishing only marginally the last few weeks, barely hanging on to third in points, while Chance had won the last two races in a row and solidified his hold on the top spot.

This weekend the races were both close to home and taking place Friday and Saturday nights. The teams would have a rare Sunday off—the only one, in fact. She knew Bryan couldn't resist going down to the shop for at least a little while that day, but he'd promised they'd spend the afternoon and evening together, doing whatever she wanted.

With that kind of relationship, what could her heart do but simply fall a little harder every day?

The secret of her feelings, the love that she felt glowed from every pore, remained unspoken. They didn't talk about the future. They didn't discuss what their relationship meant except on the most superficial of terms.

She was as happy as she'd ever been in her life, but when she stood still, when she had a few moments of quiet reflection, she swore she heard a clock ticking.

When the doorbell rang, she was in the process of setting the cupcakes on a cooling rack. She called Bryan's name, but then heard the shower running.

She wiped her hands on a kitchen towel, then walked down the hall toward the front door. They were due to leave for the Concord track to cheer on GRI's NASCAR Nationwide Series team any minute along with Cade and Isabel, who lived down the street from Bryan, but they usually just gave a courtesy knock, then walked right in.

A man in a blue jacket and khaki pants stood on the porch, holding an envelope and clipboard. "Bryan Garrison?"

"He's not available right now. Can I help you?"

"Are you…" he consulted his clipboard "…Darcy Butler?"

"Yes, but—"

"Sign here, please."

He handed her the clipboard, which she signed, noting the name at the top—Lakeside Messenger Service.

Confused, she handed back the board, and he handed her a sealed envelope made of fine and weighted cream-colored paper. "I—" She glanced up at him, knowing she needed to give him a tip. "Let me get my purse."

"The gratuity's included, ma'am." He nodded. "Have a nice evening."

As he turned away, she shut the door and stared at the envelope. Both her and Bryan's names were printed in elegant, hand-lettered calligraphy. It was sealed at the back with a gold label.

Should they open it together? Who could the note be from? And hand-delivered on a Friday afternoon? That must have cost somebody a mint.

She wandered up the stairs toward Bryan's bed-room. As she walked through the door, he strolled out of the bathroom. With nothing but a towel wrapped around his waist, his dark hair turned glossy black, his broad chest scattered with drops of water, she halted and stared, the envelope forgotten.

Wow. Swallowing, she let her gaze drift down his body.

Would he always stop her in her tracks this way? Would she always have the privilege of holding him against her? Would there be an *always* at all?

"Darcy?" he said, his voice deep, familiar and arousing.

She continued staring at his chest. "Uh-huh?"

"Do you need something?"

She watched a droplet of water roll down his shoulder. Definitely. "Ah, well…"

"Did you burn the cupcakes?"

She shook her head.

"What's that in your hand?"

"Ah…" She glanced at her hand, blinking without recognition at the envelope she held.

He moved toward her, laid his finger beneath her chin, tipping her face up for his kiss. "I invited you into the shower with me, if you remember. You said you'd burn the cupcakes."

She laid her hand against his warm, bare chest. She *really* hoped there was an always.

That murky, scary future she'd avoided facing for so long was taking shape, and Bryan Garrison was standing right in the center.

With a great deal of will, she shook aside that image and held up the envelope. "This came by messenger."

He took the envelope in one hand, then grasped her hand and led her over to the bed, where they sat side by side. It wasn't the bed he'd shared with his ex, she thought vaguely as he broke the seal. The rest of the immaculately decorated house was pretty much the same as when she'd lived here, but he'd told her he'd completely refurnished the bedroom with darkly stained oak, a navy bedspread and cool gray walls. She wasn't sure why that mattered, but it did.

Inside the envelope was an engraved card.

Mitch Garrison requests your presence for a late dinner on board Victory Lane. Lake Norman Marina. 10:00 p.m. this evening. Casual dress.

Bryan looked at her. "What's going on?"

"I have no idea. It came by a hand-delivered messenger, so I guess it's pretty important. A celebration for Cade maybe?"

"*Before* he's won the championship? And the night before an important race?" Bryan shook his head. "That's not like Dad."

As another knock on the front door sounded, Darcy rose. "Who could *that* be?"

"I'll get dressed and meet you down there," Bryan said as he moved toward his closet.

Before Darcy got halfway down the stairs she heard Cade's voice. "Everybody decent?"

"Coming!" she called. When she reached the downstairs hallway, she rounded the corner and saw Cade and Isabel. "Hey, Bryan's getting dressed."

Cade kissed her cheek, then immediately darted toward the kitchen. "Do I smell cupcakes?"

"I haven't iced them yet," Darcy called after him.

"Who cares?"

Isabel cast an affectionately exasperated look after her husband. "Men, they're always thinking with their stomachs." She glanced back at Darcy, her deep brown eyes sharp, as always. "We didn't interrupt anything, did we?"

Darcy wasn't sure she'd ever get used to Isabel's direct, uncensored conversations, yet she appreciated them at the same time. "No. I'm baking, and he's... showering."

"Uh-huh."

Alone with a woman who not only understood the magnetism of the Garrison men, but had fallen hard for one of them, Darcy walked into the living room and sank into one of the overstuffed chairs. "Do you ever get used to them? Cade, for you, of course. But Garrison men in general?"

Isabel dropped onto the sofa. "Nope."

"That's not encouraging."

"It helps if you admit you love him, can't live without him. Hard, I know, but it helps."

"Hard for you?"

"Oh, yeah." But she smiled when she said it.

Isabel was so strong and independent-minded. Tough, and some would say distant. But Darcy had seen her pacing for her husband and his team. She'd seen her compassion for sick kids whose greatest desire was to meet and talk to Cade. She'd seen her appreciation for his fans, when she'd delivered water to lines of people waiting in the hot sun at an autograph session. When she'd given private tours through the GRI shops to those who'd shown up the night before Fan Fest activities, wanting only to be the first in line the next morning.

"I'm working on admitting it," Darcy said finally. "I really am."

Cade walked into the room, a half-eaten cupcake in his hand. "What's this invitation to dinner from Dad? Is he crazy? We'll miss the end of the race."

Darcy blinked. "You got one, too?"

"Yep," Cade said, sinking onto the sofa beside his wife. "And so did Rachel and Parker. Isabel called them on the way here." He extended the cupcake toward Isabel. "You want a bite, honey?"

"No. I'd rather—"

"Why am I always the last one to get a cupcake?" Bryan asked as he appeared in the room, dressed in black pants and a white button-down shirt with the GRI logo stitched over one pocket in red.

"Oh, good grief." Darcy darted into the kitchen, her mind still on the invitation. She, Isabel and Cade wore jeans and casual shirts. Could there really be casual dress for a formal dinner invitation? What was Mitch up to?

They'd talked frequently over the last several weeks, mostly about him wanting to win back his ex-wife, but he'd given no hint about organizing a family get-together. Not that she expected him to discuss all his plans with her. He'd probably organized a nice dinner, some private time with his kids in the middle of the crazy race season. Parker had undoubtedly helped, and they both thought it would be fun to make the event a surprise.

The hand-delivered invitation and formal card-stock absolutely screamed Parker Huntington.

Bryan slid into the kitchen. "I didn't expect you to jump up and fetch me a cupcake."

She placed one in his hand. "Oh, but I know you. You'd have eaten one in here in secret, then carried one out with you, then blamed the trick on your brother."

He frowned at the treat. "Where's the icing?"

Shaking her head at her own susceptibility to that boyish disappointment, she pulled the tub of icing—homemade with artificial sweetener instead of sugar (not that she planned to tell Bryan)—out of the fridge, then smoothed on the frosting and handed it back. "Your brother didn't get icing, you know."

He wrapped one arm around her waist. "But I'm special."

She pressed her mouth to his. "Oh, yeah, you are."

"What do you think the invitation means?"

"I'm not sure. We'll talk about it in the car." She turned away and grabbed her cooler of snacks—the low-fat, actually good-for-you variety. "We need to get going. The chopper's supposed to meet us in ten minutes."

Bryan and Cade's neighborhood had the advantage of a helicopter pad. It was an odd luxury among such otherwise normal people. Most people in NASCAR were like that, actually. They had these strangely public, high-pressure jobs, yet you could hang out with them over a barbeque and a beer or a tall glass of iced tea without a moment of awkwardness.

As Isabel drove, Darcy glanced from Bryan to Cade, both still enjoying their cupcakes. "Big Dan is making chicken and steak fajitas at the track, you know."

"He got icing," Cade mumbled around his cupcake.

"Sometimes I think you guys would trade sex for cake," Isabel said.

The guys exchanged a glance. "Let's not go crazy," Cade said as Bryan nodded his agreement.

"What do you think this invitation is about?" Isabel asked.

Cade shrugged. "It's too formal for Dad. Did he and Leanne get back together?"

Nobody knew, but his suggestion got Darcy thinking all the way to the track and even during the race. She questioned Parker, but he claimed he'd had no part in the dinner party.

Darcy knew Mitch wanted his wife. He wouldn't really go back to Leanne, would he?

Though questions remained, Darcy fought to concentrate on the race, making sure the over-the-wall guys were well-hydrated, and still keeping her eye on the time.

At nine-thirty, she and Isabel dragged everybody away from the pits and into the helicopter again. There was very little said on the way to the marina. Parker had generously arranged for a limo to meet them at the GRI helipad, and popped a bottle of champagne for the ride over.

"We might as well be comfortable," he said as he filled glasses for the tense crowd.

Rachel was the first to raise her glass. "It's a party," she said, smiling bravely.

"For who?" Cade asked, though he tapped his sister's crystal to his.

Nobody knew.

Darcy clenched her hands around her champagne glass after one sip and had no desire for another. What was going on? Bryan was already cynical of commitment. Was his dad really going to jump from woman to woman forever? She'd been so sure he was sincere in wanting Barb back in his life.

And a boat? A boat you could have dinner on with formal, hand-delivered invitations was a yacht. And at night? On a busy race weekend? It all spelled something significant.

They stepped out of the limo and walked down the sidewalk to the dock. A big boat—a yacht in Darcy's mind—was pulled into the first slip with the words *Victory Lane* printed across the hull and bright red, flaming stripes along the side. Obviously recognizing the bobbing boat, the Garrison siblings headed that way.

A man in white pants, shirt and cap, reminiscent of a navy dress uniform, greeted them at the edge of the dock. "Good evening," he said, extending his hand to help Rachel, who was first in line, across the gangway. "Please proceed inside to the dining room."

"Who's that dude?" Cade whispered as they all headed in the direction indicated.

Nobody knew.

Darcy squeezed Bryan's hand as Parker slid open the door to the dining room. He glanced at her, and his usual controlled expression was gone. He was concerned. She had no idea what to say, since she felt the same.

As they stepped into the room, Darcy noted the elegant flower arrangements and flicking candles all around, throwing shadows and light on the plush gold and deep red furnishings. She saw handmade canapés on trays, champagne in a bucket…and a collared minister standing on the far side of the room.

Before she could do more than draw a shocked breath, Mitch stepped forward. He was smiling. Barb, wearing a peach silk dress, her face glowing, stood beside him. They were holding hands.

"Hey, kids. Welcome to our wedding."

CHAPTER EIGHTEEN

BRYAN FLINCHED.

When Darcy, who'd been holding his hand, squeezed his back, he realized he didn't have to deal with this head-turning, mind-boggling moment that had raced into his life alone.

"Oh, my gosh," Rachel exclaimed, embracing Mom. "This is… Wow. Oh, my gosh."

Cade and Parker stepped forward, giving Dad a brief hug. Isabel kissed Mom's cheek. Darcy, after glancing at Bryan, approached the couple, then hugged them both.

Bryan remained frozen.

"How did this happen?" he finally managed to ask.

Everybody else stopped talking, hugging and—in Rachel's case—crying. They all stared at him.

"It's kind of a long story," Dad said, clapping Bryan on the shoulder. "I'll give all the details after the ceremony."

A weird buzzing hummed through his ears. Shock, he thought faintly, he was in shock. His marriage hadn't lasted. His parents' marriage hadn't lasted.

Love wasn't forever.

Darcy laid her hand on his arm. "Bryan?"

He looked at her, her golden gaze fixed worriedly on his face. His heart contracted in a hard, almost painful squeeze. *Could I? Do I lo—*

No. Look at the pain so many people in his life had gone through on account of that single emotion.

"I—" He looked at his dad, so happy and hopeful. He cleared his throat. "Congratulations." He embraced his father, then his mother, and some part of the coldness in his heart warmed. He hadn't seen them this happy in four years.

Cade clapped his hands. "Okay, let's get married."

The ceremony was brief, but moving. The minister offered words of faith and encouragement. The ladies sniffled. The guys beamed.

Bryan was proud of himself for acting normal, for smiling, offering congratulations and even raising the first toast once the presentation of the happy couple had been made. All the while, though, buzzing panic settled in his belly.

He couldn't feel…that way about Darcy. It was simply their proximity, the bond of rehab and yoga, the shared pain of their pasts. Eventually, their interest in each other would wane, and he'd go back to—

What? What did he have to go back to?

Defensiveness and anger. Impatient surliness. Disillusionment and misery. Cold as steel.

"Nice ceremony," Isabel said, approaching him.

"Yeah," he managed to say before swigging champagne.

"You look a little pale. You're not sick, are you?"

"No. I was just thinking about tomorrow night. Cade could really use a good run."

Her direct gaze met his. "Liar."

He raised his eyebrows. "Excuse me?"

"You turned sheet-white the moment you noticed that minister, and you haven't remotely recovered since. What I want to know is—are you thinking about your wedding or your divorce?"

"Neither."

Isabel simply cocked her head.

Sighing, he leaned close. "Look," he whispered, "don't you think this is all a little too precious and perfect? Everybody wants Mom and Dad to get back together. For four, long, lousy years we've watched them fight, ignore each other and date other people. Now, all of a sudden, everything's peaches and champagne?"

"That's a strawberry," she said, pointing to the red fruit on the side of his glass. "And what's wrong with precious and perfect? What's wrong with realizing you made a mistake and doing everything in your power to make it right again?"

"Maybe it could be right. Maybe, in time, they could have reconciled. You can't tell me you don't think this is coming out of left field."

Isabel shrugged. "I told you guys I saw something between them in Richmond."

"But *this?* How can—"

"You two look way too intense over here," Cade said, sliding his arm around his wife's waist. "It's a party." He flicked his finger against the side of Bryan's champagne glass, making the crystal sing. "Or hadn't you noticed?"

Bryan drained his glass, then set it on a table nearby. "Yippee."

"What's with him?" he heard Cade ask Isabel as Bryan stormed away.

He escaped to the deck.

Mercifully, the breeze was even cooler than when they'd boarded. Was it really less than an hour ago that his parents had been bitterly divorced?

"Bryan?" his dad called.

"Up here," he answered back, bracing his hand on the bow railing.

He didn't turn when his dad moved alongside him, but he could feel his stare. "I thought you'd be happy for us. Everybody's happy for us."

"I am. I'm—" Bryan ducked his head. "It's great, Dad. It's just…sudden."

"No, it isn't. I've known for more than a year that I made a mistake leaving your mother. It's just taken me this long to figure out how to tell her and make things right again."

He turned his head and met his father's gaze. "So she just took you back?"

"It wasn't that simple." He sighed. "I made phone calls, asked her to dinner, sent flowers and gifts. She couldn't have cared less. At Richmond, after our family portrait, she slammed the door in my face, said she didn't want me to bother to apologize.

"But I refused to listen. I knew my life would never be right without her. I told her I loved her—always had, always would. Eventually, she believed me."

"Sounds simple to me."

"Admitting you've been a jerk and throwing your heart out to get stomped on by the one person you want above anyone or anything else in the world isn't at all simple."

Refusing to acknowledge the truth of that possibility in his own life, Bryan looked away. "I'm glad you're happy."

"You don't look it."

"It's the Chase. Cade's championship. It's a heavy goal on all of us right now."

"But everybody else is inside, drinking champagne, and you're out here by yourself." As they both obviously heard footsteps on the deck, he added. "Though not for long, I guess."

As his dad started to walk away, Bryan asked, "Would it be weird to get wedding gifts from your kids?"

He shook his head. "I've got everything I need already."

As he heard his father and Darcy talk quietly, her offering congratulations and him thanking her for all she'd done for the family, Bryan stared at the rippling black water.

There was an entire world of living things beneath the surface. Humans polluted their environment and dropped down baited hooks, but they kept swimming. Bigger, prettier, stronger fish came along, but they—

Stop. Stop now.

You are officially losing it.

He shook his head, then turned toward Darcy. He extended his hand, which she grasped.

She shivered, pressing her body against his, wrapping her arms around his waist. "It's cold out here. Why aren't you inside?"

"I just needed a minute to take it all in."

"Your parents—together again."

He heard the smile in her voice and allowed himself to relax for the first time since walking onto the boat. "Pretty amazing, huh?"

"Yeah."

"Stay with me tonight," he whispered against her temple.

"I thought I already was. I brought my suitcase over yesterday, remember?"

"Right." He searched his brain for a quick reason why he'd be so desperate not to be alone. But, in some ways, he *was* alone. He, alone, hadn't made his marriage work. He, alone, was terrified of commitment.

Because that's what all this ridiculous buzzing was. Fear. He didn't want to commit his heart, only to get rejected again.

And Darcy deserved so much more.

She deserved a life free from the past, unburdened by a man who'd been betrayed by love and was unwilling to risk his heart again. He didn't want to be that man anymore.

Could he find the courage to change and embrace a hopeful future with her, or would he lose her forever?

DARCY STUDIED her cookbook in vain.

There was absolutely nothing within those normally reliable pages that could substitute for a Martinsville grandstand hot dog. Nothing healthy anyway.

The GRI teams were determined to consume them, hoarding them in cardboard containers along with every man and woman on every team, retired or active, young or old.

Everybody she consulted about their ingredients just smiled. Her own team, who'd loved every meal she'd ever prepared for them, told her not to bother cooking this weekend, advised her to quit being paranoid and just eat one already.

It completely went against her grain, yet, like the chocolate breakdowns, she was tempted.

She looked away from the slaw, chili, mustard-and-ketchup-slathered dog—which was a strange shade of bright red, by the way—Rachel had brought her earlier, assuring her she couldn't truly be part of the team until she'd tasted the legend that brought fans, teams, officials and generations together.

She'd forbidden Bryan to go within fifty feet of the infield concession stands set up by the track to serve the teams, but had little doubt he was even now passing out money to GRI employees, getting them to buy his race-day breakfast.

Wincing, she ducked into the fridge for an apple. Who ate hot dogs for breakfast anyway?

She had bigger problems than hot dogs, though. Namely, the man she loved didn't know she did. And probably didn't want to know.

Yet, not telling him felt like lying.

And though she'd spent the last few years living for the moment, trying to get through each day, barely acknowledging next week, now she wanted to know…*what's happening next week?*

The season was coming to an end. Would she continue to be his girlfriend after the last race? Did their relationship have an expiration date like their employment contract? The panic over being included in family pictures and events paled in comparison to wondering what the future held.

And she wanted a future with Bryan.

As crazy as it seemed, considering how guarded and damaged she'd started the year, she wanted it all with him—marriage, kids…forever.

But was his sense of trust too damaged to take those risks? To believe in anything beyond next week? Could he ever really love her in return? His parents' wedding should have confirmed how strong love can be, yet all week he'd seemed oddly distracted and distant.

Eating her apple, she dug into her gym bag for the legal pad she'd been scribbling on for weeks.

Reasons I Love Him...

It was schlocky and silly. Like a high school girl's spiral notebook of hearts and flowers, declaring her devotion to her man. Well, *boy,* in that context.

Something had changed inside her. Darcy was through playing the rules by the whims and surges of fate, to limiting herself to what *should* be, instead of trying for what *could* be. She'd accepted her husband was gone, she'd mourned him, she'd made her peace with her past, and now she was awake again. She was completely wide-awake to the possibilities of the future.

So, she had to tell Bryan how she felt.

The timer above the stove beeped, intruding on her thoughts. Okay, she had to tell him after she lit the hauler grill. The way she had a tendency to stare into space, thinking about Bryan and what to do about him, she'd resorted to setting timers for everything.

Grabbing the long-handled lighter, she headed out

of the motor home. Surely *somebody* on the team would prefer her Cajun-spice grilled chicken sandwiches to hot dogs.

WITH ONLY a small amount of guilt, Bryan tossed his empty hot-dog wrapper in the trash. He justified his action by remembering he hadn't broken Darcy's rule—he hadn't gotten within fifty feet of the concession stand.

Sam had.

Bryan headed into Cade's garage stall, making sure Sam and the rest of his team were ready to go for the race, then he visited Shawn's and Lars's teams. Lars, himself, was standing next to his car.

After all the turmoil early in the season, Lars had spent most of his time lately either testing or following Kevin around, probing for advice and a shoulder to lean on. It had finally seemed to occur to him that next year the legendary Splash car would be his alone, and he had shoes to fill that were so large, it was likely he'd drown before he dog-paddled, much less swam.

"You feeling good about today, Lars?" Bryan asked his young driver.

He jerked his shoulders. "It's Martinsville."

The half-mile oval track was extremely tough for young drivers to navigate. Some never got the feel for the balance of speed versus brakes. But Bryan knew Lars had plenty of talent and was ready to go through those grueling five hundred laps.

"You talked to Kevin this week?" he asked.

"Yeah."

"Remember what he told you. You'll be fine."

"Yeah." Lars managed to offer a half smile. "You, too."

"Me?"

"Cade's gonna win the championship."

Bryan crossed his arms over his chest. "You're sure about that, are you?"

"Surer than I am about going into Turn One today and not hitting anything." With a final grin, Lars turned to go back to his team.

Spotting Marcus McCray, the owner of the team his dad had driven for before he started GRI, Bryan waved at him, then strode over, though part of his mind was still on that precious trophy. He wanted it for Cade almost more than he wanted to draw his next breath. This was his year. It just had to be.

You never knew when the next turn in the road was going to stop you in your tracks. You never knew when things were about to change forever.

"Hey, Marcus," he said, shaking the other owner's hand, "have you talked to my sister, Rachel, today?"

"No. Haven't seen her."

"She's looking for you. Something about a charity event at the last race. She couldn't reach you on your cell."

Marcus frowned. "Can't stand the thing, ringing or vibrating half the time. My assistant has it somewhere." He glanced around. "Though I have no idea where he is, either. I'll find Rachel or call her at the office tomorrow."

"Great. Thanks. Good luck today." Bryan smiled. "Well, sort of."

"You, too. And, hey, I hear congratulations are in order. It's good to see Mitch and Barb together again."

Marcus had been around through the building years and the glory days with his dad. They'd raced together for a decade and won two championships. Bryan knew his dad's old boss had been equally as disappointed and confused by the break-up as the family had been. "Thanks. It's still a little surreal."

"I told Mitch he blew it, not having a bachelor party. It's not every day a couple of old dogs like us get that opportunity."

"Oh, I'm sure you could talk him into a Recently Married party." He reached into his pants pocket for his phone. "I'll call Rachel and let her know." He stopped, realizing he didn't have his phone.

Marcus patted his shoulder. "I'm always losing the dang thing, too."

As he headed off, Bryan searched his memory for the last place he'd seen his phone. Between the hectic, pressure-filled racing schedule and his parents' wedding last weekend, it was no wonder he was distracted.

He'd definitely had his phone last night in the motor home, so that was as good a place as any to start. Rushing in that direction, he wondered how many people had tried in vain to reach him. Though he agreed with Marcus about the phone being a distraction and an interruption a great deal of the time, it was a vital line of communication on a race weekend.

When he reached his motor home, he called out, "Hey, Darcy! Have you seen my—" He stopped, realizing he was alone. That wasn't good. He'd been sure she was here when he was eating his forbidden hot dog. Though he supposed his secret was still safe, since, if she'd spotted him, she would have stormed over and snatched the thing out of his hands.

Speaking of spotting…

He saw his phone sitting on the side table by the sofa. Grabbing it, he noticed a legal pad and Darcy's handwriting.

Reasons I Love Him…

What was this? Reasons who loves—

Again, he stopped, and this time his heart did, too.

He looks at me as if I'm amazing. He likes chocolate. When he touches me, I tremble. He's kind and generous—though sometimes he has to be reminded he feels this way. He—

And that was as far as he got. The door swung open and Darcy stepped inside.

CHAPTER NINETEEN

"YOU WEREN'T SUPPOSED to see that," Darcy said, her horrified gaze fixed on the pad in Bryan's hand.

"How is this possible?" he asked, his voice low with shock.

"That I love you, or that I was dumb enough to write it down?"

"That—" He sank onto the sofa. He didn't look happy or even pleased. He looked panicked.

He wasn't ready to hear about her feelings. He certainly wasn't going to say the words back to her. She'd known that, even though she'd been telling herself it was deceptive to keep quiet.

Her hands trembled, so she clutched them in front of her.

"You can't," he said finally, staring at her. "We're not ready for this."

"When will we be?" she asked, her pain making her voice sharp. "A month? A year?"

He set the pad aside and stood, pacing. "It'll go away."

"It'll go away?" she repeated in disbelief.

"Why can't we be together without promises and declarations? Why can't we just enjoy each other? Why do we have to complicate things?"

Shock rendered her speechless. Who was he? This was not the man who held her tenderly at night, who brought her chocolate when she was upset, who included her in family pictures and virtually every aspect of his life.

All that was fine, she guessed, as long as she didn't expect promises or, heaven forbid, *declarations.*

Angry, embarrassed and hurt, she grabbed her cooler of supplies, then darted toward the door.

"Don't go." Bryan grabbed her arm. "We have to…settle this."

She narrowed her eyes and shook herself free of his touch. She didn't want him to touch her or look at her or say anything else that would completely shatter her already cracked, bruised and battered heart. "Your feelings on the subject are pretty clear— you don't have any."

As she flung open the door, he called after her, "Love doesn't last!"

She glared at him over her shoulder. "Yes, Bryan, it does. Unfortunately for me, it really does."

Moving briskly out of the motor home lot and into the garage area, she prayed she wouldn't see anyone she knew. She had mere minutes of holding herself together, of forcing her fury to make her put one foot in front of the other.

She handed over all the supplies to Big Dan, then she lied. She told him she had a family emergency and had to go home.

Concern darkening his eyes, he laid his arm around her shoulders. "Who's taking you home? Did you arrange everything with the boss man?"

Nodding, she swallowed a burning lump of tears. She didn't consider that a lie, since she didn't think Bryan would be surprised to find her gone. "I'll be fine," she said, then squeezed him.

"See ya!" he called after her.

She waved, but wasn't sure she *would* see him again. That thought alone sent a tear rolling down her cheek. So many people on the team had become like family to her these last several months. To think this chapter of her life was over made her stumble, though somehow she kept moving.

She couldn't stay with Bryan and love him, knowing he didn't love her in return. She had too much pride and self-respect.

When she got back to the motor home, Bryan was gone, as she'd expected him to be. It was race day after all. A small personal crisis wouldn't stop the green flag from falling in a few hours.

After quickly packing her stuff, she grabbed the rental car keys and took one last glance around.

She'd lightened the depressing darkness of the décor with some bright red throw pillows and a fleece blanket tossed on the sofa. Garrison red, of course. She'd actually consulted with the guy who wrapped and decaled the cars to be sure she had just the right shade.

She saw the pad on the sofa and considered whether to take it or leave it. In the end, she couldn't make herself go near it, so she simply turned around and walked out.

As she drove, she tried to find a reason to regret putting her feelings down on paper, but she couldn't. She'd rather be honest and alone, than with him, fooling herself.

Was she running again?

Sure.

But it wasn't as if she had anything to hang around and fight for. She loved him, and he clearly didn't love her. Case closed. End of discussion. She couldn't stay and fight for something that had never belonged to her in the first place.

So that's it, huh? her conscience, intrusive as always, asked.

The man you love, traumatized by divorces and a career-ending accident, can't say three little words, and you're going to turn your back on him?

"Yep," she announced to the empty car.

Anger had certainly driven her to leave, but even when her temper lessened, she'd still know she'd made the right decision.

As she knew all too well, life was too short to settle for good when she could have great. Maybe Bryan would eventually trust her with his heart. Maybe he would get over his issues and come after her. She didn't think it was likely, though she had hope.

And maybe she was drawing a hard line—love her wholly and forever or goodbye—but she knew she couldn't accept less. She'd had her love of a lifetime and lost it. She thought she'd somehow managed to find that miracle again in Bryan.

She couldn't pretend that wasn't what she wanted and needed.

She'd been devastated before. She ought to be used to it by now.

On that horribly bitter thought, she swung by the grocery store down the street from her apartment building. She bought two giant bags of mini chocolate bars—thank goodness for Halloween—and three bags of truffles.

She was going to need all the help she could get.

SHE'D LEFT HIM.

Bryan had no idea why he stood in his bedroom, staring in utter disbelief at the empty spot in the corner where Darcy always left her suitcase.

Why should he be surprised? When life got rough or didn't go as planned, women left. At least the women *he* got involved with.

When she hadn't appeared at lunch, he'd been concerned. When she hadn't come for the singing of the national anthem, he'd gotten seriously worried. So, while the drivers climbed in their cars, he'd run over to the motor home lot. Even now, he could hear the cars taking their pace laps.

Where had she gone?

He dialed her cell phone twice, but she didn't answer. He needed to be on the pit box, dammit, not standing around, his throat tight, his heart—

Whirling, he strode outside.

Somehow, he pretended to be fine. He held on to his anger and went through his usual race routine, visiting all the GRI teams' pit boxes, talking to crews, listening to radio chatter.

When Chance got involved in a wreck a few laps shy of halfway and had to pull his car into the garage for repairs, ruining any chance of him winning the race, Bryan felt a brief ripple of excitement. If Cade could finish in the top ten, he'd likely pull ahead of Chance in the points battle.

That excitement quickly wore off, though, and Bryan concentrated on his brother's efforts to win the race.

For about ten minutes.

After that, he wondered about Darcy. There weren't an abundance of hotels in the Martinsville area to start with, but on race weekend, there probably wasn't a vacant room in the entire state.

Where had she gone?

And how had she gotten there?

He hadn't thought earlier to look for the rental car keys. Unless she was wandering around the garage area with her suitcase, she had to have taken the car. So, where would she—

Home.

It was barely a two-hour drive to the Mooresville area from the track. They'd actually taken the helicopter up, but the GRI travel coordinator always rented Darcy a car for trips to the grocery store for supplies.

Emptiness settled into his gut at the realization of how thoroughly she'd left him. How easily and quickly. They hadn't made promises or commitments, after all. There was nothing to hold her to him.

He knew she'd been upset earlier, and maybe he'd handled things badly, but he'd been honest. Did she want him to spout pretty words he didn't feel?

His heart contracted the way it had the night of his parents' wedding, calling him a liar. He felt plenty. Maybe too much.

But he didn't want to face his emotions. He wanted to continue to repress. Keep on denying.

He failed miserably at both.

Because as Cade won the race and moved to first place in the championship standings, Bryan thought of Darcy. As the team erupted around him, he took off his headset and stared at the floor of the war wagon. All he could see were the scrawled words of devotion Darcy had written on a yellow piece of paper.

He makes me happy.

That was the last line on the list.

Yet, he hadn't lived up to that expectation. He'd

been too proud or cautious or afraid to really make her happy. Instead, he'd driven her away.

I knew my life would never be right without her. I told her I loved her—always had, always would.

His dad had said those words to him when Bryan had asked why his mom had forgiven his dad and taken him back. Would they work the same magic for Bryan? Even if they were a little late in coming? Even if the woman he wanted to say them to had, rightly, run away from him?

Well, they *had* to, because they were all he had. He clenched his fist. They called him Steel for a reason, didn't they?

He couldn't use the excuse that love didn't last, not anymore. The joy of it was everywhere around him—and not just in racing. He'd been running from his feelings, desperate to avoid being rejected.

Instead, he'd been rejected for *not* telling her he loved her.

How dumb was that?

"Where's Darcy?" he heard his sister shout over the roaring crowd and the team's whoops of excitement all around him. "I just talked to Big Dan, and he said she had to leave for a family emergency. What happened?"

"She left."

"Did something happen to her parents?"

"No." Frustrated, he pushed his hand through his hair. "At least I don't think so."

"Don't *think?* How do you not know—" She

stopped, and he looked up in time to see her plant her hands on her hips. "What did you do?"

"What makes you think *I* did anything?"

She simply stared at him.

"Okay, so maybe I did something." He shoved aside his pride and the idea that there couldn't be a worse time or place for a meaningful discussion. None of this—the victories, the championship—meant anything without her to share it. "I need help, Rach. I'm in real trouble."

"Finally realized you love her, huh?"

Smugness was not a state he normally encouraged in his sister, but there was no point in denying the truth. "Oh, yeah."

Sitting in the seat next to him, she grasped his hand. "You've got to tell her."

"Gee, that's a good idea. Wish I'd thought of it when she told me, and I told her love didn't last."

She cringed. "You actually said that?"

"Hell, I shouted it."

"*O-kay.*" Pausing, she patted his hand. "Well, don't worry. We'll figure something out."

He recalled Isabel telling him he loved Darcy— only to have him argue, of course—but how had she known? He met his sister's gaze. "Obviously, you know I lo—" He stopped.

"Good grief, Bryan, if you can't say it to me, how are you going to say it to her?"

"No, it's not that. I just—" He felt a flush rise up his neck. "I just want the first time I say it out loud to be to her."

She blinked, then tears filled her eyes. She pressed her lips together briefly. *"Awww."*

"Yeah, I'm a real romantic." Since he so completely wasn't, he knew he had to figure out how to become one. Fast. "So you know how I feel about her, and so does Isabel. But *how* did you know?"

"Oh. Pretty much when you started doing yoga."

"But—yoga? That was eight months ago."

She angled her head. "Has it been that long?"

"Yes. How could you possibly have known when I only figured it out ten minutes ago?"

"I saw you in the Real Men Do Yoga shirt."

It was no wonder he was lousy at romance. He was more confused than ever. "What does that have to do with anything?"

"The Bryan 'Steel' Garrison I grew up with would never, *ever* wear that shirt. Even in private," she added before he could argue that very point.

"So T-shirt equals love?"

She nodded. "See, you *do* have a romantic side."

"Mmm." He didn't think telling Darcy the proof of his love rested on a screen-printed T-shirt would get him very far. "I think we're going to need more of an expert than you or me. How about—"

"Parker," they said together.

Rachel stood. "Come on, let's go to Victory Lane,

do the interviews, hugs and the hat dance, then we'll figure out a way to get her back."

For the first time in hours, a spark of hope surged through him. "*We* will, huh?"

"Sure." She tugged him to his feet. "No offense, brother dear, but you've screwed this up in a big way. We'll call a family meeting."

"OKAY, PEOPLE, let's get on with this." On Monday morning, his sister stood at the head of the conference table in his office. "Operation Get Darcy Back will now commence."

Bryan winced. "Do we need a name?"

Rachel winked, obviously enjoying herself to a ridiculous degree. "Be glad that Isabel talked me out of the idea of team T-shirts."

Sending Isabel a grateful glance, he leaned back in his chair. He should have known his family would go full out. They never did anything halfway. If you were going to race, you raced to win.

They were all present—his parents, Cade, Isabel, Parker and Rachel. They had his grandfather on alert for a call should they need his expertise— He was entered in a fishing tournament for the next three days.

When one Garrison was suffering, they all suffered until the problem was solved.

For once, instead of being aggravated that he had problems or embarrassed that he'd confessed them, he was happy to see them all. Love surrounded him. Every day. All the time.

Love of a sport. Love between families. Love between siblings. Love between couples.

He couldn't imagine it would be long before that love extended to a new generation of Garrisons. Kids running around again, learning the turns and nuances of the go-kart track, finding their way in the world, whether it was on the track, in the business office or in a whole new venture—doctors, lawyers, owners of dry cleaners.

The idea of that future—marriage, kids and whatever else came his way—didn't scare him anymore. If Darcy was beside him, he could overcome any fear or obstacle.

Rachel was right. He'd loved Darcy for a while, since wearing that silly yoga T-shirt, while insisting she be included in team and family pictures, since she'd trusted him with her pain and her body. Her leaving had forced him to face his stupid fears and denials.

Now, if only she'd forgive him for forcing her to take such a drastic action. If only she'd believe in their love and future.

"Grand gesture," Parker said definitively, then sipped his coffee as if the matter was settled.

Isabel glared at him. "I say simple is best. If Bryan shows up at her door in a tux, she's going think somebody died."

"Can we do grand *and* simple?" Rachel asked.

"No." Cade frowned. "We have to pick. Remember Mom and Dad's wedding—big boat, moonlight, champagne. That was grand."

Mom patted his hand. "Thank you, dear."

"But it was also simple," Isabel argued. "Family only. No organs, bridesmaids or gobs of people."

"Is that a dig on our wedding?" Cade asked.

"No, of course not." Isabel sighed. "I only meant Darcy is a one-on-one person. She isn't comfortable in crowds."

"I agree," Dad said.

"It wasn't the crowd that caused her to faint," Rachel said to him. "Can we move into the present?"

As his family debated around him, Bryan wished Darcy was there. After less than a day, he missed her calmness, her touch, her smile, the scent of her tropical-vanilla-tinged lotion, the commanding way she warned him away from cheeseburgers and Martinsville hot dogs.

But if she was beside him, there'd be no reason for a meeting.

Even better.

Despite Rachel's advice to keep silent until she'd helped him formulate a plan, he'd called Darcy after the race and left messages on both her cell and home phones, apologizing for the things he'd said and asking her to call him, so they could talk.

She hadn't.

"What about Richard Childress's winery?" Parker suggested into the mix of voices.

Everybody fell silent.

Rachel smiled. "It's certainly grand."

"But it's also simple," Isabel said, her eyes sparking. "Elegant and simple."

"He has that lovely barrel room," Mom added, "where he ages the chardonnay. There's a waterfall and these amazing iron chandeliers that give off a glow of intimate lighting. He rents it out for small parties. I'd be glad to call him."

Dad shifted his glance to his bride. "You're close buddies with Richard now, huh?"

Mom lifted her chin. "He invited me to parties when you were being a jerk."

Dad covered her hand with his. "And I'm grateful to him."

Bryan stared at his dad in amazement. The man he knew was totally focused on racing, on making his team the best in NASCAR. And while, given Cade's current position, he'd clearly accomplished that, he hadn't forgotten what was truly important.

Well, maybe he had for a while.

Everybody was entitled to a stumble. To going off-track. To crashing, then making repairs and finishing the race. The key was finding a way back without a DNF.

And racing metaphors weren't going to impress Darcy.

He leaned forward, his shoulders slumping, his

hands cupping his coffee mug. He had to find some-thing else, something tangible and profound that would prove his love and his regret for how he'd treated her.

Though Cade and Isabel had snapped at each other during the discussion, Bryan wasn't surprised to glance out of the corner of his eye and see his brother whispering in his wife's ear.

Love *could* last forever.

"Whatever the location," Rachel said with a defini-tive nod, "he needs to bring chocolate."

"And champagne," Parker said.

Isabel shook her head. "What does he need to bring champagne for? He'll be in a room surrounded by wine barrels."

"If it's okay with you people, I think I'll just bring a ring."

Everybody stared at him.

Parker smiled. "Now, *that* would be a grand gesture."

"Propose?" Cade asked, staring at Bryan in shock. "You're going to propose?"

"Marriage is all the rage in this family," his mother said, her eyes gleaming with pride.

"Yeah." Rachel nudged Cade. "We got you to the altar. How hard can it be to get Bryan there?"

Bryan kept waiting for the idea of marriage to sound wrong, but he was through with panic and denial. His only concern was wondering if he'd be rushing Darcy. Would she balk at the pressure of such a big decision?

On the other hand, what was he waiting for? He wanted Darcy with him, committed to him. He didn't want her to leave, and while vows didn't always hold forever, he knew they would with her. If she said yes, he'd have her by his side—always.

Hadn't they been coasting long enough? Hadn't his suggestion that they not complicate their relationship led to her leaving?

Still, proposing was a little crazy.

He would either win it all, or lose her in an instant.

Isabel held up her hand. "*Hello*...people. Back to reality here. Don't you think he should probably get her to talk to him again first?"

"That particular question would require a response," Parker said.

"If we're having a wedding, the boat's available," Dad said.

"No boat." Rachel shook her head. "This plan has to come from Bryan. Besides, Darcy was on the boat for the wedding. We should at least be original."

"I agree," Isabel said. "We're taking over, not helping."

Rachel looked at Bryan. "Are we helping?"

"Yes."

"But?"

"No but." His gaze swept his family. "I just want her back. Whatever we have to do to make that happen, I'm ready."

As the discussion resumed, he slid his hand into

his pocket, fingering the folded piece of yellow paper he'd tucked there. No matter what happened, what was decided or planned, he had a tangible reminder that she loved him.

He only hoped he wasn't too late.

CHAPTER TWENTY

DARCY HALTED at the bottom of her apartment building steps. "A limo?" She turned to the elegantly dressed man next to her. "What are you up to, Parker Huntington?"

"Many things." He laid his fingertips on the small of her back and urged her toward the door being held open by the chauffeur. "Right now, I'm taking you out for a drink and sympathy conversation."

With a sigh, she slid into the limo and glanced over at him as he joined her. "When women have a bad breakup, they eat ice cream—chocolate, of course— watch chick movies and drink too much wine. They do not get dressed up in designer clothes and ride in limos to undisclosed locations with their ex-boyfriend and employer's brother-in-law on Wednesday nights."

"The dress is lovely on you," he said. "Green is definitely your color, and Rachel did a superb job with the sizing."

"Why am I wearing it?" she asked, fingering the silky fabric, but still feeling silly.

He grasped her hand and squeezed it. "Because you're my friend, and you're hurting."

Not at all fooled by his smooth manners, she narrowed her eyes. "You're not plotting anything?"

His eyes widened. "What would I be plotting?"

"To get me and Bryan in the same place at the same time."

"While I would certainly love to see you two work through your problems, you give me too much credit. Trust me, I could never get Bryan Garrison to anyplace at anytime without his total cooperation."

She watched the lights of the freeway fly by out the window. She didn't like thinking about Bryan, much less talking about him. Yet she knew she had to talk to somebody. She couldn't sit alone in her apartment and shed another tear.

Not answering his messages had probably been cowardly, certainly unprofessional. She was supposed to be working for him, after all. But she'd deleted them without even listening. She simply couldn't hear his voice, couldn't bear to hear him tell her that love didn't matter or last. Again.

Would he love her someday? Would he wake up one morning and think, *Gee, I really love that Darcy. Maybe I oughta set aside my ridiculous pride and fear long enough to tell her.*

Even if he did, she wasn't sure they could go back to before the hurtful words they'd said on Sunday.

"There are a lot of charismatic men in stock car

racing," she said quietly, still watching the flickering lights.

"Are there?"

She looked over at Parker. "You could be their Grand Poobah."

"I should tell you my wife is a very possessive woman, and she might be offended by your compliments." His smile lit up his green eyes. "However sincere."

"My point is…you're trying to pull one over on me."

"I am?"

"And it isn't going to work."

"It's not?"

She clenched her jaw at his transparently not-so-innocent tone. "I'm not going back to him."

"Okay."

"You're not going to try to talk me into forgiving him?"

He smoothed the lapels of his dark blue suit coat. "Certainly not. You're capable enough of making up your own mind about your relationships."

"Yes, I am." She nodded, crossing her arms over her chest. "He doesn't want all of me, then he gets none of me."

"Amen, sister."

"I laid out my heart and soul, and he stomped on them, trod around for a while, then sailed out the door."

Parker lifted his finger. "Technically, you were the one who sailed out the door."

"How do you—" She pressed her lips together to keep from saying something hurtful.

While she'd been holed up, alone with only her chocolate for comfort, in her apartment, he'd been sharing all the intimate details with his family. She'd been discreet, telling everybody they broke up, but offering nothing more. It was nice to know that same courtesy had been returned.

"Well, I had plenty of reason—" She halted as the limo turned in a grand iron gate. "What's this?"

"A winery."

"A...what?"

"Don't worry. They have drinks, and my ear is feeling very sympathetic tonight."

Mouth open, she stared out at the landscape. Muted lighting caused the twisting vines to cast shadows along the valley of land below the winding path the limo took.

"It's beautiful," she managed to say through the tears clogging her throat.

"Very Tuscan, don't you think?"

She watched the stacked stone and red tile roof of the main building come into view, and though she'd never been to Italy in person, she had a general idea of the architecture. "I guess so."

"But all the grapes for the wine are either grown on site or at other local vineyards. Everything from North Carolina. Amazing, isn't it?"

Darcy looked away from the setting long enough

to meet Parker's gaze. "Thanks. Thanks a lot. This is just the distraction I needed."

"The evening's not over yet," he said as the limo rolled to a stop in front of the building.

They were whisked through the lobby by the attentive and friendly staff and led downstairs to a room with iron chandeliers and old-fashioned bulbs that simulated flickering candles. Wine barrels were scattered in the front of the room, while a rock wall waterfall dominated the back. A single table, set for two with elegant china and real candles, sat just beyond the waterfall.

A fracture of unease worked its way through her body. "Ah, Parker...I don't think this is appropriate for—"

"Hi, Darcy."

She closed her eyes for a moment, then opened them and turned back toward the door she'd just walked through.

Bryan, ridiculously handsome, dressed in a dark gray suit and silver tie, stood in the opening of the room. He held a dark brown package with a gold ribbon and had the nerve to smile at her.

She whirled toward Parker. "You set me up."

"I did indeed." He kissed her cheek. "I hope forever." He pulled back and studied her at length. "You, more than anyone I know, deserve to be happy. Give him a chance."

"I—" She fought for a smart retort, some way she

could call him out for lying to her, but he was already striding out the door, and as she quickly ran through their conversation, she realized how careful he'd been to be endearing, say little and promise nothing.

"He could patent that charm," she muttered, "and make another fortune."

"I brought chocolate."

Darcy jumped, realizing Bryan had moved across the room. She turned her back on him, though she could smell the dark cocoa and coconut. The man played dirty. She needed to remember that. "I'm not interested."

"But I love you."

Heart pounding, she jerked her head toward him. "You—"

"Love you." He set the box on the table and slid his arm around her waist. His eyes, usually smoky and cloudy, burned blue and bright. "Always. Forever."

"But—"

"But nothing. I was an idiot for the things I said on Sunday. I was scared." He smoothed her hair away from her face, then pressed his lips lightly to her temple. The warmth slid through every part of her. "I was stupid, too. But I won't be anymore. I need you more than I've ever needed anyone."

She forced herself to meet his gaze. "You said you didn't believe in love."

"Did I mention I was stupid?"

"I—" She swallowed. Everything she wanted was

being handed to her. All the dreams she'd had could come true, the man she loved could be hers.

And yet she doubted the gift.

Bryan hadn't done all this. Even without Parker bringing her, there were too many details for him to have managed on his own.

"This is all—" she glanced around at the romantic room and fought the pleasure over intimate details, over him arranging something so amazing "—nice, but you literally woke up this morning and decided you love me?"

He shook his head. "Nope. Rachel says it was the moment I wore the yoga T-shirt. Isabel thinks it was at my parents' wedding. Dad decided I couldn't resist your grilled chicken. Mom thinks it was your compassion. Cade thinks it was your strength, and Parker somehow knew we were right for each other from the very beginning." He gestured to the room. "Then they all helped me arrange this."

Tears gathered behind her eyes. Her heart trembled. The man she'd known was hiding behind disappointment and betrayal had fought his way out. "And you? What do you think?"

Grasping her hands, he pulled her close. "I've been fighting my feelings for you for months. Fear again, thinking I could float along and not face my feelings, not consider the future and really let go of the past. But you changed all that." He handed her a folded piece of yellow paper. "You made me realize I couldn't care less about trophies or trips to Victory Lane unless you're there."

Her hands shook as she unfolded her list.

Reasons I Love Him.

"I've been carrying around that list since Sunday," he continued. "And I know I didn't arrange this on my own. Parker thought I needed a grand gesture. Rachel wanted simple. Mom suggested the winery.

"But this…" Wrapping his fingers around her wrists, he dropped to one knee and opened the dark brown box. "This is all mine."

Nestled in the center of four chocolate truffles was a sparkling diamond ring. Her gaze jumped to his.

"Will you marry me?"

She blinked. Diamond still there. Man of her dreams still kneeling. "I—"

The diamond shone; the chocolate glistened. A million negative reasons for taking such an abrupt leap into the future raced through her mind.

But she'd learned a great deal about racing in the last year. Opportunities didn't come along every day. Momentum was critical. Risks were tempered against rewards. Families raced together.

Besides all that, she was through being cautious. She was going to close her eyes and jump. She had no idea what awaited her, but she knew Bryan would stand by her side as they faced the future together.

Forever in love.

Pressing her lips together to stem the tide of

emotions, and failing miserably as a tear tracked down her cheek, she simply nodded.

With sure and confident hands, he slid the ring on her finger, then rose and yanked her against him. His heart beat wildly against her chest.

She knew she'd cherish that sound, just as she would always long for the roar of the crowd, the growl of the engines and the laughter the Garrison family would share far into the future.

CHAPTER TWENTY-ONE

RACE MORNING in Homestead, Bryan leaned against his motor home counter and sipped coffee.

Today the championship would be decided, and his brother and everybody at GRI would either walk away elated or devastated. With Cade in the points lead, the trophy was theirs to lose. Any mistake—from a bad spark plug to a missed lug nut on pit road—could cost them everything.

The whole season was down to four hundred miles. Anticipation over the gravity of what the next few hours would bring tightened his stomach muscles.

"Morning."

He glanced down the hall as Darcy walked toward him. "Morning," he said, feeling that tightness loosen a bit.

Dressed in one of his old souvenir T-shirts, she shuffled toward him.

Since she was rarely the slow-moving one in the morning, he savored the pleasure of watching her wake up.

She slid her arm around his waist and leaned against him. "Couldn't sleep?"

He kissed the top of her head and inhaled her vanilla-touched scent. "It's a big day."

"When does the garage open?"

He glanced at his watch. "In twenty minutes."

"I'll get in the shower, so I can come with you," she said as she pulled away.

"You don't have to do that."

She tossed a grin over her shoulder. "Who's gonna feed all your guys, then? I'm betting you're not the only one up before sunrise."

Fifteen minutes later, she was pouring coffee in her bright red No. 56 Huntington Hotels travel mug and ready to head out the door.

Self-conscious, but not so much to resist the impulse, he stared at that number and said a silent prayer. There wasn't much left he could do now. The day was up to Cade, Sam and his team.

He focused on Darcy. At least she was a sure thing. "Is this speedy getting ready stuff part of the honeymoon period, or can I count on this for the next sixty years?"

"Honeymoon period? We're not even married yet."

Grabbing her by the waist, he pulled her against him. "I told you we should have gotten the minister to do the ceremony in Victory Lane last week."

"Oh, no. I want a ceremony on the beach and a real honeymoon—with no race cars, wrenches or dyno numbers in sight." She slid her hand up his chest. "And you all to myself."

"You will. After today."

"For a few days. Until you start thinking about Daytona next year."

Feeling guilty, he nodded.

"And I know you're doing that already." She kissed him lightly. "Hey, I've got this owner's wife thing down pat."

Wife.

She'd only been his fiancée a few weeks. But nobody, including them, thought they were rushing into a commitment. Darcy had really been a member of the family for months. Making their bond official was easy.

Which they were doing behind Parker's oceanside hotel tomorrow afternoon. As long as the team, their friends and family were around, they might as well take advantage of the moment.

If the beach was what Darcy wanted, then she'd get it. As long as he had her, Bryan wasn't worried about anything.

Well…except today's race.

Cade had to finish ninth or better and lead a lap to win the championship.

Seemingly reading his thoughts, Darcy squeezed his hand. "He's going to w—"

He laid his finger over her lips. "Don't jinx it."

"Fine," she mumbled.

"Aren't you the one always talking about not upsetting the universal balance?"

She pulled his hand away so she could talk. "You're the one who said he was going to w—" She stopped, clearing her throat. *"You know,"* she whispered, "at Indy. And look what happened there."

"Maybe so, but I'm not risking anything today."

"What about tomorrow?"

His gaze searched hers. The golden sparks that he knew he'd see the rest of his life were shining bright and sure. "No risk there, either. You love me."

"I certainly do." She puckered her lips. "One last kiss for luck."

No way he was turning down an invitation like that.

"Poor Parker," she said when they reluctantly separated.

"Parker?"

"Yeah. He probably didn't get any sleep last night with Cade calling every five minutes to make sure he still had the lucky penny."

Bryan felt the blood drain from his face. "He *does* have it, doesn't he?"

Laughing, she steered him out the door. "I'm sure he does, but let's go make sure."

EPILOGUE

Fall, two years later

AMID THE CELEBRATION in Victory Lane, Isabel Garrison pulled her vibrating phone from her pocket.

Baby coming. Get here ASAP.

—P

She glanced at the date and time the message was sent. Today, basically ten seconds ago. That couldn't be right.

Even though Parker was a new dad, she couldn't imagine him forgetting his son arrived yesterday. In fact, he, Rachel and Patrick Mitchell Huntington—named for both grandfathers—were still at the hospital in Charlotte. What baby could—

Oh, boy.

Or, more accurately, *oh, girl.*

Darcy's in labor?!? she texted back to Parker.

For forty humming seconds—which she counted, one-by-one—she tapped her foot and looked up at the risers, watching her husband and his team take another picture and switch ball caps to yet another sponsor for the next picture. It was a ritual they'd shared many times over the last three years. In fact, she was usually next to him in those pictures. Just not today, when—

Yes! was Parker's response.

On our way… she sent back, then stuffed the phone in the back pocket of her jeans. She had to get this circus moving. Racing was their business, but family was their life.

All the grandparents, aunts, uncles, cousins, in-laws, etc. were at home, cooing over baby Pat, so there was only her and Cade to get to the new birthing party. And they needed to get moving.

For the first time ever, she wished Cade wasn't so skilled behind the wheel. If he'd finished a little farther back in the field, they'd already be on their way to the airport by now.

"Let's go, champ," she said in her husband's ear after working her way through the jubilant crowd. "We have to go meet your niece."

Cade's trademark Garrison blue eyes widened. "I just met my nephew yesterday. Or did I dream we were in the hospital last night?"

"These things apparently happen in pairs."

"I thought it was threes."

"Bite your tongue."

To avoid NASCAR's wrath for her taking their race winner without completing his media obligations, she invited other drivers, officials and several reporters onboard the Garrison Racing Incorporated jet for the flight back home. Though her thoughts and her heart were with Darcy and Bryan, she knew her role as PR director for the company. She kept everybody in the party mood with food and champagne, while she encouraged Cade to entertain with stories of tough-as-nails champion Mitch Garrison misty-eyed over his first grandchild. When he included the tidbit that she'd cried more than anybody, she retaliated by sharing the story of Bryan and Darcy's beach wedding two years ago, during which her newly crowned NASCAR Sprint Cup Series champion husband had spent so much time staring at his trophy the rest of the family had threatened to chuck it in the Gulf.

Heading into the hospital with every kind of media trailing in her wake—including a live TV crew, which Bryan certainly wasn't going to be happy about—Isabel was thankful she'd had the foresight to send a message ahead, telling Parker to warn the medical staff about her unusual entourage.

"When are we going to do this?" Cade whispered in her ear as they rushed down the hall toward labor and delivery.

"Win another race or disrupt a major medical center?"

"Have a baby?"

Isabel felt the blood drain from her face.

Raised by drug addict parents who'd cheat their

own grandma out of her last buck to get their fix, Isabel didn't think she was too well qualified to be a parent. But Parker and Rachel, and now Bryan and Darcy, seemed to think they were ready.

Maybe, after she'd watched her in-laws for a while—a decade or two—she'd find the courage to take that step.

"Ah, sure...eventually," she hedged.

Cade slid his arm around her waist. His lips brushed her cheek. "Don't go into panic mode, Izzy. I've got to win at least one more championship before we start our family. I can't tie Bryan. I have to beat him."

This wasn't a comfort. The man was more than two hundred points ahead with four races to go until the end of the season.

Then she remembered something important. Bryan had one championship, so two would best him. But Cade's father had two, so only three would get Cade to the top of his family.

She ground to a halt. "Don't you think you should not only beat Bryan, but your father, as well? Think of the accomplishment, the family legacy, the pride of your fans...the glory at Thanksgiving."

Cade cupped her cheek. "If I didn't know you better, baby, I'd think you were scared of motherhood."

She shook her head briskly. "But you know me better than anybody, so that can't be possible. I'm just..." She searched her brain frantically for a logical argument—which should have come naturally. "Thinking of you, and your career, of course."

"Babies? Careers?" A reporter stuck a microphone near Isabel's and Cade's faces. "Do you two have an announcement to make?"

Though the reporter was a friend, Isabel glared at her. "We're about to announce the arrival of another Garrison. You guys—" she pointed at the crowd behind her, then the waiting room off the hall to their left "—stay here until we do."

Since laughs and cash were exchanged during the seconds when Isabel and Cade turned right and the media turned left, Isabel knew she'd been had. She was the most notorious control freak in the garage, so dealing with situations—like birth—where she had absolutely no say, was predictably driving her just a little bit crazy.

In the L&D wing of the hospital, they inquired about Darcy's room and were told she was in 409. Only a few steps down that hall, Isabel realized she hadn't needed to ask. All the Garrison men—Mitch, Parker, Grandpa Jack, even Bryan—were pacing outside the room at the end of the hall along with Darcy's father and uncle.

"What's going on?" she asked as she approached them. She popped Bryan lightly on the shoulder. "What're you doing out here?"

"She threw me out!" Bryan shouted, throwing up

his arms, then tossing a dark look at the closed door a few feet away. "She said this was all my fault, and I should be suffering as much as she is." In a desperate and uncharacteristic move, he grabbed Isabel's arms. He clutched her tight and bared his teeth. "You've got to go in there. I went through all the classes, all the disgusting and terrifying videos, I *have* to see my daughter born."

She cast a glance at the men pacing—like some eerie 1950s flashback. Cade eased their anxiety a bit by handing out pink ribbon-decorated bubblegum cigars. They could probably all use a shot of whiskey or at least the promise of champagne, but she'd leave that in her husband's capable hands.

Instead, she focused on the immediate crisis.

Holding Bryan's desperate and bloodshot gaze, she nodded and pulled open the door.

She'd kick some butts. At the very least, she'd find the anesthesiologist and get him to tranquilize anybody who argued or who was in pain.

Inside, two L&D nurses and a doctor were hovering near Darcy's feet, intermittently consulting about her legs bent in the stirrups and the electronic equipment standing nearby. Barb Garrison and Darcy's mother, Hannah, were wiping Darcy's brow and spouting encouragements, while Rachel, dressed in her bathrobe, held a blanketed bundle of newborn son and rocked back and forth, keeping up constant verbal encouragement.

Worse, Darcy looked scared.

"What the hell are you people doing?" Isabel burst out.

They all stopped and stared.

"You—" she pointed at Rachel "—get back to your own room. We'll send Parker down to let you know when the baby is here."

Rachel shifted her son upright to her shoulder, then nodded and headed out the door Isabel held open.

Isabel extended her hand in the direction Rachel had disappeared. "Grandmas, go outside with the grandpas." When she saw the mutinous look in her mother-in-law's eyes, she simply shook her head. "Out."

With the room nearly clear, she pointed at one of the nurses. "You, go get the anesthesiologist."

"Mrs. Garrison refused all pain med—"

In two short strides, Isabel had closed the distance between her and the nurse, during which the other woman had paled and stopped speaking. It was possible she'd stopped breathing. "You know what, Nurse…" She flicked a glance at her name tag. "Nurse Ellen, I think she's changed her mind."

Urged by common sense or the fire that blazed from Isabel's eyes, Nurse Ellen nodded. "I thought she needed something an hour ago." She rushed from the room.

Isabel caught the door before it snapped closed. She thought for a half a second and remembered to gentle her voice as she spoke to the man in the hall whose whole life had been racing, then, after rediscovering his family, now knew his life could be both. "Bryan, your wife needs you."

The doctor looked relieved and the remaining nurse sent her a wink as she waved Bryan in, then sailed out after a brief stroke of her hand against her sister-in-law's sweaty cheek.

Once in the hall, Isabel joined the anticipatory pacing. Very little was said. After an hour, she joined Cade, leaning against the wall. They held on to each other, much as the rest of the family was doing. She checked on the media members a couple of times, who seemed perfectly happy to use the hospital's wireless Internet connection to file their stories while they were hot on the scene, witnessing the next generation of Garrisons springing to life, undoubtedly destined to change racing's next incarnation.

At 2:02 a.m., Hallie Barbara Garrison was born.

Dad Bryan burst from the delivery room with a light in his eyes and a flush on his face that Isabel was certain hadn't been seen since he'd won the championship back in '04. The family was ecstatic. The team, including Big Dan—who'd shown up during the wait with barbeque dinners, beer and sweet tea—vowed to party until 7:00 a.m., their report time for the next prerace meeting. The media sent out firsthand pictures for their reports, then relaxed into the plush leather limo seats provided by Huntington Hotels for their journey home.

Isabel, tears in her eyes, clutched her husband's hand and followed the rest of the Garrisons into Darcy's room. Looking down on the blue-eyed, pink-cheeked bundle, who would someday grow into a strong, compassionate woman worthy of the Garrison name, then around at the men and women she loved as she'd never imagined she could, she was certain they were all thinking the same thing—how lucky they were to have not only success but the bond of family they'd all cherish for generations to come.

* * * * *

ACKNOWLEDGMENTS

It's hard to believe our journey with the Garrison family is coming to an end. We've loved, laughed and cried with them, and we know their future is as bright as the championship trophy they strive for each and every week.

There have been so many people who've helped us bring this series to life it's hard to formulate a list—but we're still going to try. So, here goes…

Thanks to our hubbies, Ryan and Keith, for their constant support and inspiration. And a special thanks to the all the kids—Krista, Robbie, Bella, Caitlyn and Grace—for hanging in there when Mom is on the phone talking about the wild mix of plots, characters and racing details.

Thanks to all our supportive friends and fellow writers who help dig us out of the holes we often find ourselves in: Jean Brashear, Jacquie D'Alessandro, Jennifer St. Giles, Rita Herron and Stephanie Bond.

Thank you to the amazing editorial staff we've been privileged to work with over the last few years, including Stacy Boyd, Tina Colombo, Tracy Farrell, and Marsha Zinberg at Harlequin and John Farrell, Catherine McNeill and Jennifer White at NASCAR.

Also at Harlequin we owe a great debt to everyone in the PR and art departments for taking such great care of our trilogy, giving us fantastic covers and sharing their generous enthusiasm. We're especially grateful for Michelle Renaud. We had the best marketing guru in Michelle and an even better friend.

Thanks to our fantastic agent, Pamela Harty and The Knight Agency, who's stood right beside us through every crazy moment and God knows there were plenty of crazy moments to go around.

A great big hug to Russ Thompson and Bobby Hamilton Jr. for all of the great gearhead info. We can't think of two better guys to get under the hood with. Nobody knows race stats like Russ. Thanks, Russ, for always keeping us on track.

Smoke, you inspired us while writing this trilogy. You'll have to guess why.

Everybody at Sirius NASCAR radio and especially the gang at Tradin' Paint. The producers always have on great guests, who make our research process easier and fun. Postman *is* the man, and Chocolate, you definitely know which character you are!

The webmaster of Jayski.com. Whenever we needed a fact, a historical tidbit, statistic or detail, we knew where to go. Thanks a bunch!

And finally thanks to the racers who've inspired us, the people in front of and behind the scenes who bring us the show and the fans who remind us why we love this crazy sport.

Love and gratitude to you all!

Liz & Wendy

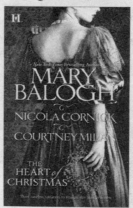